# Going, Going, Gone: Susie's Story

# ALSO BY BARBARA L. CLANTON

## THE CLARKSONVILLE SERIES
*Out of Left Field: Marlee's Story (Book One)*
*Tools of Ignorance: Lisa's Story (Book Two)*
*Going, Going, Gone: Susie's Story (Book Three)*
*Stealing Second: Sam's Story (Book Four)*
*Out at Home (Book Five)*
*Tools of the Devil (Book Six)*
*Going Under (Book Seven)*
*Stealing Hope (Book Eight)*

## THE WHICKETT SERIES
*Art for Art's Sake: Meredith's Story (Book One)*
*Dani's Story (Book Two)* ... <Coming Soon>

## THE GRASSE RIVER SERIES
*Quite an Undertaking: Devon's Story (Book One)*
*Rebecca's Story (Book Two)* ... <Coming Soon>

## THE GIRLS' SPORTS SERIES (Children's Books Ages 9-12)
*Bases Loaded*
*Side Out*
*Live, Love, Lacrosse*

# GOING, GOING, GONE

## Susie's Story

### BOOK THREE IN THE CLARKSONVILLE SERIES

## BARBARA L. CLANTON

eBook ISBN    978-1-953734-18-1


Revised First Edition 2021

9 8 7 6 5 4 3 2 1


Cover design by Sarah (Forcoverservice)


Published by:
Bibi Books Publishing Company, LLC

# Dedication

To the memory of my mother-in-law Mamie Victoria Weathers.

# Acknowledgments

I'd like to acknowledge many people who have supported me while writing this story. Big giant humongous thanks go out to Sheri Milburn, Mary Jane Ambrico, Carmen Roldan, and Diana Schnitzer for being ever ready to help critique my words whenever I called, texted, or emailed. I also want to thank the fabulous Regal Crest team for their help and support – Mary Phillips, Trinka Kittle, Cathy LeNoir, and Donna Paw oski.

I also need to thank my ever-supportive family: My parents – Paul and JoAnne Clanton, my brothers –Paul and John Clanton and their respective families, and my partner's family—Mamie, Joe, Joey Weathers.

And then there is Jackie, my granite, who once said, "Life is like putting on 501 button jeans. You close one button at a time, rest, and then work on the next. It takes work, but you can do it." Life is so much fun with a built-in philosopher in the house.

# Table of Contents

## Author's Note to the Revised Edition

I was gifted the chance to go back and revise my earlier writing and have delighted in revisiting the gang in Clarksonville, who wanted their individual stories told. "Going, Going, Gone: Susie's Story" is Book Three in the Series and was initially published in 2011.

At the start of this story, it is no secret that the main character, Susie, is in love. As the story progresses, we see how that relationship grows and how Susie deals with others as they find out she is a lesbian.

This is a *revised* edition, not a second edition. Nothing major has changed in the story plot. Only the grammar, punctuation, and awkward things (to my current ears and eyes) have been changed, updated, or eliminated.

I'm confident that the emotions and situations will stand the test of time and that you, dear reader, will enjoy Susie's coming-out story.

Cheers,

Barb

Central Florida (March 2022)

# Chapter 1

## No One Would Care

Susie smacked a fist into her glove. The East Valley Nor'easters needed one more out to beat the Elmhurst Rage, and then she could whisk Marlee away to their private place. No one would miss them for two, maybe three hours.

"C'mon, Marlee," Susie yelled from left field. "Fire it in there." She leaned back on her heels and breathed in the sweet July air. Without thinking, she tucked a lock of escaped hair under her hat. *Dios mío*, Saturday morning games took forever.

When school had ended, Susie figured they would have all the time in the world to be together, but Marlee worked at D'Amico's restaurant in Clarksonville, and Susie babysat for Mrs. Johnson's kids in East Valley. Susie wanted to ditch the kids that summer so that she could get a real job, but her mother wouldn't let her. Mrs. Johnson was her mother's boss, after all. *Aay*, but why worry about that *mierda* when it was Saturday and Marlee was there.

Susie cheered when Marlee pitched the second strike to the batter. "One more, pitcher," she called. *One more, and we're out of here.*

Susie admired the sleekness of Marlee's cat-like grace as she pitched, the way her athletic body moved so effortlessly. Susie stood in the outfield and watched Marlee go from standing completely still to exploding off the pitching rubber toward the plate, throwing her whole body toward the catcher. Marlee expended so much energy in that one fluid motion that Susie almost felt guilty standing in one spot in the outfield. Somehow that didn't seem fair.

Susie rubbed the heel of her glove. She couldn't wait to run her fingers through Marlee's short silky blonde hair and then pull her down on the blanket. She'd rest her head on Marlee's chest and run her fingers over Marlee's tight abs. Marlee would hold her close and stroke her back. Was it possible to stay that way forever? Safe and secure? She closed her eyes and took a deep breath. *Dios*, she needed this game to be over.

Susie's eyes flew open when she heard shouting. Crap, a line drive was heading right for her. She made a split-second decision to dive, but as soon as she was airborne, she knew it was wrong. The ball careened off the grass just in front of her outstretched glove and whizzed by her head.

She landed with a thud. With a grunt, she pulled up to her knees and leaped to her feet to chase the ball down. Rachel, the center fielder, was already tracking it down at the fence. Rachel picked up the ball and heaved it to the shortstop. Abby held on to the ball as the runner glided easily into third base with a stand-up triple.

"Shit!" Susie muttered under her breath. She hated making errors, especially in front of Marlee. She slammed her glove against her thigh in frustration.

"Where's your head, Torres?" Coach Gellar called out to her. "No more bonehead mistakes."

Out of the corner of her eye, Susie watched her coach pacing in the dugout. What was the big deal? They were winning by a score of 3-1, and it was only the second game of their six-week summer season anyway.

Marlee grinned at Susie. Susie shrugged back and pounded her glove. She felt her cheeks get warm. "My bad, Marlee. My bad. Pick me up."

As Susie had hoped, Marlee struck out the next batter and sealed the Saturday morning victory for the East Valley Nor'easters.

"Ball game," the home plate umpire announced and took off her face mask.

Susie sprinted toward the pitcher's circle to join the infielders already in celebration. She patted Marlee on the back. "Way to go, Marlee."

Marlee's crystal blue eyes and devilish smile melted Susie down to her toes. Susie wondered if Marlee truly knew the physical effect she had on her. Later. She'd show her later when they were finally alone.

Susie and her teammates lined up for the high-fives with the other team. Susie got in line behind Marlee and pushed her ever so gently on the back. Marlee pushed back. It was their way to make physical contact in public, to say, "Hey, I like you," to hug each other with the whole world watching.

Once they got through the high-five line and huddled up for their team meeting with Coach Gellar, the razzing began.

"Nice catch, Susie," Rachel said with an exaggerated eye roll.

Susie felt the heat rising in her cheeks. "The sun. It got in my eyes."

Coach Gellar raised an eyebrow. "I'm sure that's exactly what happened. I'm sure it had nothing to do with daydreaming."

"Nope," Susie said but could tell that her coach wasn't amused. At all.

"Mm hmm." Coach Gellar pursed her lips together. She shook her head in clear disapproval, her short salt and pepper hair barely moving. "Anyway. Nice win, girls. Elmhurst is usually a pretty tough team, they travel all over the state, but their pitcher seemed kind of green today."

Marlee leaned against Susie ever so slightly. The bare skin on her forearm sent tingles up Susie's arm. Her heartbeat quickened, and she had trouble focusing on their coach.

"We're undefeated, but if some players don't start taking summer softball seriously, that'll change quickly." She looked each one of her players in the eye, but Susie was sure Coach Gellar glared at her for an extra-long moment. "But," the coach continued, "I'm going to challenge that. Most of you want to play softball in college. In order to do that, you have to play on a traveling team like ours. You have to compete with the very best. We've got mostly East Valley High School players on our team—"

"Panthers! Whoop whoop!" Abby started a chant, and most of the team enthusiastically joined in. All except Marlee.

Marlee leaned over and whispered to Susie, "Hey, Panther, you'd better stop hooting if you know what's good for you."

Susie clamped her lips shut but couldn't help the smile creeping up her face.

"And," Coach Gellar gestured toward Marlee, "since we've

invited McAllister and her catcher Lisa Brown from Clarksonville to play with us this season, it behooves us to put in a hundred and ten percent during every game. Their team, after all, knocked us out of the North Country playoffs to go on and win the state title."

Marlee was the only one to whoop, but her teammates smiled their admiration.

Coach Gellar's gaze again lingered on Susie for a moment. "We don't want them thinking we're a bunch of slackers on the other side of the county."

The team chuckled, but Susie sighed. Coach Gellar never let anyone forget a mistake. It would be a while before Susie would be able to accrue enough *atta girls* to combat her *bonehead mistake.*

"All right, girls," Coach Gellar continued, "our next game is Tuesday. Six o'clock sharp. Those of you who can get here by four will be able to take batting practice."

Susie groaned. What Coach meant was that she wanted every one of them there by four o'clock for batting practice. That was going to be tough because Mrs. Johnson didn't get home until four. Sometimes later.

The coach dismissed them but then turned back and added privately to Marlee, "Nice pitching, McAllister."

"Thanks, Coach." Marlee hesitated for a second and then added, "I don't want to seem rude, but I kind of miss Lisa."

Coach Gellar nodded as if she understood. "Back when I pitched at Cortland, I had a favorite catcher, too. You're stuck with Baxter for now until Lisa's hand heals."

"That's at least two more weeks." Marlee groaned.

"You'll live." Coach Gellar smiled and turned to yell to her team, "Everyone's back here Tuesday at 4:00 sharp!"

Susie and Marlee headed back to the dugout and sat hip to hip on the bench. Susie grabbed her bag and tossed her glove inside. She wanted to take off her hat, but that would have to wait until she got in Marlee's van and brushed her hair. No sense scaring the rest of the free world with hat head.

"Hey," Marlee said with a tap on Susie's thigh, "are we going to the usual spot?"

Susie stopped untying her cleats and sent Marlee a smoldering glance. She nodded once.

Marlee sucked in her lower lip. "Hurry up, then, slowpoke," she whispered. "It's bad enough we didn't see each other on our anniversary yesterday."

"*Aay, mi vida,* you're so impatient."

"Three-month anniversaries don't come along every day, you know." Marlee flashed a smile.

Susie melted. She lived for that smile because it was just for her.

Marlee threw her cleats into her bag and put a pair of flip-flops on over her white socks. "Are you going to finish taking off your cleats today or what?"

Susie whispered low, "I'll take off anything you want."

Marlee moaned just loud enough for Susie to hear.

Susie yanked off her shoes and threw them in her bag. She put on a pair of red crocs and stood up. "Ready to go?" If the team hadn't been milling about, she would have reached for Marlee's hand. She didn't think anybody knew that she was seeing Marlee, but she wasn't ready for them to find out yet. Neither she nor Marlee had come out of the closet to their respective families either. If Susie's parents ever found out, it would be as bad as the time she backed the car into the garage door. *Aay*, who was she kidding? This would be way worse. This would be off the Richter scale of disasters in her mother's life. She would never be able to show herself at another family reunion again.

Marlee sprang up off the bench, threw her bag over her shoulder, and winced. "Yee-ouch."

"Shoulder?"

"Mm hmm. Sometimes it gives me trouble."

"I'll rub it for you later," Susie said with a seductive grin.

"Promise?"

"*Sí, claro.*" Susie nodded. "Here, let me carry your bag for you."

"You sure?"

"Yeah." Susie shouldered Marlee's gear. "And now we need to go talk to the one who sent you to the hospital with that shoulder injury in the first place."

Marlee looked up and grunted. Christy Loveland was sitting on the first row of bleachers. "I forgave her for that a long time ago."

"I know. C'mon." Susie reached for Marlee's hand but then pulled back in frustration. Someday maybe they'd have the courage to hold hands in front of people.

Christy stood up when they opened the gate from the field. "Yo. What's up, chicklets?"

"Hey, Christy," Marlee said.

Susie gave Christy a quick hug. "Thanks for the ride today."

"No problem. I hear Puerto Ricans are bad drivers, so I'm making the roads safe for—"

Susie whacked her in the arm so that she couldn't finish her sentence.

"Can't take it, Rican?" Christy smiled as she backed away out of whacking range.

"*Chistosa.* Very funny." Susie rolled her eyes.

They headed toward the parking lot. "Where are Sam and Lisa today?" Christy asked.

"Oh," Susie said, "they're at Lisa's dad's wedding."

Christy cocked an eyebrow. "Are Lisa's parents divorced?"

"Not exactly." Marlee exchanged a look with Susie. "It's kind of a long story. One that we just found out about, actually. Apparently, Mr. Brown, the man we thought was Lisa's dad, is really her step-dad."

"No shit?" Christy's eyes grew wide for a moment. "I'm not the only one with issues then, am I?"

Susie shook her head. "Apparently, Lisa's biological father wanted to get back into her life, so there you go. She's at his wedding, and Sam's with her."

"Cool. Tell Lisa I said, uh…" Christy furrowed her brow. "Are congratulations in order? Well, whatever, tell her I said hi. Hopefully, I'll get to see her and Sam before I split for the golden land. And Jeri, too. I haven't talked to her since our last game. I don't know what Clarksonville's going to do for a center fielder now that Jeri's graduated."

"Me neither," Marlee said with a sigh.

"Hey, come to our game Tuesday," Susie said. "Sam'll be back, and I think Lisa's coming to meet the team."

"I'll get Jeri to come, too," Marlee added.

"Yeah, I can do that. I'm not leaving until Wednesday."

"*Qué bueno.*" Susie threw Marlee's softball bag in the back of the van and threw her own on top. She unzipped a side pocket and pulled out her hairbrush. She brushed her hair into a reasonably manageable mess. It would have to do for now.

Marlee asked Christy, "Are you all set for your big California move?"

"Just about." Christy nodded. "It's funny. My mom's been all teary-eyed about me going away to college."

"Pfft," Susie spat. "Why? Is she actually going to miss you? She wasn't around for most of your life."

"Yeah, really. I think she's finally facing the fact that I'm all grown up. And she's coming to terms with the fact that she's the mother of two college-aged girls."

Susie laughed. "You're probably right. She's crying over her lost youth."

Marlee grinned. "Sounds like you two are psychologists or something."

"Hey," Christy said with a laugh, "when you've gone to as much therapy as I have in the last two months, it wears off on you. And, you know what?" Christy asked, a grin spreading on her face.

"What?" Susie leaned against Marlee.

"I think I'm going to major in psychology once I get to UCLA. Maybe then I can analyze my stupid family."

Susie clapped Christy on the back. "Hey, don't forget you can always call your best friend."

"Who would that be?" Christy tried to keep a serious face.

"Cut it out, *chica*." Susie stuck out her lower lip. "Just for that, I may change my cell phone number."

Christy didn't banter back but smiled the sad sort of smile she'd been wearing since the night she threw the pitch at Marlee that sent her to the hospital. "I'd ask you guys to go to Stewart's for ice cream or something, but I know you kids want to be alone and get it on."

"Shut up." Susie smacked her friend good-naturedly on the arm. She briefly considered delaying their alone time to go with Christy, but she didn't think she could wait much longer. "Hey, why don't I come over tomorrow after I babysit the Johnson kids?"

"Johnson brats, you mean?" Christy rolled her eyes.

"Yeah, something like that." Susie smiled. The Johnson kids weren't brats. Nine-year-old Bethany was kind of bitter ever since her dad moved out, but overall, she was a good kid. And how in the world could the precious one-year-old baby Emma ever be considered a brat? She hadn't logged enough time on earth to even qualify.

"Oh, hey," Christy pulled out her phone, "let me take a picture of you guys. I don't have one."

"Okay." Susie and Marlee stood as close together as they dared in the busy parking lot and posed while Christy took their picture with her cell phone.

"Thanks. I'll send it to you when I get a sec."

"Cool," Marlee said. "We don't have many pictures of the two of us."

"All right, chicklets. I'm outta here."

Susie gave Christy a quick hug. "*Hasta mañana, chica.*"

"Yup, I'll see you tomorrow." Christy headed toward her car. "Don't do anything I wouldn't do," she called back over her shoulder.

"Hmm," Susie said with a laugh, "that leaves it wide open, doesn't it?"

Marlee smirked and shot Susie a suggestive look.

They were about to get into the van when someone called Marlee's name.

They turned to see a pretty blonde girl about their age walking toward them. Susie recognized her as the pitcher from Southbridge. When the girl reached them, she completely ignored Susie but looked Marlee directly in the eye. "Nice game, Marlee."

"Oh, thanks."

"I'm a pitcher, too."

"Oh, yeah?"

"Yeah, but I don't have near your speed. And how do you get so much movement on the ball?"

Marlee shrugged, but Susie could tell she was enjoying the attention.

The Southbridge pitcher took a step closer. "So, uh, think you could show me some pitches? You know," she gestured toward the field, "sometime?"

"Sure," Marlee answered quickly. "What d'ya want to learn? What's your name? You know mine. It's only fair I know yours."

The girl flicked her long, poorly dyed blonde hair behind her shoulders and giggled. "Bree."

Susie's stomach churned. How dare this chick from Southbridge flirt with her Marlee. She was skating on thin ice.

Marlee smiled and leaned ever so slightly closer to Bree. "That's a nice name."

"Marlee's a nice name, too. I saw that article about you winning States in the Clarksonville Courier. That was so cool."

"Thanks."

*Okay, that's enough.* Susie cleared her throat. "Marlee, we gotta go."

"Okay, yup." Marlee seemed to snap out of the spell Bree had captured her under. She pulled the van keys out of her pocket. "We'll talk later, Bree."

"Count on it."

Susie felt her face flush with anger. She glared at the girl, but the girl either didn't notice or didn't care. She apparently only had eyes for Marlee.

# Chapter 2
### Heart-Stealing Pitchers

Marlee pulled the van onto the barely discernible dirt road off County Road 62. Susie's heart sped up the closer they got to their hidden spot tucked away under the weeping willow tree between two cornfields. Sam had taken Susie there once during the brief time they were seeing each other. Marlee turned off the engine, and they undid their seatbelts.

Susie turned toward Marlee. "I wish we didn't have to hide like this."

"It's okay." Marlee swung around to face Susie. "I like being alone with you."

"You know that's not what I meant. I mean, we have to hide and—"

Marlee put a hand on Susie's arm. "I know what you mean, Jelly Bean."

"You knew what I meant, Jelly Bent?"

Marlee nodded and added a seductive smile.

Susie picked up the hand still resting on her arm and kissed each one of the fingertips in turn. "I need to thank this pitching hand personally for getting us out of that game."

"Yeah," Marlee laughed, "what was up with you missing that

line drive?"

Susie groaned. "I was thinking about you."

Marlee burst out laughing. "Oh, man. Are you kidding?"

Susie shook her head. "*Aay, Santo,* I'm afraid not. I thought you would strike out that girl, and then we could get out of there. I didn't even see the ball coming until I heard somebody yell."

"You're lucky Coach Gellar didn't chop your head off."

Susie sighed. "I know. I think it's my season to get picked on. Every season she picks somebody new to harass. Last season, it was Christy."

"Yeah, I saw that at our last game against you guys last spring. Coach Gellar really lit into her." Marlee reached behind her seat and pulled a Styrofoam cooler closer. "Do you want a coke or water?"

"Water."

Marlee handed her a bottle of water and took one out for herself. "You know, you only have one more school season left with Coach Gellar, and then you're free."

"I don't know if I'm going to survive it. I hope my coach in college isn't like that." Susie desperately wanted to go to the same college as Marlee, but Marlee never brought up the topic. Susie took a long pull from the bottle hoping Marlee would take the bait and mention college. No such luck.

"I like Coach Speers," Marlee said. "She's calm but smart. She knows how to motivate us without yelling."

"Your coach is cool." Susie rolled her eyes, "Coach Gellar's philosophy is what doesn't kill you, makes you stronger. You know?"

"Tell me about it." Marlee rubbed the shoulder on her pitching arm.

"Hey, I promised to rub that out for you." Susie tossed her bottle into one of the van's cup holders. "C'mere." She gestured for Marlee to lean in closer. Marlee started to turn around to present her shoulder, but Susie said, "Nuh, uh. We've been here for over three minutes, and you haven't even given me my three-month, one-day anniversary kiss yet."

Marlee whipped back around and murmured, "Happy anniversary, sweetie."

Susie's heart swelled. "You called me sweetie." No one had ever called her that before.

"Less talking. More kissing," Marlee said and leaned forward, her face mere inches away from Susie's.

Susie closed the gap and kissed Marlee's soft and tender lips. She put a hand behind Marlee's head to pull her closer and ran her fingers through Marlee's hair. Marlee put a hand just below Susie's throat and rubbed the fabric of the uniform jersey.

Susie groaned when Marlee pulled out of the kiss.

Marlee looked at Susie with longing. "Let's get out of these seats."

"Okay."

Marlee pointed to the blanket in the back of the van placed there for their private moments. "Inside or outside?"

Susie grinned. "I remember when you used to be the shy one."

Marlee smiled but repeated her question. "Inside or outside?"

"Outside. It's July. We'll be stuck inside the van or worse, my car when it gets colder."

Marlee nodded in agreement. They met on the passenger side, and Marlee spread the blanket under the tall willow tree.

"Here," Susie said, "sit down, and I'll massage that shoulder for you."

"Mmm," Marlee moaned in agreement and sat down cross-legged on the blanket.

Susie sat behind her and placed both hands on Marlee's pitching shoulder. "The usual spot?" Susie began to rub the strong shoulder muscles.

Marlee nodded. "All those playoff games in a row messed me up."

"Christy hitting you with a pitch is what messed you up."

"Yeah," Marlee agreed. "That feels so good. Can you go for the knots next?"

Susie dug her thumbs in at the hard knots in Marlee's back. "I'm sure being New York State champs was worth all that extra pitching."

"Yeah. Coach Gellar must have been pissed when we knocked your powerhouse East Valley team out of first place."

"*Dios mío*," Susie said, remembering the day they lost. "She reamed us out good, but she took it mostly out on Christy."

"Christy didn't need that, especially with all that stuff she was dealing with back then."

"I hope she finds what she's looking for in California," Susie said and hugged Marlee from behind and kissed the shoulder she had been massaging.

Marlee moved her shoulder around. "Ah, that feels so much better. I should probably put ice on it."

"I know something better than ice." Before Marlee could ask, Susie trailed several kisses along the newly massaged shoulder. The trail continued up Marlee's neck. She suckled the soft skin of Marlee's earlobe.

Marlee moaned and reached overhead and behind to stroke Susie's head. It wasn't long before Marlee turned around, and they kissed again under the shade of the willow tree. Susie put a hand on Marlee's chest and gently pushed her down on the blanket. She lay on her side and stroked Marlee's stomach as they kissed. She reached lower and ran her hands from hip to hip.

Marlee moaned and pulled away.

"Too much?" Susie stopped her hand motions.

"You—" Marlee cleared her throat. "You make me feel so much. I just, I—"

"It's okay, *mi vida*." Susie gave her a reassuring smile knowing that they had to go at Marlee's pace. She twirled a lock of Marlee's short blonde hair around her finger. "You have the prettiest color hair."

"I love yours, too." Marlee reached up and ran her fingers through Susie's long auburn tresses. "I love it when you wear your hair loose like this."

Susie smiled without breaking eye contact.

"Oh, God," Marlee shut her eyes for a moment. "You suck me in with those brown eyes of yours every time."

Susie's smile grew wider. "Let's not even go there, Miss crystal-blue eyes."

Marlee pulled Susie closer, and Susie laid her head on Marlee's chest. Susie was dying to take their relationship to the next level, her body ached for it, but Marlee obviously needed a little more time before they went further. For now, Susie would have to ache in silence.

Marlee stroked the head resting on her chest. "So, tell me about the first time you knew."

"Again?" Susie lifted her head to look at Marlee and grinned.

"Again." Marlee pushed Susie's head back down.

"Okay." Susie draped an arm across Marlee's tight stomach like she had imagined doing just before she made the error in the game. "Well, you know about Sam's yearlong crush on Lisa, right?"

"Yeah. Well, I didn't know about it back then."

"Okay, so Christy and I are totally teasing Sam on the bus, and I said something like, 'So are you going to get her phone number this time?'"

"And what did Sam say?"

"She told me to shut up," Susie said with a laugh. She trailed her fingers gently along Marlee's stomach. "She turned beet red, though, and then Christy said something like, 'Lisa's probably going out with that cute blonde pitcher of theirs.' Sam looked so devastated. It was as if the thought had never occurred to her."

"Did you think I was cute?"

Susie picked her head up and flashed Marlee a look of disbelief. "Of course, I did. All Sam and I ever talked about was the Clarksonville softball team, so I thought about you a lot, actually."

"I thought about you, too, but you didn't know I had a major league crush on you then, did you?"

"Nope. And especially not when you threw that pitch at my head."

"Ahh, c'mon," Marlee groaned. "It slipped. Am I ever going to live that one down?"

"Probably never, *mi vida*, but, hey, it kind of brought us together."

"I guess."

"So, anyway, you knocked me down, I picked myself up, and got right back in the batter's box. You were turning the most glorious shade of red. You were so cute that I think I fell in love with you right on the spot."

"You grinned at me. I thought you were plotting your revenge."

"No way. I was plotting how to get your phone number. I asked Christy if I could invite you guys to hang out with us at her house. She was cool with that. You know how she likes to party."

"Yeah, really."

"So, I gestured for Jeri to come over. I feel bad. I kind of used Jeri to get to you. I didn't really know her that well. My dad knows her dad and all, but I was desperate. I said, 'We're having a party at Christy's on Friday. Why don't you guys come out? The more the merrier.' Then I nodded my head toward you and Lisa."

"I saw Jeri talking to you guys," Marlee said. "I should have walked over. I was too shy, I guess."

"If you had, we could have saved a whole lotta time and gotten together so much sooner."

"The whole world would have seen how much we liked each other."

"No kidding, but don't forget that somebody had *un novio*."

Marlee inhaled through her teeth. "I know. Me having a boyfriend must have been totally confusing for you."

"Yeah, just a bit."

"One time when I was kissing Bobby, I imagined I was kissing you."

"You did?"

"Yeah." The embarrassment was clear in Marlee's voice. "I started getting excited and kissed him harder."

"*Dios mío.*"

"Yeah, he thought I was totally responding to him. When I realized what was happening, I made him take me home."

"What a tease," Susie said with a grin.

"I didn't mean to be." Marlee grimaced. "He pretty much broke up with me right after that."

"Sorry."

"Nah, he moved on right away, and it gave you and me the green light."

"Ahh, very nice." Susie reached under Marlee's shirt and ran her fingernails lightly across her stomach. "You know what?"

"What?"

"I saw you watching me talk to Jeri that day."

"You did?"

Susie nodded. "I smiled when you glanced over, but you looked away so fast you must have gotten whiplash."

"I didn't want you to catch me staring."

"Again, you might have saved us some time."

Marlee laughed. "After the game, when you whispered in my ear about serving you up a grand slam pitch? I just about had a coronary."

"I remember how good you smelled."

"I did? You never told me that. I was all sweaty and gross from the game."

"Mmm. You don't smell bad after games, Marlee. You smell like…"

"What?"

"You smell like *you,* my heart-stealing pitcher." Susie burrowed her nose into Marlee's uniform jersey.

"Is that a good thing?"

"Mm hmm." Susie sat up on one elbow and gazed into Marlee's eyes. "A very good thing." She brushed a lock of hair off of Marlee's face and caressed her cheek. She let her fingers move over Marlee's mouth. Marlee opened her mouth slightly as her breathing got heavier. Susie traced Marlee's lips with a finger and then slid her finger in slightly. Marlee caught the finger in her teeth and ran her tongue along the tip.

"Kiss me," Marlee said around the captured finger.

Susie scooted up higher on the blanket and gently extracted her finger. She pressed down gently on Marlee's lips with her own. Marlee threw her arms around Susie's neck and pulled her closer. Susie felt the blood rush to her face when their bodies pressed together. *Dios mío,* how she wished she could feel Marlee's actual

21

skin against hers, but she wasn't going to rush her.

Marlee pulled Susie away for a moment, her breathing labored. "I want…"

"What, baby, what do you want?"

"I want you on top of me," Marlee whispered shyly.

Susie didn't hesitate and threw her leg on the other side of Marlee's. She let the weight of her body fall gently.

"Mmm," Marlee moaned. "That's so nice."

Susie held herself up with one arm so she wouldn't mash Marlee to bits and leaned closer for more kisses. She felt Marlee move rhythmically beneath her. A rush of heat flushed Susie's body as they rocked together.

"Oh, God," Marlee said. "I want to feel more of you." She tugged on Susie's uniform jersey.

Susie shifted her weight off Marlee and sat up. She encouraged Marlee to help tug the shirt off. Susie felt the warm July breeze on her bare torso, covered only by her sports bra.

Marlee ran her fingers over Susie's bare stomach sending delicious shivers through Susie's entire body. Just as Susie leaned in for another kiss, Marlee jerked her head to the side. "Do you hear that?"

"What?"

"It sounds like a car."

They sat stone still for a moment.

Susie heard the distinctive rumble of an engine approaching. "¡Mierda! It's heading right for us. C'mon."

Marlee threw Susie's shirt at her and leaped up. She grabbed the edge of the blanket in panic and pulled at it before Susie finished putting her shirt back on. Susie leaped off the blanket and couldn't help the nervous giggles bubbling up from her stomach. Marlee started giggling, too, as she balled up the blanket. Laughing hard, they flew toward the van, tripping over each other on the way. Once inside, Marlee gunned the engine, threw it into reverse, and took off as if their lives depended on it.

# Chapter 3

### We Saw You Kissing Her

"*Dios mío*," Susie said in frustration. "I can't believe we almost got caught by that farmer."

"You don't think he saw us, do you?" Marlee slowed the van down. She had been speeding down C.R. 62 as they made their getaway.

"Nah. I'm just glad his stupid tractor was slow, 'cuz that gave us time to get the hell out of there."

They drove around East Valley for a while trying to find a good spot to be alone, but every time they thought they had privacy, a car would pull up, or somebody would walk by. The last place they tried was an elementary school parking lot, but apparently, there was some kind of school function going on that afternoon, and their privacy was, once again, invaded.

Marlee banged the steering wheel in obvious frustration. Susie figured Marlee was as frustrated as she was. After a while, Marlee pulled the van onto Susie's street and then into her driveway. The three-bedroom, two-story house sat on an acre of land, giving the house and yard plenty of elbow room between neighbors.

Marlee grinned. "We have to find a new spot now, you know."

"I know."

Marlee put the car in park and turned off the engine. "Oh, your house is so cute."

"Thanks. A whole acre is a bitch to mow, but it's nice."

"Can I come inside?"

"Umm…" Susie hesitated.

"C'mon. You met *my* mom."

A thousand thoughts rushed around Susie's brain, and she couldn't think of a single response.

"Are you ashamed of me?"

"Never, *mi vida*, never."

"Then what is it?"

Susie looked away and undid her seatbelt. She didn't know how to tell Marlee that her mother would kill her, probably kill them both, if she found out her daughter was *una lesbiana*. She had no idea how her father would react. "You have to give me time, *mi amor*. I need to break it to them gently."

"You can tell them I'm your friend. They don't have to know anything else."

"My mother will know instantly that we're more than friends."

Marlee pressed her lips together as if she were holding back something she really wanted to say. After a moment, she nodded and looked away.

Susie opened the passenger door and went around to the back of the van. She pulled out her softball bag and then closed the door gently. She took a deep breath, walked up to the open driver's side window, and leaned her elbows on the frame.

"I'll see you on Tuesday?" Susie flashed her toothiest grin at

Marlee.

"I guess."

"Don't be mad."

Marlee took a deep breath. "It doesn't seem fair. I mean, I've talked to your mom, your brother, and even your *abuelita* on the phone, but for some reason, I'm not allowed to meet them."

Susie checked the time on her cell phone. Her mother wasn't due home from work for at least another hour. If she could get Marlee out of the house and headed back to Clarksonville before then, it might work. "Okay."

"Okay, what?"

"Come on in."

"Really?"

Susie's heart leaped when she saw Marlee's blue eyes brighten. She leaned in the driver's side window and kissed Marlee quickly, wishing it could be more. "Really. C'mon."

Marlee whipped her seatbelt off and scampered out of the van. They walked up the driveway toward the two-story colonial. Susie turned around and pointed to the second floor of the detached garage. "That's my room."

"Can I see it?" Marlee grinned.

"Sure." Susie frantically tried to remember the state she'd left her room in before Christy picked her up for the game. Did she make her bed? Did she put her dirty clothes in the hamper? She couldn't remember. "Let's go inside the house first."

Susie heard the blaring television even before she opened the screen door to the mudroom. Dark wood paneling and winter coats hung in wait for the inevitable cold to return to the north country of upstate New York. The room was almost depressing. She kicked her thirteen-year-old brother Miguel's muddy sneakers out of the way and shook off her crocs. She gestured for Marlee to take off her flip-flops.

"Oh, man," Marlee grinned sheepishly and slid them off, "I hope my socks don't have holes in them."

Susie laughed. "*Aay*, no worries, but that orange clay line on them is quite attractive."

Marlee looked down and brushed at her socks. "Oh, great. That's going to make a really good impression."

Susie pointed to her own socks. "I've got a matching pair right here, so don't worry about it." Susie stroked Marlee's reddening cheeks. "Ready to meet *mi abuela*?"

"Your grandmother?"

Susie nodded. "C'mon." She stepped up from the mudroom into the front hallway. She wondered what Marlee thought about the shrine to the Virgin Mary that her *abuelita* had set up in the entryway. Her *abuelita* never failed to cross herself and mumble a prayer of thanks to the blessed Virgin at least once a day.

"Susana?" Susie's *abuelita* called from the living room.

"*Sí, soy yo. Y tengo una amiga conmigo, también.*"

Marlee raised an eyebrow in question.

"I told her I had a friend with me." Susie led the way past the shrine to the living room.

Susie's *abuelita* sat on the couch, crocheting a sweater.

"*Abuelita*," Susie said, "*ésta es mi amiga*, Marlee." She turned to

Marlee. "This is my *abuelita*."

Susie hid a smile as Marlee's cheeks turned bright red. It was one of the things Susie loved about her.

"It's nice to meet you," Marlee said and smiled.

Susie's *abuelita* peered at Marlee over her glasses. "*Ah, tu eres un querubín.*"

Susie burst out laughing.

"What did she say?" Marlee shot a wide-eyed glance at Susie.

"Tell you later." Susie reached over the couch and grabbed the remote control to the television. She turned the volume down to a more human level.

Susie's *abuelita* put her crocheting down, stood up to her full height of not quite five feet, and smiled at Marlee with a twinkle in her eye. "It nice to meet, Miss Marlee."

Susie coughed into her hand to hide the surprised grin at her *abuelita's* attempt to speak English.

"It's so nice to meet you, too, finally." Marlee bowed slightly and added, "It's been nice talking to you on the *teléfono*."

"*Ah, sí, sí, muy bien.*" Susie's *abuelita* sat back down on the couch and picked up the remote control. "*Un querubín,*" she mumbled to herself as she turned her attention back toward the television and cranked the volume to maximum.

Susie steered Marlee through the doorway into the kitchen. When they were out of view from her *abuelita*, she leaned back against the countertop and pulled Marlee to her. She held Marlee by the hips and leaned in for a kiss.

Marlee hesitated and looked back toward the doorway. "Where

are your parents?"

"Oh, don't worry. They're at work. *Mi hermano* is around here somewhere." At Marlee's confused expression, Susie clarified. "My brother Miguel. He's around here somewhere, probably playing games on his computer or out skateboarding with his friends."

Susie pulled her closer. Nervous as she was having Marlee in her house, Susie lost herself in the kiss. After they separated, Susie pointed out the kitchen door. "So that was *mi abuela.*"

Marlee's eyes sparkled. "She's so cute. You didn't tell me she knew English."

Susie laughed and stroked Marlee's back. "She doesn't. I don't know what that was all about back there." She shrugged, "Maybe she remembered that you're not too fluent in Spanish."

"I know three whole words in Spanish. That's about it."

Susie grinned. "I'll teach you more if you want."

"Hey what did your *abuelita* call me? *Un querubín?*"

"She called you a little angel."

"A little angel?" Marlee laughed. "I'm pretty sure I've never been called that before."

Susie reached for Marlee's hand. "C'mon, let me show you my room."

They made their way to the mudroom, donned their respective shoes, and headed to the garage.

"This is so cool," Marlee said. "I can't believe your room is in a separate building. It's like you have your own apartment."

"Yup, it's kinda like that. Remember that weekend you almost got to stay over?"

"Thanks to Christy, I spent the night at East Valley Hospital instead."

Susie opened the door to a set of stairs leading up to her bedroom.

Marlee followed right behind. "Don't you think your mother would have been suspicious with me staying over, though?"

"Yeah, she would have. Obviously, I wasn't thinking clearly."

At the top of the stairs, she opened the door to her room that spanned the width of the two-car garage below. Susie made a quick scan. No dirty clothes in sight and her bed was made. Thank goodness she'd decided to be neat that morning.

"Nice weight set." Marlee ran a hand over the barbell resting on the bench press. A rack of hand weights lined the wall next to an exercise ball and a jump rope. Marlee eyed Susie up and down. "So this is how you got so strong."

Susie flexed her muscles and then laughed. "Yeah, I like lifting. It helps me hit grand slams off Clarksonville pitchers."

Marlee laughed and then smacked Susie playfully on the arm. "Shut up. I'm never throwing you a hittable pitch again. Ever."

"*Aay*, we'll see about that, now won't we?"

"Oh, wow." Marlee walked over to the bookshelf and laughed. "Most people put books on their bookshelves."

"Not rocks?" Susie put an arm around Marlee's waist while Marlee picked up her rocks one by one.

"What's this pretty pink one?" Marlee held it up so the light would shine through it.

"That's my favorite. It's rose quartz. Silicon dioxide."

"Isn't silicon what they make breast implants out of?" Marlee looked confused.

Susie laughed. "I think that's silicone, with an *e* at the end. It's made with silicon and a bunch of other stuff, too. Sand is silicon dioxide but in a granular form. Do you know how they make glass?"

Marlee shook her head.

"They basically melt sand. Silicon's in toothpaste, too."

Marlee's eyes widened. "There's sand in my toothpaste?"

"Kind of. It helps remove plaque and stuff." Susie picked up a piece of granite that Sam had brought her from Maine, "Granite is an igneous rock." She felt shy all of a sudden, and her cheeks got warm. "Sorry, I'm a rockhound."

"That's cool that you want to study geology." Marlee put down the rose quartz and reached for the small piece of granite. She examined it and a few of the other rocks for a few minutes while Susie explained each one, and then she wandered around Susie's room checking out the stuff on Susie's dresser, nightstand, and desk.

Susie sat on her bed. With anyone else, she might have felt that her privacy was being invaded, but she knew Marlee just wanted to know more about her. It was, after all, the first time Marlee had been up in her room. "Do you still want to be an engineer?"

"Yeah, I think so. Maybe environmental engineering. Maybe physics. My math teacher is pushing me to apply to Cornell. I think she went there, but I don't know. We'll see." She stopped in front of a closed door but didn't open it. "Is this your closet?"

"Nope, that's the bathroom." Susie pointed toward the door near her rock collection. "That one's the closet."

"That's so cool that you have your own bathroom."

"Shower, too."

Marlee blushed and sat down in the desk chair. She swiveled around in the chair to face the desk and ran her hands along the old wood. "Is this where you do your homework?"

"Mostly. Sometimes I sit on the bed." She smoothed the bedspread with her hand. "This is usually where I am when I call you." She raised a suggestive eyebrow.

"Oh, yeah?" Marlee's expression spoke volumes.

Susie patted the bed in invitation.

Marlee stood up, never losing eye contact. She sat next to Susie and leaned in for a kiss. Susie put her arms around Marlee's waist and met soft, receptive lips with her own. Still holding on by the waist, Susie fell back against the bed and pulled Marlee on top of her.

Marlee put her hands out to brace herself. "Am I squishing you?"

"Not a chance." Susie pulled her down again, enjoying Marlee's weight on her. She shimmied her body so that her thigh landed strategically between Marlee's.

"Ooh," Marlee moaned and increased the pressure. Susie was a little surprised by Marlee's boldness but didn't question it and lost herself in Marlee's kisses. Marlee kissed Susie along her jawline to her ear. She suckled Susie's tender earlobe sending delightful shivers down Susie's body, and then continued her exploration, kissing Susie's neck and collar bone. She pulled the collar of Susie's shirt down and kissed the tender skin underneath Susie's throat.

Susie heard herself moan. She was reaching the point of no return, so she clasped her arms around Marlee's back and then, with one swift movement, rolled Marlee onto her back. She put her own weight on top but leaned on one elbow so that Marlee would be able to breathe. She left a trail of kisses copying Marlee's path and was just about to pull the neck of Marlee's shirt lower when she opened her eyes, and her clock came into view. "*¡Aay, mierda!*" She bolted off of Marlee. "C'mon, get up. You have to go."

"Why?" Marlee sat up quickly and raked her fingers through her hair. "What happened?"

"My mother."

"What about her?"

"She should have been home by now." Susie leaped off the bed. Marlee stood up, and Susie grabbed both of her hands. "*Lo siento, mi vida,* but…"

"Okay, okay. I'm going."

The dejected tone in Marlee's voice made Susie's heart clench. *Aay, Dios,* there was no way she could make it right. She'd call her later and beg for forgiveness.

They hurried down the stairs, but Susie stopped at the bottom and opened the outside door a crack. She sighed in relief. Her mother's car wasn't in the driveway.

"Okay, c'mon." Susie opened the door, and they hustled to Marlee's van.

Once Marlee was safely inside the driver's seat with her seatbelt fastened and the engine running, Susie leaned in the window, "Please forgive me, *mi vida.* I'll make it up to you."

"Promise?"

"Yup." Susie gave Marlee a quick kiss and stepped back, hoping Marlee wouldn't hate her.

"Bye." Marlee waved and turned her head to back the car out of the driveway. Marlee stopped at the end of the driveway because a car was heading her direction on the road. Susie groaned. It was her mother. Her mother's car slowed down and then stopped. Marlee, obviously confused, looked to Susie for guidance. Susie waved the back of her hand toward the road, indicating that Marlee should continue to back out. Marlee nodded, and Susie held her breath, waiting to see what would happen. Marlee backed out, put the van in drive, and headed down the road past Susie's mother.

Susie wasn't sure if Marlee waved back one more time or not. She couldn't think over the pounding of her heart as her mother pulled into the driveway. Susie uprooted her feet and went over.

"*Hola, Mami.* You're late today."

"*Aay,* Mrs. Johnson gave me a ton of things to do just as my shift ended."

"She works you too hard."

"It's okay. I enjoy my work." She opened the trunk of her car. "Ah, Susana, can you get the bags from the trunk? I went shopping on my lunch break, which is probably why my boss made me work late."

"Because you didn't work through your lunch break like you usually do?"

Her mother shrugged.

She reached into the trunk for the Walmart bags. One was

heavy with cans of condensed milk. Ooh, maybe her *abuelita* was going to make flan for dessert. Susie breathed a sigh of relief as she pulled out the bags. At least her mother wasn't giving her the fifth degree about who Marlee was.

"They had the cutest little sundresses at Walmart today. You should stop by and get one."

Susie groaned. She wasn't out of the woods yet. "Okay, *Mami.*" She had no intention of going to Walmart to shop for sundresses. She had enough in her closet already and only wore those occasionally, like the one she'd just worn to Christy's graduation.

They headed toward the front door. Her mother reached for the handle but didn't open it. A lump formed in Susie's throat. Here it was.

"Who was that girl?" Her mother pointed toward the end of the driveway where Marlee had stopped the van.

Susie swallowed hard and cursed herself for doing it because her mother had seen. "Oh, she pitches for my summer team. She gave me a ride home from the game." *And she's just a friend, Mami, just a friend.*

"Was that Marlee?"

Susie willed herself to get her nerves under control. "*Sí, Mami.* Should we go in now?"

Her mother looked at her hard and steady as if trying to read her mind, but just when Susie was about to crack under the pressure, her mother turned toward the door and opened it.

Susie breathed a slow sigh of relief and followed her mother into the kitchen. She put the bags on the kitchen table. "I'm going to my room to take a shower, okay?"

"Come back and set the table for dinner in an hour."

"Okay."

Susie turned around, thinking she was free and clear when her mother blurted, "I want to meet this Marlee girl."

"Okay." Susie didn't wait for her mother to add anything more and bolted toward the garage like an antelope running from a lion.

She reached for the garage doorknob but stopped when she smelled cigarette smoke. Miguel. It had to be. She sneaked around the back of the garage, the side hidden from the house, and found her brother and his friend Scott. Each of them held a cigarette inexpertly in their hands, trying to look cool.

Susie stomped her way toward them. "Miguel Rafael Torres, put that cigarette out." She stood over the two barely teenage boys.

Miguel looked up at his sister and took another puff, which infuriated her. She reached down and swatted the cigarette out of his hand. She stepped on it with her crocs.

"Scott," she shook a finger at him, "you'd better get outta here before I kick your ass, too." She glared at him and tried not to smile when his eyes grew wide.

Scott mashed his cigarette out on the ground and leaped up. "See ya later, dude," he said to Miguel and scooped up his skateboard before scurrying away.

"What the hell are you doing?" Susie pointed to her brother. "Trying to ruin your life? You're thirteen." She glared at him.

Her brother glared back. "Oh, yeah? Well, we saw you kissing her."

## Chapter 4

### A Real Job

Susie snarfed her dinner, reheated *arroz con habichuelas* from the night before. They were having leftover rice and beans again because her father wouldn't be home from his Vermont business trip until much later that evening. It was one of his quirks; he didn't like leftovers. Susie tapped her finger on the table, lost in thought. She and her brother had reached a tentative truce behind the garage. He would keep her secret about Marlee, and she would keep his about smoking. Of course, expecting a thirteen-year-old boy to keep a secret was risky business, and Susie knew it.

She wished her family would hurry up and finish so she could do the dishes and then bolt to her room to see if Marlee had texted her back yet. Earlier, when Marlee left, Susie ran back to her room and sent a text that read, "Love you," but Marlee didn't respond right away. Susie took a shower, threw a towel around herself, and grabbed the phone off the bed. Still no text. She got dressed, blow dried her hair, and even did a few sit-ups to pass the time, but her phone remained agonizingly silent. Her mother had a strict rule about cell phones at the dinner table, so she left it on her bed when it was time to help with dinner.

After setting the table and eating quickly, Susie sat as patiently as possible. She faced her brother but didn't really see him. That is until he stuck his tongue out at her. She didn't take the bait. She just rolled her eyes. Maybe she could bribe him to help her in the kitchen, but she doubted he'd go for it. Her parents never made him help out in the kitchen, so why would he bother? Especially when he had Marlee to hold over her. Her *abuelita* would probably try to help, but Susie never let her almost seventy-year-old *abuelita* do dishes. She had earned the right to go back to the television after dinner. Most of the time, her *abuelita* made dinner anyway, since both her parents worked long and sometimes strange hours.

Susie drank the rest of her milk and half-listened to her mother tell a story about a woman who got to the hospital so late that they didn't have time to get her up to the neo-natal ward where her mother worked. The woman gave birth in the emergency room. Susie wasn't interested in babies or children. That's why she found it weird that her mother insisted she babysit for Mrs. Johnson's kids again that summer. Kids weren't her thing. Unless Marlee wanted kids. Susie's eyes grew wider. What if Marlee wanted a houseful of kids? *Aay, Dios mío. I'm going to have to learn to like them.*

Her mother's laughter brought her back to the present. "Susana, you look horrified."

"Hmm?" She frantically scanned her brain for a lie. "Oh, I was thinking about that lady giving birth." She shivered. "¡*Uf*!"

"It's a beautiful thing," her mother said. She turned to Miguel, "Are you finished?" He nodded. "Go outside and play." He threw his napkin on his plate and bolted out the front door.

Susie's *abuelita* stood up and reached for Miguel's plate.

38

"*Aay, no, no, Abuelita,*" Susie admonished. "I'll get the dishes. Isn't *Sabado Gigante* on TV?"

Her *abuelita's* eyes lit up. "*Aay, me gusta Don Francisco.*"

Susie hid a smile behind her hand.

Susie's mother laughed. "We all know about your crush on Don Francisco." She waved her mother-in-law toward the living room. "Go on. We'll do the dishes."

Susie exchanged an amused glance with her mother and then gathered the dirty dishes from the table. She headed into the kitchen where, a few short hours earlier, she had kissed Marlee passionately. She prayed that Marlee had texted her back. C'mon, she should be home already. It only took about forty-five minutes to get to Clarksonville from East Valley. Her eyes widened. What if Marlee had been in an accident with the van? Marlee had only gotten her license in June, about a month ago, and C.R. 62 could be tricky if logging trucks or Amish buggies were on the road.

Trying her best not to let her anxiety show, Susie threw her dish rinsing and pot washing skills into overdrive.

"Slow down, Susana," her mother admonished. "Where's the fire?" Her mother took the rinsed dishes and placed them precisely into the dishwasher.

"Sorry." Susie forced herself to slow down. Before starting on the pots, she put the remaining rice and beans into a plastic container. She snapped the lid tight and tossed it into the fridge. "I guess I'm still energized from my game today."

"Did you win?"

"Mm hmm." Susie nodded. "M—" She stopped herself short.

She was just about to say that Marlee had pitched a good game, but bringing up Marlee might bring her mother's suspicions to light. "My coach said we have a long schedule ahead." She rejoiced silently that she'd found a suitable M-word to start the sentence with.

Her mother shot her a sidelong glance. "Why do you play that game?"

"*Mami*," Susie said with a disapproving groan, "you know I like to play. And…"

"What?"

"I'm pretty good at it." She washed and rinsed the last pot and put it in the drying rack. She reached out and dried her hands on the dry end of her mother's towel. "Not to mention that all my friends play."

"Does that include Marlee?"

A warning shot of adrenaline hit every nerve in her body, but she stayed cool. "Yup. Marlee, Sam, Lisa, Rachel, and Abby. They all play on the summer team." She threw in a string of names, hoping Marlee's wouldn't stand out as much that way. Susie regarded her mother, careful not to ignite whatever was brewing just below the surface.

Her mother nodded knowingly, but Susie wasn't sure just what it was her mother knew. Susie breathed an inner sigh of relief when her mother released her gaze and reached for the last pot to dry. "So," her mother asked, "when does Christy leave for California?"

"Wednesday. I'm going over tomorrow to hang out with her after Mrs. Johnson's."

Her mother glanced at the kitchen clock. "Your father should be home in a few hours. He'll expect you home tomorrow for Sunday dinner. Your *abuelita* is making *arroz con pollo*."

"And *flan* for dessert?" Susie liked her *abuelita's* chicken and rice, but her flan custard dessert was out of this world.

Her mother's warm smile sent Susie right back to childhood wrapped in her mother's arms. Susie didn't want to disappoint that smile or risk never seeing it again. Introducing her parents to Marlee might just do that.

Her mother patted Susie on the arm. "I bought the rest of the ingredients for flan at Walmart today, so it's up to you to persuade *tu abuela* to make it."

Susie squealed like a little girl, put her hands together, and looked skyward, praying to God to make flan happen on Sunday. "I won't stay long at Christy's. She's busy packing anyway."

"What is she going to study at UCLA?"

"Psychology, I think." Small talk was good. The longer they stayed away from the subject of Marlee, the better.

Her mother made a tsk sound and shook her head. "That's a waste."

"Why?" Personally, Susie thought it would do her friend good.

"What kind of job is she going to get with a degree in psychology? *Aay Santo, estos niños hoy en día no tienen sentido común*."

Susie took offense at her mother calling her best friend senseless but knew better than to challenge her.

"And, what, *Dios dame paciencia*," her mother looked skyward, "have you decided to study in college?" Before Susie could answer, her mother added, "Clarksonville Community College has one of the state's best registered-nursing programs, and after two years, you'd not only have your RN but an associate degree, too." She peered at Susie as if it had already been decided.

Susie leaned back against the counter. The way her mother was gearing up, it looked like they might be there for a while. "You know I want to study geology or earth science. Maybe even meteorology."

Her mother looked skyward again, and her lips moved silently. Susie looked down at the linoleum, knowing not to interrupt her mother as she prayed. After what seemed like an eternity, her mother finally said, "Susana."

Susie looked up.

"What kind of job will you get studying rocks or the earth or meteors?"

Susie tried not to laugh. She didn't dare correct her mother that meteorology was the study of the weather, not meteors. She decided on a safer road. "Geology's more than just rocks, *Mami*. Geologists study earthquakes and volcanoes and floods and stuff. Geologists help us understand the Earth and global warming. Brockport has a really good geology—"

"What kind of living are you going to make?" her mother interrupted. "No. You need a real job after college."

It was not the first time she and her mother had the nurse versus geologist argument and, something told Susie it wouldn't be the last either. Susie steeled her chin. She was going to study geology or earth science in college even if she had to pay for it herself.

"*Mami*, can I go now?" Susie desperately wanted out of the

conversation and back to her room. She had a cell phone to check.

Susie's mother glared at her as if trying to figure out a way to talk some sense into her. "Get the laundry out of the dryer first, okay?"

Susie took a slow and careful breath. "Okay." What her mother really meant was to fold the clothes and put them away in each person's room where they belonged. She headed for the door to the basement on the far side of the kitchen, determined to make quick work of her task and then fly back to her room. She flicked the light on in the stairwell and descended the steps as quickly as she could.

The basement was unfinished, so she kept an old pair of crocs down there so she wouldn't get her socks filthy. She slipped them on and opened one of the windows to get some air flowing in the stuffy basement. She opened the dryer and groaned. Whites. Why did it have to be whites? It was going to take her forever to match up all the stupid socks and get them to the right room.

Midway through her drudge work, she jumped when her brother started singing, "Susie and Marlee sittin' in a tree. K-i-s-s-i-n-g." He knelt outside by the open basement window.

"Shut up, jerk." She slammed the window shut and went back to her folding.

Once the clothes were folded and delivered to the proper rooms, she slithered back to her room over the garage. Luckily her brother was nowhere in sight. Just in case, she locked both the outside door and the door to her room at the top of the stairs.

She forced herself to pick up her cell phone calmly. She held it to her chest and whispered a quick prayer. "Please let there be a text from her." She slowly turned the phone over and looked at the display. No text. No voicemail. No missed call, either. She sat down hard on the bed, her disappointment deep.

There must be some mistake. Marlee always texted her back. Maybe the phone wasn't getting a signal. Nope. Strong signal. Susie powered down her phone and then turned it on again, hoping to hear the chime of an incoming text. She groaned when she heard nothing.

She stood up with her phone in one hand and ran her fingers over the rose quartz with the other. "I'm sorry, *mi vida*." She looked in the direction of Clarksonville. "I'll make it up to you, I promise."

She hit the voice dial button and said, "Marlee" into the phone, and it dialed Marlee's cell phone number. "C'mon," Susie pleaded. "Pick up." She groaned when the call went straight to voice mail. "Hey, Marlee. Sorry I had to rush you out of here today." A few seconds ticked by as she tried to figure out what to add. "My mother is giving me grief about college again." Another few seconds went by. "Call me later if you want. I'll be home." *Duh.* Susie rolled her eyes at her lack of phone skills. "Okay, I love you. Bye."

Susie clicked her phone shut and pouted. This was how things had started when Sam was about to break up with her. No returned texts or phone calls. She paced for a while until a brilliant idea came to her.

She reopened her phone and scrolled through her contacts. She found the entry for Marlee's home phone and hit the talk button. She was proud of her ingenuity and smiled. Her smile was short-lived when Marlee's mother told her that Marlee had come home from the game, showered, and then bolted right back out the door.

Where could Marlee have gone? Lisa and Sam were at that wedding, and Jeri was working at her family's restaurant. She sat on the bed again.

"Bree. It has to be." Susie slumped back against her pillows. "Marlee went to see that *idiota estúpida* from Southbridge."

# Chapter 5

### She's in Love. With a Girl!

Susie rifled through the mound of laundry on the coffee table as Bob the Builder and his Can-Do Crew built an athletic field on the television screen. Luckily, she'd only seen that particular episode twice before, so it wasn't that bad. Susie hated Sundays at the Johnsons. Sundays were laundry days. She had to make sure she timed everything right so all the laundry would be washed, dried, and folded before Mrs. Johnson got home. All that and she had to make their dinner too, like she did every night. She folded one of baby Emma's bibs. Actually, now that she thought about it, house cleaning days were worse than laundry days. Mrs. Johnson was particular about everything. Leave one speck of dust, and she cried foul. Susie dusted all day long on house cleaning days, just to make sure Mrs. Johnson wouldn't give her grief about it. The only day Susie could kind of slack off was on Fridays, mowing and weeding day. Although Mrs. Johnson inspected the lawn with a critical eye, she usually ignored the gardens.

Baby Emma had just turned a year old and was happily sitting on the floor chewing on the end of a toy cell phone, the kind that made real cell phone noises when the buttons were pushed. Emma's nine-year-old sister, Bethany, had holed herself up in her room to play games on her computer. She was convinced she didn't need a babysitter, and Susie was just fine letting her do whatever she wanted. One less kid to worry about.

Susie folded a onesie and placed it in the laundry basket. She picked up her cell phone to check the time. That's what she told herself anyway. It wasn't to see if Marlee had finally texted back or anything. It was five minutes before four o'clock. Susie had been there since seven that morning, and if she were lucky, Mrs. Johnson would be walking in the door any minute.

Susie jumped when the phone rang in her hand. Joy ran through her heart when she saw her favorite pitcher's name on the display.

She flipped open the phone. "Hey, stranger." She anticipated the smooth timber of Marlee's voice and wasn't disappointed.

"Hey," Marlee said. "I'm on my break. I can't talk too long, though. The Sunday dinner rush will be picking up soon." Marlee worked as a waitress at D'Amico's, her friend Jeri's family restaurant in Clarksonville.

"That's cool," Susie said. "Mrs. Johnson should be home any second now, and then I can get out of here."

"How were the brats today?"

"Aw, they're not br—," Susie was about to call them brats but changed her mind just in case Bethany was listening. "They're not really the b-word. Christy calls them that 'cuz she doesn't like kids. They were good today. Baby Emma *es muy preciosa*. She's walking now. She's still kind of shaky, but she gets around." Susie smiled at the baby now draped over Max, the family's goofy yellow Labrador. She was drooling into his fur.

"Wow," Marlee said, "and she's only one year old? Actually, I have no idea what babies are supposed to do when."

"Me neither." Susie wanted to ask, *needed* to ask, why Marlee hadn't returned her texts or phone call from the night before but didn't want to sound desperate. The fact that she was so desperate scared her a little. She'd always been like her parents, her mother especially, when it came to strength and confidence. Puerto Rican pride, her mother called it, but being with Marlee had reduced her to a quivering ball of need and insecurity.

There was a rustling sound, and then a new voice spoke into the phone. "Hey, Susie, how's it shakin'?"

Susie laughed. Jeri had obviously hijacked the phone. "Hey, Jeri. How's the restaurant today?" Jeri was Marlee's best friend and the recently graduated center fielder from the Clarksonville softball team.

"I don't know what's up or down today," Jeri said. "We've been swamped, but tips have sucked major big-time. Must be a weather front coming through or something."

"Sorry. That does suck."

"It was crazy here last night, too. Everybody in Clarksonville was starving for Italian."

"Good for business, but more work for you, I bet." Susie didn't really want to hear about D'Amico's Restaurant at that moment. She wanted to talk to Marlee.

"Girl, you're not kidding," Jeri agreed. "Thank God Marlee dropped everything and came in to help us out last night."

Susie fell back against the couch in relief. "That's my Marlee, the girl I'm in love with." So that's why Marlee hadn't returned the call or texts.

The rustling sounds returned, and then Marlee was back on the phone. "Sorry about that. Some people can be so rude!" The last was obviously directed at Jeri. "So, where were we?"

"I miss you."

"Me, too," Marlee said low, "but I'll see you Tuesday. Coach Gellar said we have the early game, so we'll have more time after. We could, uh, continue what we started yesterday."

Susie couldn't help the wicked grin on her face. "I'd like that." She felt her cheeks flush and figured that Marlee was probably turning ten shades of red, too. "We have to find a new spot, though."

Marlee laughed. "Yeah, and you have two and a half days to figure that one out." Susie laughed, but before she could say anything, Marlee added, "Jobs suck. They get in the way of me seeing you."

"You're preaching to the choir, but it keeps gas in my car so that I can drive to Clarksonville."

"Oh, hey, speaking of cars, my mom said she's going to help me buy a used car. That way, she can have her van back."

"Too bad. I kind of like that van."

"Mmm, me too," Marlee purred into the phone. "Oh, hey, Bree called me this morning."

Susie's stomach knotted. "She did? How'd she get your number?"

Marlee laughed. "Same way you did. Phone book."

"What did she want from you?" Oh, Susie knew exactly what

Bree wanted. She just hoped Marlee didn't want it back from Bree.

Susie didn't hear Marlee's answer because the sound of breaking glass had her on her feet in an instant. Baby Emma started crying somewhere in the distance. Max's barking added to the mayhem.

"Dammit! Crash and cry. Gotta go." Susie headed toward the sound of the crying; the phone still held up to her ear. She was angry at herself for not keeping a more attentive eye on the baby. "I love you," she blurted into the phone.

"Me, too. Bye."

Susie slammed her phone shut and stashed it into the pocket of her jeans. Bethany stood in the door to her mother's room, looking inside wide-eyed.

"What happened?" Susie rushed past her, not waiting for the answer. She danced around the hyper dog and squatted in front of the crying Emma. No blood. *Thank God.* She brushed away the shards of glass from what used to be the lamp on the nightstand. A perverse side of her was happy. Now she wouldn't have to dust that stupid thing anymore.

"Bethany," Susie called to her without looking up, "get that dog out of here." When she didn't move fast enough, Susie barked, "Now!"

"Whatever," Bethany said and called for the dog.

Relieved to have the barking dog gone, she scooped up the baby and continued to brush away possible glass shards.

Susie groaned when she heard the unmistakable sound of a familiar car door slamming shut. "*Dios mío,*" Susie mumbled, "your timing sucks, Mrs. Johnson."

Susie examined the crying baby from head to toe. No cuts, no blood. Oh wait, a bump on her forehead was starting to swell. The lamp must have hit her there.

"C'mon, little one. Let's get a cold pack on that."

Susie hoped to get the baby into the kitchen and the ice applied before Mrs. Johnson got in the door. No such luck. Susie walked by the front door just as Mrs. Johnson opened it.

"What happened?" Mrs. Johnson closed the door behind her. Before Susie could answer, Mrs. Johnson dropped her purse and work bag and held her arms out for Emma. Susie handed her over. Mrs. Johnson rocked the crying baby and shush-shushed her.

Susie stood there feeling like a school kid before the principal. "She's not cut, but somehow the lamp in your bedroom fell on her." She cringed, waiting for the rebuke that was sure to follow. There wasn't a week that went by that Susie didn't get reprimanded for one thing or another. When one didn't come, Susie mumbled, "I'll get some ice."

She moved as quickly as she could without breaking into an out-and-out run. She had just opened the drawer for a plastic bag when Mrs. Johnson called, "Just bring me an ice pop."

"Okay," Susie called back. She flung open the freezer door and mumbled, "Ice pop. Ice pop," as she searched under the frozen vegetables. When she finally found them, she blew out a nervous breath. She truly hoped Emma was okay. She had only been on the phone for a couple of minutes. With a groan, she pulled out two pops—one for Bethany, too. As an afterthought, she grabbed a clean dish towel, remembering what Coach Gellar told them about not putting ice bags directly on skin. Susie hoped that she would get extra brownie points from Mrs. Johnson, but she seriously doubted it.

By the time Susie got back to the living room, baby Emma had quieted down and lay in her mother's arms tearfully sucking her thumb. Susie handed the ice pop and towel to Mrs. Johnson and tossed the second pop to Bethany, who stood leaning against the wall near the back door.

"Here," Susie reached down for the mound of laundry on the coffee table, "let me get these clothes folded and put away."

"Just leave them."

"Are you sure? I can—"

"I'm sure."

"Well, let me at least clean up the broken lamp."

"Leave it."

Susie felt helpless at that moment, an unusual feeling for her. She nodded her head toward baby Emma now sleeping in her mother's arms. "How is she?"

"Oh, she's okay." Mrs. Johnson's voice softened. "Good thing I'm a nurse, right?"

"Right." Susie wanted to sigh in relief but kept her nerves in check. She stood there as an awkward silence fell around them. "Uh, well, I guess I'll get going now. The lasagna I made is in the oven on low."

Mrs. Johnson nodded once without looking up. She lifted the ice pop from the baby's head to examine the bump. "You're okay, Pumpkin." She rocked the sleeping baby. Bethany came over and sat on the couch next to her mother, obviously concerned about her little sister.

Susie reached for her car keys on the coffee table and slid them into her pocket. "See you tomorrow, Bethany." Bethany didn't acknowledge her, not even with her usual grunt.

Susie let herself out and hadn't quite gotten the front door closed when Bethany blurted to her mother, "Susie was on the phone when it happened. She's in love. With a girl!"

Susie groaned and pressed the front door firmly shut behind her. Could her day get any worse? Maybe Christy was right, after all. Maybe Bethany was a brat. She shuffled to her car, grateful when the engine started on the first twist of the key. According to her father, the starter needed replacing. Maybe she'd talk to him about getting it fixed when she got home, but she was afraid he might make her pay the entire bill herself. Five months from now, in December, she would turn eighteen, the magic age in the Torres household when all of her car expenses, including insurance, would become her responsibility.

She pulled the Toyota onto the street and meandered the back roads toward C.R. 62, which would take her to Christy's house. She'd only be able to spend about an hour there since her mother wanted her back home for Sunday dinner.

She pulled her phone out of her pocket. The dinner rush had probably already hit D'Amico's, so Marlee wouldn't be able to talk. Instead, Susie hit the text button and typed, "Crash & cries suck!" She wanted to continue their conversation about Bree, but that would be hard to do in a text. She looked up at the road. There weren't any cars on the two-lane highway, so she looked back down at her phone and typed, "baby Emma's ok. My nerves fried. Can't wait to see you —"

A car horn blared. Susie shot to attention. She was on the wrong side of the road. She jerked the steering wheel to the right but overcompensated and fishtailed the back end into the other lane. Somehow the other car swerved around her, and they didn't hit. Even though her heart was in her throat, she got her car headed in the right direction.

With her heart pounding, she looked in the rear-view mirror. The driver of the other car was flipping her the bird. Normally that would have sent her blood boiling, but she couldn't react to it. She could only sigh in relief. An agricultural feed and supply place came up on the right, so she pulled into the lot to catch her breath. She rested her head on the steering wheel. Once her jangled nerves were somewhat settled, she sat up and laughed when she noticed that she still held her cell phone in a death grip.

"That's it," she said to the universe. "No more texting in the car." She knew the universe doubted her sincerity, so she repeated her conviction. "I mean it. No more texting and driving. I promise."

She finished the incomplete text to Marlee on the screen, "Can't wait to see you Tuesday. I love you," and hit the send button. She smiled. Marlee would have a text waiting for her when her shift ended later that night. Susie carefully laid the phone on the passenger seat, took a deep breath, and headed back out onto the two-lane road. She laughed because she'd actually come to a complete stop and signaled out of the parking lot. She usually didn't have time for that sort of thing.

After only two more minutes on the road, Susie's heart leaped again when her phone rang. She remembered her recent vow, but since the vow hadn't included sneaking a peek to see who was calling, she picked it up. If it was Marlee, she'd pull over and answer it. No such luck. It was her mother. She toyed with the idea of letting it go to voicemail, but that was never a good idea when Isabella Maria de Fatima Torres called.

Susie pulled the car over on the shoulder, well off the road. She smirked up at the universe. See? She could keep a promise. She flipped open her phone, "¿*Aló, Mami*?"

"What happened at Mrs. Johnson's?"

Susie flopped her head back against the headrest. Yeah, the day had just gotten much worse.

# Chapter 6

### Going, Going, Gone

Susie held the cell phone away from her ear. Her mother finished her tirade about the baby Emma incident and hung up before Susie could seriously defend herself. She stared at the silent phone, wondering how much trouble she'd be in when she got home. She flipped her phone shut as gently as she could as if not wanting to rile her mother any further. What she really wanted to do was hurl the phone into the ditch alongside C.R. 62, where she sat in her car. She closed her eyes for a minute, knowing she would have to defend herself again when she got home, but she had one thing she needed to do first.

She flipped the phone back open and said, "Christy," into the voice dial. After a couple of rings, Christy picked up.

"Where are you?" Christy asked, obviously knowing it was Susie.

"Nowhere. Isabella wants me to come home instead of going to your house."

"Since when does your mother care if you come to my house? You can't catch clinical depression." Christy grunted into the phone, half serious.

"*Aay*, no. I'm afraid I messed up at Mrs. Johnson's." Susie relayed the whole unfortunate incident. "I feel bad that baby Emma got hurt, but *Dios mío*, Mrs. Johnson's making a mountain out of it."

"It was big to her, I guess."

"I wish that brat, Bethany, hadn't ratted on me for being on the phone." Her car shook as a cement truck rumbled past her on the highway.

Christy grunted on her end of the phone. "Hang on a sec." She grunted again, this time with satisfaction.

"What are you doing?" Susie frowned. Christy always had a way of not quite listening whenever Susie wanted to talk about her troubles.

"I was trying to fit way too many clothes into this suitcase. I finally got it closed."

Susie laughed. "You can always buy more clothes once you get there, *muchacha*."

"Oh, believe me, I will." Christy laughed. "You should see it in here. Wall-to-wall boxes and suitcases. I didn't realize I had so much stuff."

Susie felt her chest tighten. Her best friend was moving away. "Are you taking everything? Are you moving away for good?"

Christy didn't answer right away. She was probably trying to find a way to break the news gently. Eventually, she sighed into the phone. "I don't know. I'm gonna miss you. I definitely want you to visit me, but I have to start myself over, you know?"

"I get that." Susie stayed quiet, letting Christy direct the conversation.

"I used to resent you, you know."

"Why?"

"Because you were the one that found me and didn't let me—"

"Yeah," Susie interrupted, so Christy didn't have to say the word *die* out loud.

"Yeah."

They were silent together, each lost in her own thoughts. It wasn't something Susie ever liked to think about, but she remembered when they were fourteen and fifteen respectively, and she had gone to Christy's house. Christy's parents weren't home, but they never were. Susie let herself in when there was no answer at the front door and eventually found Christy in the upstairs bathroom. There was a lot of blood. Christy apparently hadn't had the nerve to cut her wrist too deeply, so Susie managed to stop the bleeding and nursed Christy through the entire weekend. Christy still had the scar on her left wrist but lately wore it like a badge of strength, showing the world that she had bounced back from one of her lowest points.

"So, uh," Christy began, "thanks for breaking up with Marlee that time."

"What do you mean?"

"I mean, not many people would break up with somebody they so obviously loved just to keep me calm."

"I was lucky." Susie shrugged even though Christy wouldn't be able to see it. "She took me back."

"And you got me help. Not that I was happy about it at first."

"I know, but you're working through stuff with your therapist, right?"

"Yeah, I guess," Christy said. "So, how's Marlee?"

Susie welcomed the change in conversation. "She's good. She's working at D'Amico's today with Jeri."

"I love that."

"What? Marlee working at a restaurant?"

Christy laughed. "No, dork. I love when your voice lights up when you talk about her. You've got it bad, girl."

Susie's heart warmed over. "I know."

"Susie steps up to the plate, bat in hand," Christy said in an announcer's voice. "She takes one look at the cute pitcher in the circle, and she's going, going, gone!"

"Shut up!" Susie couldn't help the smile that took over her face.

"But it's so true, my friend. You hadn't even hit your grand slam yet, but, bam, you were in love with the cute blonde pitcher from Clarksonville."

Susie laughed with her friend. "I was." She groaned. "I'm so head over heels about her. She drives me crazy."

"In a good way?" Christy laughed suggestively.

"Hey, I don't kiss and tell."

"Maybe someday I'll find a guy that makes me happy like that."

"You will."

"That's why I'm getting the frick out of here."

"Maybe I'll come with you." Susie sighed into the phone.

"You can't avoid Isabella forever."

"Pfft," Susie grunted. "I know. That's not all. Marlee's got a not-so-secret admirer."

"Ooh, besides you? Do tell."

Susie told Christy about the Southbridge pitcher, Bree, who had oh-so-obviously flirted with Marlee after the game the day before and even had the nerve to call her that morning.

"The way I see Marlee look at you, I'd say you have nothing to worry about."

"I don't know." Susie's nagging doubts came back to the surface from where she'd stuffed them.

"You know what?"

"What?"

"I've never seen you back down from a fight. Ever. Even when I was beating the crap out of you in the dugout, you stood your ground until I was done being a maniac."

"You weren't beating the crap out of me. You hit me once. You beat up the dugout more than me."

"Yeah, well, my point is that if you love her, you'll fight for her." Christy grunted again.

Susie chuckled. "Another suitcase closed?"

"Yup, you're supposed to be here helping me."

"I know. I'm sorry." Susie glanced at the time on her cell phone. "Shit, I have to go. See you at the game on Tuesday?"

"Count on it."

"I love you." Susie meant it. They had been as close as two best friends could get.

"Me, too."

Susie clicked her phone shut and laid it on the passenger seat. She checked the traffic on the two-lane highway, and once it was clear both ways, she did a U-turn and headed home.

Susie pulled her car into her usual spot on the side of the garage and toyed with the idea of bolting to her room to hide for a while, but it was best not to keep her mother waiting.

She took off her sneakers in the mudroom and headed into the house. She paused in front of her *abuelita*'s shrine and crossed herself like a good catholic girl. She kept her eyes closed and murmured. "Blessed Virgin Mary, my dear heavenly mother, take me under your protection, for I am about to be slaughtered." She wanted to smile but couldn't find the strength.

With a deep breath, she headed into the main part of the house. Her mother held a handful of plates and silverware and unceremoniously dumped them on the table with a clatter. "Finish that." She didn't look at Susie.

Susie scurried over and set the table without a word. She felt her mother's anger all around her like a thick fog, but there was nothing she could do about it until they had another one-sided discussion about her thoughtless mistake at Mrs. Johnson's. Susie slunk into the kitchen. Her *abuelita* stood at the stove checking the rice. Her mother wiped the counter with short, swift movements and looked like she could blow at any moment.

Taking a chance, Susie asked, "What else can I help you with, *Mami*?"

"Go get your brother and father for dinner," came the terse answer.

Susie spun on her heels and fled the kitchen as fast as her feet would take her.

Once the Torres family was seated at the table and had said

grace, Susie's father smiled sympathetically like she was a prisoner about to be sentenced. "So, how's the traveling team this summer, *mi mariposita?*"

She loved it when he called her his little butterfly and bless him for trying to change the mood at the table. "We're good. Christy's not pitching, but we have the Clarksonville pitcher this summer."

"Marlee," Miguel singsonged, and Susie shot him a warning look. He made a face back at her but didn't press it.

"*Ah, sí,* I remember her. You always complained about that pitch she threw you—what was it?"

"Her rise ball." Susie chuckled. "I can't hit that thing to save my life."

He grinned at her sympathetically. She appreciated the attention-diverting small talk but knew the clock was ticking down on the head-handing discussion with her mother. Susie mostly pushed the food around on her plate, having lost her appetite. Susie perked up when her *abuelita* went into the kitchen and came out with the flan for dessert. Apparently, her loss of appetite didn't apply to dessert, and she savored every bite like a death-row inmate eating her last meal.

"*Mami,*" Miguel said as he pushed his now-empty dessert dish away, "can I go outside and play?"

Her mother nodded once, and he bolted from the table, almost knocking his chair over. Susie frowned as he left. When he wanted something from his parents, he used his little-boy voice. It worked on their mother every time. Susie wondered if that would work for her. Not a chance. She was almost eighteen.

Susie cleared the dishes while her mother took care of the leftover food. Her *abuelita* and father retreated to the living room to watch television. Her *abuelita* turned the volume up extra loud as if not wanting to hear the slaughter that was about to begin.

Susie stood at the sink rinsing the dishes thinking how alike she and her mother were. Susie even resembled her mother, although Susie towered over her by about five or six inches. They had the same brownish-auburn colored hair, although her mother's mostly came from a box these days. They had the same brown eyes, too, except at the moment, her mother's eyes were dark, a gathering thunderstorm.

"Susana," her mother said abruptly, making Susie jump, "why did you put baby Emma in such danger?"

"*Mami*, I didn't." Susie turned off the faucet and spun around to face her mother. "I would never put the baby in danger. *Sí*, I was on the phone, but I had just looked at the baby. I only looked away for a—"

"*Ella es un bebé*. You can't take your eyes off a baby for a second. Ever!" Her mother's voice rose steadily in volume. "Especially once they learn to walk. They're curious about everything."

Susie knew better than to try and defend herself any further. "*Lo siento, Mami*. I'm sorry I wasn't paying close enough attention."

Susie's mother sighed and leaned back against the counter. "People like us," she said tersely, "can't afford to mess up in the slightest. We have to be twice as good as them to be thought half as good. People like us aren't good enough to check the *White* box on those forms." She stared into space as if forgetting that Susie was even there. "No, they have that special little Hispanic box just for us. And it wouldn't matter anyway, have skin that's a little darker, and the whole world judges you immediately."

Susie glanced down at her forearm. Yeah, she was darker than all of her friends. Christy said once that it looked like she had a year-round tan. And now that summer was there, she was even darker.

"So," her mother looked back at her, "it didn't matter that you cleaned her house, washed her clothes, did her gardening, made her family breakfast, lunch, and dinner." Her mother's voice was increasing in volume again. "No, all that doesn't matter, because you had to be on the phone not paying attention to the one thing that was most important. The baby could have been seriously hurt."

Susie felt terrible. Her mother was right. She vowed to leave the cell phone in the car the next day so that it wouldn't be a distraction. "I won't let it happen again, *Mami*. I won't. I promise."

"No, it won't." Her mother took several steps closer. "It won't because Mrs. Johnson fired you today."

"What?" Susie gasped. "What do you mean?"

"What do you think it means, *hija*? It means you won't be working for Mrs. Johnson anymore. The job I bent over backward to get for you. It also means that you'll be grounded for the next two weeks and doing all those jobs here that you did for her. You'll clean the house, do the laundry, mow the lawn, and weed the flower beds. And you can say goodbye to softball for the next two weeks, too."

Susie started to protest, but her mother cut her off.

"Mrs. Johnson is my boss," her mother said in clipped tones.

"You've single-handedly jeopardized this whole family by your indiscretion. I don't know how I'm going to face her tomorrow."

"But *Mami*, I have a game on Tuesday," Susie said weakly.

"You should have thought about that before you put that baby in danger."

Susie didn't really care about doing the household chores, but she couldn't stand the thought of not seeing Marlee for two whole weeks. And Christy. Christy was moving away. Forever.

"But Christy's moving on Wednesday."

Something like compassion flickered across her mother's face, and Susie held her breath. Her mother said, "I'll discuss that with your father, but for now, I'm going to leave you with the rest of this kitchen to clean up." She flung the dishtowel on the counter and headed out the door. She turned around at the last moment and pointed a finger at Susie. "Think about what you've done."

"*Sí, Mami.*" Susie turned and gripped the edges of the sink until her knuckles turned white. She wanted to grab the nearest plate and fling it against the wall. Instead, she flung her mother's dish towel, but it barely made a sound. It was quite unsatisfying. She wanted to roar but could only squeak.

# Chapter 7

## Visiting Day

Susie checked the time on her phone. The game had to be over by now. They had to be on their way. Susie hoped her friends hadn't done something silly like gone into extra innings. Through much pleading and tears, she convinced her parents to let Christy and some other friends, including Marlee, come over for a farewell party for Christy.

The day before, her mother pounded on the outside garage door at six-thirty in the morning before heading to the hospital for work. Apparently, she wanted to make sure Susie was up and ready to tackle the list of chores waiting for her on the kitchen table in the house. Monday had been filled with house cleaning. This, of course, included Miguel's room. He took great delight trying to sabotage her efforts by shooting toilet paper wads at the garbage can and missing most of the time. Susie didn't give him the time of day, waited until he got bored of his game, and simply cleaned up after him when he left. In addition to the usual dusting, vacuuming, and cleaning the kitchen, Susie's mother made her scour all three bathrooms, including both tubs. She had worked so hard cleaning that she didn't have the time or energy to get in a decent workout with her weights. She'd done a hundred sit-ups, but that was it.

Susie took it in stride, though, because she had earned the punishment, and there was no sense complaining. She simply kept her focus on the end of her two-week sentence. That's when she'd look for a real job. Sam's family probably owned a business or two that would hire a seventeen-year-old with no skills other than knowledge of rocks and softball.

Susie stretched her aching back. In addition to mowing, edging, weed whacking the lawn, her mother's list for Tuesday had included weeding the rose gardens. There were no less than five separate rose beds around the property. She'd finished the two beds in the front of the house and had a good start on a third but didn't have time to finish before she had to go inside and make lasagna for her family, ironically the same meal she had cooked for the Johnson family the day *la mierda* had hit the fan.

Susie couldn't wait to see her friends. She'd only been incarcerated for two days, but she felt like a prisoner on visiting day. Her head jerked when she heard a car door open and slam shut. She looked out her bedroom window to the driveway below.

"Hi, guys," Susie called out the open window and waved. Marlee, Christy, Sam, Lisa, and Jeri stood on the driveway below. "C'mon up. The door's unlocked."

"Be right up," Christy said and led the way.

Marlee lagged behind on the driveway and threw Susie a smoldering glance.

Susie's eyes grew wide. "Get up here," she hissed. She hoped she'd have time to spend a couple of minutes alone with Marlee before everyone had to leave.

Christy burst into her room. "Yo, what's up, jailbird?"

"Shut up." Susie hugged her best friend.

Sam flipped her blonde ponytail behind her and was next in line for a hug. "Sorry to hear about your, uh, incarceration."

"You shut up, too."

Sam laughed and made way for her girlfriend Lisa to greet Susie.

Lisa gave Susie a quick hug. "Good to see you again, Susie." She gestured to the weight bench. "Nice weights."

"I wish I had time to use them. My mother's keeping me way too busy. I'm surprised she let you guys come over."

Jeri grabbed Susie in a quick bear hug. "The way Marlee gossips, it sounds like you're on a chain gang living on bread and water."

Susie laughed. "It felt like it today." She grabbed her lower back and stretched again.

Jeri nodded. "I feel your pain." She jumped when Marlee poked her in the back.

"Do you mind moving out of the way?" Marlee grinned behind her.

"Oh, excuse me." Jeri slithered off to the side. "Let me not stand in the way of love." She clapped her hands twice and said, "Everyone, let's please turn around and give the lovebirds a moment of privacy."

Sam and Lisa laughed but did as Jeri asked and turned away.

"Oh, how sickening," Christy joked as she turned around.

Once they had a second of privacy, Susie threw her arms around Marlee's neck and kissed her as if she hadn't seen her in months instead of days.

Marlee leaned her forehead against Susie's. "I've missed you, too." She whispered in Susie's ear, "I wish we could be alone." She nipped at Susie's earlobe, causing Susie to jump.

Christy, or maybe Jeri, cleared her throat suggesting the couple's alone time was over.

Still facing the other direction, Sam said, "Uh, Susie? P? We're burning daylight here. Can we turn around?"

"Yeah." Susie laughed but didn't let go of Marlee.

"Two, you always ruin my fun," Marlee said to Sam using the nickname she'd made up after Sam started calling her P for pitcher.

Christy groaned. "Somebody get a crowbar to separate those two."

"Shut up," Susie said and released Marlee. Her heart fluttered when Marlee seemed reluctant to go.

"Hey, Sus," Sam pointed to the food laid out on Susie's desk, "is this for us?"

Susie nodded. "A going away feast."

"Great. I'm starved." Sam picked up a small plate and loaded veggies, crackers, and dip on her plate. She grabbed a bottle of water from the cooler on the floor.

"Hey, guys," Susie gestured for the others to help themselves to the snacks, "did we win the game?"

"Oh, yeah," Lisa said, loading her plate with broccoli florets. "They spanked Mohawk."

"We," Sam turned her gray-blue eyes on Lisa.

"What?" Lisa turned to look at Sam, her long black braid

swinging behind her.

"Just because you can't play yet, doesn't mean you're not part of the team. You should say, '*We* spanked Mohawk.'" Sam crossed her eyes at Lisa.

Christy laughed. "Hey, I don't know what you girls do in your spare time, but I don't want to hear about who spanked who."

Both Sam and Lisa stuck their tongues out at Christy.

"Or what you do with your tongues, either." Christy squeezed her eyes shut and covered her ears. "La la la la la la la," she singsonged.

Susie pulled Christy's hands off her ears, causing Christy to stop la-la-la-ing. "You know we queer girls don't kiss and tell."

"Yeah," Sam agreed and pulled Lisa into a tight embrace. "We kiss, but don't tell."

Everybody laughed and then settled into filling up their plates with veggies and dip and crackers and Susie's *abuelita*'s *mantecaditos* cookies, the little butter cookies that Christy loved. Susie's mother hadn't let her drive to Price Chopper to get real party food, so Susie had to raid the kitchen for anything she could find. Getting permission to throw a party for Christy had been a major feat in itself, and Susie knew not to push her mother further.

They sat in a circle on the rug on the floor, and Susie was glad she had included her own room in her cleaning assignment the day before. Her friends talked about their slaughter win over the Mohawk All-Stars.

"All-Stars," Christy spat. "Yeah, right."

"Hey," Lisa chimed in, "they have potential."

Christy looked at Sam. "Is she always this optimistic?"

Sam nodded and reached for Lisa's hand.

Susie smiled at the obvious affection between them. "Hey, Lisa, when can you play?"

Lisa held up the hand she'd broken during the spring school season. "My doctor said I can start throwing next Tuesday. Good news, eh?"

A cheer went up in the room. Marlee's eyes widened, and she sported one of the biggest grins Susie had ever seen.

"I'm getting my catcher back." Marlee looked skyward. "Thank you, Lord."

"It's good to know you missed me." Lisa grinned back at her pitcher.

"More than you know," Marlee said.

"Hey," Lisa's tone turned serious, "I meant to ask you. Who was that girl you were talking to after the game tonight?"

"Oh, that's Bree."

Susie almost choked. Marlee hadn't hesitated. Marlee hadn't asked, "What girl?" or said, "She's nobody." No, Marlee answered right away as if Bree was an old friend as if they'd known each other for years. Susie tried not to let the alarm bells sounding off in her head get any louder. She cleared her throat and asked, "How'd you pitch today?"

"Oh, good," Marlee began, but Susie half-listened to the words because, in the back of her mind, she wondered if the threat was real or if she had just imagined Marlee's ease with Bree.

Christy's laugh brought Susie back to earth. "And here's the ironic thing," Christy said. "You guys were ahead by eight runs, right? So, Coach Gellar puts Mary in to pitch. Mary is obviously Marlee's back up this summer, but she'll be the starting pitcher for East Valley next spring."

Sam groaned. "I think we're gonna be in trouble next spring."

"We totally are." Susie looked at Sam. "Does Coach Gellar hate me?"

"Yes." Sam didn't hesitate.

Susie waited for Sam to say she was kidding, but she didn't. "What do you mean?"

Sam exchanged a glance with Marlee, one that Susie couldn't read. "Oh, you know how she is. She made some snide comment today about being responsible for your actions on and off the field and how some people didn't do that."

"Meaning me." Susie's heart sank.

Sam and Marlee nodded.

Christy patted Susie on the knee. "Looks like you're Coach Gellar's new target, buddy. Sorry to hand that off to you, but I'll gladly give up my crown."

Susie groaned and fell forward into her circle of friends. "*Aay*, my life sucks."

"Nah." Sam pulled Susie back up to a sitting position. "You have us."

The others agreed, and Susie nodded. "Yeah, you're right. If I can only break out of my cell, then I can hang with you guys."

"Next time, I'll bring you a cake with a file baked in it," Marlee offered.

"Sounds good, but make it flan, and you've got a deal."

They talked briefly about the circumstances surrounding Susie's unceremonious firing from the Johnson's and her subsequent prison term, but after a while, Susie needed to change the topic. She sat up tall and raised her bottle of water. "Hey, *chicas*, I want to make a toast." The others raised their respective bottles of water as well. "Christy," she looked at her best friend, "we're gonna miss you when you go to the sunshine state of California, although technically Arizona gets more sunshine than either California or Florida, which is called the Sunshine State—"

Sam poked Susie. "Okay, science geek, we get the picture. Get on with it."

Susie playfully scowled at her friend at the interruption but continued. "We're all going to be thinking of you this winter when we're freezing our asses off here, and you're tra-la-la-ing around the beach with your blond boy-toy."

Christy snorted. "I wish."

Jeri grabbed Christy's arm. "Take me with you."

Susie raised her water bottle higher. "To Christy."

"To Christy." Everyone held their water bottles up and then tapped them together.

Many toasts and good luck wishes were shared, but all too soon, it was time for Susie's friends to go.

"Don't go," Susie pleaded. "Visiting days in this prison are so short." She stomped her feet in protest as any mature seventeen-year-old would do.

Lisa hugged her first and then Sam. Sam said she'd stop by the next day to keep her company during her prison work program.

"You're a true friend," Susie whispered and gave Sam another hug.

Jeri hugged her next. "I wish you lived closer. My Dad would probably hire you for the restaurant."

"That's okay. Marlee would distract me, anyway."

Marlee hit Susie gently on the arm in protest. "Would not."

"Not intentionally, *mi vida*, not intentionally." She flashed Marlee a suggestive look.

"Oh, get a room." Christy groaned and then laughed. She grabbed Susie in a big hug. "Keep in touch, okay? You're probably the only thing I'm going to miss around here." Christy pulled out of the hug and reached into her shirt pocket. "Here." It was a picture of Susie and Marlee—the one she'd taken at the ball field the weekend before.

Susie hugged Christy again quickly. "Very cool. Thanks."

"I know how much you mean to each other." Christy spun around and wiped at her eyes. "C'mon, gang, let's wait downstairs and give the lovebirds some private time." She barreled out the door. Sam, Lisa, and Jeri followed.

As soon as the last one was out the door, Marlee flew into Susie's arms. A look of frustration overtook her face. "I wanted tonight to be so much more."

"I know what you mean, Jelly Bean."

Marlee grinned. "You knew what I meant, Jelly Bent?"

Susie nodded and let herself get lost in Marlee's soul-swallowing blue eyes.

Marlee whispered, "I want to continue what we started on Saturday."

Susie raised an eyebrow. "Oh," she said with understanding. "Me, too." She leaned her face down to within an inch of Marlee's. They breathed each other's breath for a moment, enjoying the closeness until Susie couldn't stand it anymore. She closed the gap and pressed her lips against Marlee's. Marlee groaned and pulled Susie tighter. She rubbed Susie's back but then let her hands reach lower.

"Ooh," Susie moaned, wishing Marlee didn't have to go.

"Susana!" her mother's voice called from the driveway, piercing their quiet moment.

"Shit!" Susie recoiled from Marlee's arms as if scalded.

"Get down here." Her mother's voice was designed to get immediate results.

Susie rushed to the open window. "Okay, *Mami*." She spun back around to face Marlee. "She knows. *Dios mío*, she knows you're up here alone with me."

"How does she know?"

"She knows everything." Susie ran to her closet and grabbed the Clarksonville softball sweatshirt that Marlee had given her a while back. "Here, take this and run out with it. Pretend you forgot it up here or something and had to run back up for it." She thrust the sweatshirt into Marlee's hands.

"It's, like, ninety degrees outside. She's not going to believe I wore a sweatshirt."

"I know, but, uh, you're a pitcher, and pitchers wear sweatshirts sometimes." Susie nudged Marlee toward the door. "It doesn't matter. Just go, go, go!"

Susie paced the floor of her room, listening to Marlee run down the steps. She spied out the window and grinned when Marlee said, "I got it." She held up the blue sweatshirt to her teammates assembled on the driveway. "I can't believe I almost forgot it."

"Yeah," Jeri said obviously confused, but apparently understanding that she needed to play along. "Good thing you remembered it."

Susie was about to race down the stairs but realized she was still holding the picture Christy gave her. She carefully placed it in her top desk drawer and then ran down the stairs at full steam. She couldn't keep her mother waiting any longer. Once she got to the bottom, she waved at her friends pulling away in their cars. Sam and Lisa in Sam's Sebring convertible. Christy was in her brand new Jeep Wrangler, a graduation gift from her parents, or, as Christy called it, a going-away present. Marlee and Jeri were last in Jeri's convertible Mustang, also a graduation present.

Susie's mother stood in the driveway with her arms crossed. It looked as if she wanted to scold Susie for something but stayed silent until the cars were well out of sight. She turned to Susie and said, "Come inside. I have your list for tomorrow." She headed toward the house.

Susie hung her head and slinked behind her mother like a scolded puppy dog.

# Chapter 8

## A Miracle

Susie climbed the ladder. "¡*Aay!*" She pounded the top rung. "Sam, I forgot the damn sponge."

"I'll get it." Sam pulled the sponge out of the bucket and wrung it out. "I'm tired, too. You must be exhausted."

Susie nodded. "I have to keep going, though. I have to get this done before Isabella gets home."

Sam nodded. She tossed the sponge toward Susie, who caught it deftly with one hand. "What are we on? Our fifteenth window?"

"Yup, something like that." Susie soaped up the second-story window, one of her parents' bedroom windows. "And get this. I don't even get to rest when we're done, either. I have to drive *mi abuela* to her friend's house to play cards."

"Wow. No rest for the weary."

"Nope." Susie washed the grime off the window and then tossed the sponge back down to Sam. She then said, "Sprayer," like a surgeon asking for a scalpel. Sam snaked the hose up the ladder, and Susie sprayed the soap off the windows. "Look out below," she called before dropping the sprayer back to Sam. Susie snatched the squeegee from her back pocket and finished off the window. She wiped up a few residual drips with a dry rag. "Screen," she called.

"Okay, hang on." Sam scurried to the garage where the screens lay drying in the late July sun. She grabbed one, ran back over to the ladder, and climbed up a few rungs.

Susie climbed down one rung, grateful she didn't have to climb down all the way. She took the screen and then pressed it securely in place. She trudged down the ladder and moved it to the next dirty window. With a sigh, she decided that she just couldn't bring herself to do one more window until she rested. "I call a break." She undid her ponytail and raked her fingers through her hair. "Ugh," she flopped to the ground. "I hate this."

Sam handed Susie a cold bottle of water from the cooler. "Me, too." She sat down next to her and took a swig from her own water bottle.

"Thanks."

"No problem."

"No," Susie said, "I mean, thanks for wasting a whole freakin' day helping me."

Sam frowned. "I got your back, Sus. You know that. You'd have mine."

"Yeah, I would." Susie drank some of the cool water. "I wish Mrs. Johnson had come home five minutes earlier or five minutes later. But, no, she had to come home at just the wrong moment. She probably thought I was beating her kids."

Sam laughed. "I doubt that."

Susie shrugged without smiling.

"Hey," Sam said, "you never liked that job anyway."

"So?"

"So, the universe is helping you move on."

"Yeah, but—"

"You're the one that's always talking about the universe." Sam clicked her tongue in disapproval. "How much was she paying you, anyway?"

"Fifty bucks."

"That's not too bad. Fifty bucks a day—"

"A week."

Sam's jaw dropped.

"You're, uh, mouth is open."

"Susie." Sam's voice was disapproving.

"What?"

"Fifty dollars a week is way below minimum wage. That's ten dollars a day. For the hours you spent there, that's, like, a dollar an hour." Sam shook her head, obviously appalled. "She took advantage of you, Sus."

"I never wanted to babysit for Mrs. Johnson. My mother negotiated everything. She's my mother's boss." Susie took another long drink from the water bottle.

"Oh, I forgot about that. I see why your mom's so crazy about all of this."

"I swear I looked away from baby Emma for a second. It was an accident." Susie pulled her knees up and hugged them tightly.

"I know." Sam smiled sympathetically. "And the baby's fine, so you need to let yourself off the hook about it."

"I guess." Susie regarded her friend and attempted a smile. She was lucky to have Sam in her life. Maybe Sam would step into the best friend role with Christy moving away. Could an ex-girlfriend turn into a best friend? What about Marlee? Could a girlfriend be a best friend, too?

"So, how're things with Marlee?" Sam asked as if reading Susie's mind.

Susie smiled. "Great. I like her so much. I just wish…"

"What?"

"I wish we lived closer. I wish I weren't grounded. I wish my stupid car worked." She glanced at her old rusting Toyota looking pitiful next to Sam's shiny red Sebring convertible.

Sam followed her gaze. "Is your car still giving you problems?"

"Yeah, my dad thinks it's the starter. But he's never home long enough to do anything about it." Susie sighed. "Whatever. I'll get it fixed soon. But to answer your question, Marlee's *magnifica*. I can't believe the way I feel when I look at her."

"Oh, God."

"Don't make fun."

Sam smirked. "I'm not. It's just that I know what you mean. I feel the same way about Lisa. She's so tall and strong. And you don't even understand what goes through me when I undo her long braid and run my fingers through her hair." Sam closed her eyes and tilted her face toward the sky as if in rapture at the thought.

"You've got it bad, Sam."

Sam opened her eyes and grinned. "I can't help it. I've had a crush on her for a year and a half. Try and live with that kind of desperation."

"Try this stupidity. Break up with the girl you're in love with

80

and then beg her to take you back."

"Why'd you break up with Marlee, anyway?"

"Because I'm *muy loca*." She twirled her finger in a circle near her ear.

"Yeah, I agree."

"Oh, shut up." Susie swatted her friend playfully. "If I had any strength at all, I'd punch you."

Sam smiled. "Well, I'm glad you came to your senses and begged Marlee to take you back. Christy clung to you way too much. I mean, c'mon, you finally found somebody who loved you for all the right reasons. Your best friend shouldn't try to take that away from you. She shouldn't have gotten in between you and Marlee."

"That still pisses you off, doesn't it?"

"Yeah," Sam snorted derisively. "I watched her slap you in the dugout. I guess I'm still a little protective of you."

Susie's heart warmed. "Being best friends with Christy meant being there for her all the time. *All* the time. I don't think she understood my need to, my need for..."

Sam put a hand on Susie's wrist. "I know."

They exchanged a knowing look and sat alone in their own thoughts for a moment. Susie hoped that Christy would find happiness in sunny California that she had never managed to find in upstate New York.

"I think my mother suspects something about Marlee and me, though."

"Ooh." Sam took a sharp intake of breath. "That's gonna be rough."

Susie chuckled and gestured toward the window cleaning equipment spread around them. "It already is. You know how she always takes things to the extreme."

"No kidding. Like the time she supported that Republican running for the school board? What was his name?"

"*Dios*, how can I forget?" Susie rolled her eyes. "Joe Wilson."

"Oh, right. Your lawn was plastered with those 'Elect Joe Wilson' signs."

"She made me hand out leaflets to kids at school to give to their parents."

Sam laughed. "There was no way I was going to wear that button you gave me."

"I didn't expect you to, but, *Dios*, I had to give it to you, or she'd know I didn't."

"That's true." Sam nodded. "She's a mind reader."

"But then she changed her mind when she learned that grand and mighty Joe Wilson wanted to cut funding to the nursing classes in the BOCES program."

"Yeah, I remember that. She did a complete one-eighty on him and supported the Democratic candidate with just as much, if not more, fervor."

"That's my *mami*." Susie laughed. "She goes full force with everything. Those 'Elect Joe Wilson' signs on the lawn were yanked out so fast, it made my head spin."

"So, do you think she grounded you because of Marlee?"

Susie nodded. "Partly. Well, supposedly, I'm grounded for being *irresponsible* at Mrs. Johnson's." She made air quotes around the word irresponsible.

"But you think it's more than that?"

"Yeah, if she grounds me, then I can't see Marlee at softball or in Clarksonville. Thank God she didn't take my phone away. At least Marlee and I get to talk every day."

"She probably didn't think of it," Sam said. "Have your parents even met Marlee? She's nice. She's cute. She's charming. What's not to like?"

"I'm scared to death to introduce them. She's pushing, though."

"Marlee?"

"Yeah." Susie scratched her knee absently. "She wants to meet them. You know her dad passed away a while ago, right?"

"Yeah, Lisa filled me in."

"So now that I've met her mom, Marlee thinks it's only fair that she meets my folks, too. *Aay, Dios mío*, that's going to be a tough day."

"Tell me about it. Lisa's bugging to meet my parents, too. She met Helene, though."

"Your nanny?" Susie teased.

"Shut up. You know Helene's not my nanny anymore."

Susie raised an eyebrow.

"Not really. Okay, whatever." Sam's cheeks turned a slight shade of crimson. "Do you think your parents ever knew about us?"

"What? That we were seeing each other for two minutes last summer?"

"Hey," Sam smacked her friend on the arm. "It was two whole months."

Susie grinned. "No, I don't think they knew. They'd never suspect Samantha Rose Payton of such depravity."

"Oh, please."

"C'mon. You're Samantha Rose Payton of the East Valley Paytons. You own most of East Valley and half of Clarksonville County. You're above reproach."

"And you know how much I hate that shit."

Susie softened her gaze. "I know."

"So why do you think they know about you and Marlee?"

"I don't know. They just do." Susie looked down. She really didn't want to talk about it anymore.

"All right. Forget I asked. C'mon," Sam said with a tap on Susie's knee and stood up. "We have seven more windows to go."

Susie wanted to confide in Sam that Bree was sniffing around Marlee but was too tired to even think about it. She reluctantly got to her feet and stretched. "Thanks for helping me. I think I'd still be doing the windows on the first floor if you hadn't come over."

"Anytime, Sus. You know that."

"Why don't you go home. I can finish up on my own."

"No way. I told you last year when we broke up—"

"*We* didn't break up," Susie said semi-seriously. "You broke up with me." It still stung a little.

"Yeah, you're right. Last year when *I* broke up with *you*," Sam amended, "I told you we'd still be friends and that I'd always be there for you. I meant it."

Susie regarded her friend for a moment. "Me, too."

"Good, and since I already have a thousand hours logged in

today, I need to see this job through." Sam headed toward the ladder. "C'mon. Let's finish this puppy."

Susie's heart swelled. Sam had once told her that they made better friends than girlfriends, and she was right. She was lucky to have such a supportive ex-girlfriend.

~~~

Susie towel dried her hair and tossed the wet towel on her bed. She should have hung it up but was too tired to care. She grabbed her car keys and phone off the dresser, plunked her wallet in her back pocket, and lumbered down the stairs. After three days of solid work, she was sore in spots she hadn't known she had.

She stepped inside the mudroom of the main house but didn't bother to take her crocs off. She leaned in the door and called, "*Abuelita? Está lista?*"

"*Sí, sí.*" Her *abuelita* shuffled toward the front door struggling with an equally enormous box in both hands. Her massive purse slung over one wrist. Susie relieved her of the box, and one whiff told her that *abuelita*'s famous *mantecaditos* cookies were inside.

"*Abuelita*, can I steal one?" Susie grinned at her *abuelita* as she made a show of sniffing the box.

"*Aay, no.*" Her *abuelita* swatted her hand. She reached inside her purse and pulled out a plastic bag stuffed with the treasured butter cookies. "These for you."

Susie's eyes grew wide at the sight. She tucked the box under her arm and snatched the bag from her *abuelita*'s hand. She pulled one out and stuffed it in her mouth. "Mmm, *muchas gracias, Abuelita.*" Next to flan, *mantecaditos* were her favorite dessert. At that moment, she realized her *abuelita* had spoken English, something she never did.

Susie held the outside mudroom door open for her *abuelita*, and they headed toward the car. Even though she was only driving her *abuelita* to a weekly card game, it felt good to get out of the house after three solid days of confinement. The *mantecaditos* didn't hurt either.

Susie turned the key in the ignition. The car engine made a high-pitched whine but didn't catch. Susie turned the key off and prayed that the starter would catch the next time. With eyes closed, she turned the key gently and was rewarded when the engine roared to life. "All right," she patted the front dash. "Good girl."

They headed onto C.R. 62 toward the outskirts of town, where her *abuelita*'s friends gathered for their weekly Wednesday card game. After a mile or two, Susie's muscles stiffened up. She groaned and tried to stretch in the cramped car.

"Are tired you, Susana?"

"*Sí, muy cansada.*"

"You *mamá* work you too hard."

With a yawn, Susie nodded but then whipped her head around to look at her *abuelita* with narrowed eyes. "*¿Estás hablando inglés?*" Susie's *abuelita* had never seriously tried to speak English before.

"Yes, I is."

"Am," Susie corrected. "Yes, I am."

"*Aay, inglés es difícil.*"

"Yup," Susie laughed. "English can be hard, but if you keep at it, you'll be speaking like me soon enough."

"*Aay, sí.*" Her *abuelita* laughed.

"But why are you speaking English, *Abuelita*?"

"I learn English to speak to your *querubín*."

The warmth that overtook Susie came straight from the center of her heart. In the seventeen years her *abuelita* had been in the states, nothing had motivated her to learn English. Not answering the telephone, not shopping in stores, not communicating with the family's English-speaking friends. Susie took her eyes off the road long enough to smile. "Thank you, *Abuelita*. That's really nice."

"Marlee is nice girl. *Un querubín.*"

Susie grinned. "A little angel." *I think so, too.*

"*Sí,*" her *abuelita* tapped her on the arm, "you happy glow when you talk of your Marlee."

Susie gulped. How much did her *abuelita* know?

"*Tu mamá,* she no see yet. She no see that you fall in love with *el querubín.*"

Susie swallowed hard. Her *abuelita* knew she had fallen in love with Marlee. Maybe she had been too careless the other day when Marlee came to the house. Miguel figured it out, too. *Aay*, but then again, he had seen them kissing. That was kind of a dead giveaway. She'd have to be much more careful in the future.

But wait, Susie thought, her *abuelita* wasn't freaking out. She sounded, what was the right word? Supportive. That was not a word she ever expected to use when her family found out she liked girls and liked one blue-eyed blonde-haired girl in particular.

*Abuelita* tapped Susie's arm. Susie jumped at the touch; she had been so lost in thought. "You *mamá* will see the light soon. She no want you take tough path in life. She no want you hurt. You," her *abuelita* wagged a finger at her, "be honesty to self, then all is good."

Susie took a deep breath and willed herself not to cry. If her *abuelita* accepted her, could her mother and father? For that, she needed a miracle.

# Chapter 9

## In the Closet

The next couple of days were filled with a ton of chores. One day Susie pressure washed the driveway, and the next, she started cleaning out the basement. The basement job would take at least three days, but since the late July days were beginning to heat up, she didn't mind having to spend time in the cool space.

It was Saturday, her third and, hopefully, final day in the basement. Susie looked at the clock on the wall over the washing machine. It was a few minutes past noon. The Nor'easters' game had started at ten o'clock and should be over soon. She'd wait a few more minutes and then call Marlee to see how the game went. She took a cardboard box off the dusty shelving unit and brought it to the now cleared worktable to sort through it. Half the stuff in the basement was junk, which most likely included the things in the box. She was just about to toss a broken toaster into the trash bag when her phone rang.

She shoved the toaster aside and squealed at Marlee's name on the caller ID. She flipped open the phone.

"Marlee?"

"Hi! How're you holding up in that musty old basement?"

Susie could hear Marlee's smile through the cell phone. "It is what it is. I wish you were here. Or I was there."

"Me, too. I miss you. The Nor'easters miss you, too."

"Uh, oh." Susie leaned her head on her hand. "What happened?" Through the phone, she heard a car engine start up and figured Marlee was heading home.

"Coach Gellar moved Rachel from center to left, but Rachel complained that the balls came to her faster in left than in center."

"Did she make an error?" Susie cringed.

"More like three."

"Three? *Aay,* Coach Gellar's probably so pissed at me that she can't even think straight."

"We won, though, so it worked out."

"Oh, good." Susie sat up straighter, and they talked about the game, how Marlee pitched, and how Marlee couldn't wait for Lisa to play the following Tuesday.

"Sam'll be ecstatic to have Lisa on the team. They're so in love," Susie teased.

"I know. Are we all gushy and icky sweet like Lisa and Sam?"

Susie laughed. "I don't know. I think maybe we are."

Just then, Susie heard a voice in the background yell something like, "Life is good!"

"Who was that?" Susie asked.

When Marlee didn't answer right away, Susie's radar went on high alert. *Was it Bree? Was Marlee driving her home or something? Was Marlee driving her to some secluded place to be alone?* Susie kicked the worktable. "Ow," she said.

"What happened?" Marlee asked. "Are you okay?"

"Just banged my foot. I'm fine." *But not really.* "Are you on your way home?"

"I'm on the road, yeah."

Susie frowned. Her answer sounded kind of evasive. "Call me when you get home. Unless you're working at D'Amico's?"

"Nope. No D'Amico's today. Tomorrow."

"Cool. I need a real job, too."

"You'll get one. Once you're off restriction, that is."

"Oh, hey, Christy called last night. She made it to California in one piece and moved into her apartment."

"That's awesome. I'm glad she's getting settled."

They talked a bit more about Christy, but then Marlee said she needed to hang up in order to concentrate on the road. Susie hung up reluctantly. She rubbed her eyes, wondering if the voice she thought she heard had been her imagination. Maybe it had been the radio. But why didn't Marlee just say it was the radio, or someone in the next car, or whatever?

Her phone rang again, jolting her out of her spiraling depression. "What's up, Sam?" There was no enthusiasm in her voice.

"Oh, that's nice. You sound like you lost your best friend."

Susie sighed. "I just talked to Marlee on the phone."

"You just talked to Marlee?"

"Yeah, I think she might be interested in that Bree girl."

"Bree? Who's that?" Sam sounded perplexed.

"That Southbridge pitcher."

"Oh, yeah," Sam said. "She was at the field today."

"See?"

"I'm coming over."

"Why?"

"You need cheering up," Sam said. "I'll meet you in your room."

"I'm in the basement."

"Just go to your room."

"Why?"

"Just go," Sam demanded. "I don't want to go into that yucky basement."

"Okay, fine. Whatever." Susie thought Sam was acting really weird. Maybe there was some truth to Bree turning Marlee's head. Maybe Sam, good friend that she was, wanted to break it to her gently. "I'll see you in a few." Susie made her way up the basement stairs.

"*Ciao.*" Sam hung up.

"*Mami,*" Susie called, "I'm taking a break in my room for a minute. Sam's coming over."

"Not too long," her mother called back from her bedroom, where she was organizing her closet. Apparently, watching Susie work so hard had motivated her as well.

"Okay." Susie was too tired to care, but she'd have to make sure Sam didn't stay too long.

Susie trudged up the stairs to her room and washed her hands and face in the bathroom. She was about to throw herself on her bed in exhaustion when she noticed the rose quartz on the rock shelf. She held it up to the light and thought about Marlee. She gripped it tightly in her hand, letting misery wash over her. She crumpled onto the bed, her back to the door, and tried not to think about Marlee alone with Bree.

After a while, she heard the unmistakable sound of Sam's Sebring pulling into the driveway. The car door opened and then shut, but Susie didn't bother to roll over. Sam knew the way to her room and would let herself in. Susie stroked the smooth surface of the quartz she still held in her hand. "Marlee, don't break my heart."

"I won't."

Susie bolted upright off the bed. "You'd better not be a hallucination." She raced into Marlee's open arms. She kissed her lips and then held her face so she could kiss every square inch of it. "What are you doing here? How did you..." She glanced out the window toward the house.

"Don't worry. They don't know I'm here. Sam went inside to keep your parents occupied and give us some alone time. I snuck out of her car and then up here."

"I didn't even hear you." Susie drank in Marlee like she hadn't seen her in months instead of days. "I thought you were on your way home."

"No," Marlee smiled and pulled Susie closer, "we just made you think that. I was in Sam's car when I called you."

"That was Sam's voice I heard?"

Marlee nodded.

"Not Bree?"

Marlee shook her head. "Susie, I'm not interested in Bree. She keeps calling me at least twice a day, sometimes more, but I keep blowing her off. I told her not to call so much, that my mom needed the phone for business." She ran a finger down Susie's cheek. "I want to be with my *Latina* girlfriend, Susana. Perhaps you've heard of her? Gorgeous girl, a woman actually, with long brownish-reddish hair and biceps like granite?"

Susie put her arms around Marlee's waist. "Never heard of her, but you can be with me if you want."

"I want." Marlee pointed to the bed. "We've got five minutes, tops. Let's not waste it."

Susie's growl came from somewhere deep within. She grabbed Marlee's hand and pulled. Susie flopped on the bed and pulled Marlee on top of her. If her mother found Marlee there, especially like this on the bed with her, Susie was sure she'd be dead meat or worse. But at that moment, she didn't care.

Marlee nestled herself on top of Susie and stroked her face. She leaned down to kiss Susie's cheek and then kissed her way to an ear. She suckled the delicate skin of Susie's earlobe and then kissed her way along Susie's jawline to repeat the torture on the other earlobe.

Susie, meanwhile, stroked Marlee's back and let her hands reach just above Marlee's butt. Oh, how she wanted to reach lower, grab two handfuls, and press Marlee against her, but Marlee was in charge, and she couldn't rush her. Susie's breathing got heavier as Marlee's lips trailed a path along the soft skin of her neck. She couldn't stand it any longer and pulled Marlee front and center for a full kiss on the lips. Marlee moaned, which sent Susie's stirred up libido into overdrive. Taking charge, she grabbed Marlee by the waist and then flipped her over and scrambled on top in one swift move. She strategically placed her thigh where Marlee would appreciate it most and applied a little pressure. Marlee's moan meant she'd hit the mark.

Susie kissed the same path Marlee had taken. She revered Marlee's sweet, chiseled face as she went but didn't stop there. She kissed her way down Marlee's neck trailing kisses along her collar bone, Marlee's moans spurring her on. She was just about to pull Marlee's shirt collar lower so she could kiss the sensitive skin there when Sam's voice in the driveway stopped her.

"Okay, Mr. Torres, I'll tell her. It was nice to see you all again."

Susie heard the mudroom door slam and then Sam's footsteps on the driveway heading toward the garage.

Susie stopped her trail of kisses and groaned. "*Aay*! There's never enough time."

Marlee smiled sadly. "I know. We'll more than make up for it next time we're alone."

Susie pushed herself off of Marlee and then helped her sit up. They sat on the bed and laughed as Sam made her presence known. She stomped on the bottom stair and called up loudly. "Susie, are you home? It's me, Sam. I'm coming up the stairs now." Bam, she pounded her foot on the stair. "One stair." Bam. "At a time." Bam, bam, bam. "Okay, I'm at your door." She stood on the other side but didn't open it.

Susie laughed. "Sam, it's okay. Come on in."

"Okay." Sam opened the door, let herself in, and shut it quickly. She smiled at Marlee and then at Susie. "I wish I could have given you more time."

"I'm happy for the time we got." Susie snuggled against Marlee.

"Thanks for smuggling in my girlfriend."

"See? I told you I had your back." Sam sat in the desk chair. "I just couldn't tell you I was bringing Marlee here because, well, you'd get all goofy, and then your mother would know."

"I would *not* get goofy," Susie protested.

Sam raised an eyebrow in disbelief.

"Okay, whatever." Susie rolled her eyes for Marlee's benefit. "Isabella has amazing mind-reading skills."

As if to prove Susie's point, they froze when they heard the mudroom door open in the main house. The sound of short quick footsteps on the driveway immediately had Susie on her feet. "Shit! It's my mother. What do we do? What do we do?" She searched her room frantically for somewhere to stash Marlee in case her mother came up the stairs.

The outside garage door opened, and the quick steps were on the stairs.

Susie sprang into action and pushed Marlee toward the closet. "Get in," she hissed. Thank God Marlee didn't protest. "Hide behind my clothes in case she opens the door."

Marlee's eyes grew wide in disbelief, but she didn't protest. Susie closed the door just as her mother jerked the bedroom door open and marched past the weight set toward Susie. Susie leaned against the closet door, trying desperately not to telepathically give away that the love of her life was hiding right behind her. She casually pushed off the door and headed back to sit on her bed, hoping to divert her mother's attention.

As soon as she sat on the bed, she regretted the decision. Did the bed look tumbled, like she'd been rolling around with somebody on it? She resisted the urge to fix her hair, fearful that she had bed head and totally give herself away.

"Susana, I need you to get some groceries at Stewart's."

"Stewart's?" Susie had no idea what her mother was talking about.

"Oh," Sam said to Susie's mother, "I didn't get a chance to tell her." She turned toward Susie. "Your dad wants you to take all the garbage from the basement to the Waste Management place."

Her mother threw up her hands. "He insisted you do it today. I told him you weren't done yet, but you know men." She looked at Sam, who was trying not to break out laughing. "They get something in their head, and you can't stop them." She turned back to Susie. "So, as soon as Sam leaves, get the trash out of the basement."

"*Sí, claro.*" Susie hated the way her voice sounded so meek. Marlee must think she was a sniveling coward in front of her mother. Which she kind of was.

"Get milk, eggs, and butter."

Susie sprang off the bed and grabbed a pad and pen from her desk. She wrote down the list with a shaking hand. "Anything else?"

Her mother remained quiet for a moment. Susie's heart beat so loudly she was sure everyone could hear it. *C'mon, Mami, I can't take this.*

"No," her mother said, "that's all I can think of. Bring your cell phone in case I think of anything else."

"Okay."

"And you go nowhere else." She poked the air with a finger to solidify her point. "Just to Waste Management and then to Stewart's."

"Yes, *Mami.*"

Her mother turned on her heels and headed toward the door when the unthinkable happened. There was a noise in the closet. "What was that?" Her mother whirled around.

Sam sprang to her feet and pointed to the ceiling. "Are those squirrels back, Susie?"

"What squirrels? You never told me about squirrels." Her mother looked up where Sam was pointing.

Susie couldn't help the look of panic on her face. She tried to act natural but saw her life flashing before her eyes as the seconds ticked on.

"Susana," her mother put a hand on her hip. "What's going on?"

"Nothing, *Mami.* I promise." She swallowed guiltily and knew her mother saw it. "The squirrels sometimes—" Susie didn't get to finish her sentence because there was a shout from the driveway.

"*Mami,* oww!" Miguel's baby voice called. "I hurt myself."

Susie's mother flew to the door and down the stairs instantly. Susie raced to the window to see what had happened. Her brother Miguel sat on the driveway clutching his ankle in obvious pain, but when he saw his sister at the window, he flashed her a conspiratorial smile. The downstairs garage door flew open, and his smile was gone instantly.

"*Mami,*" Miguel cried, laying it on thick, "I fell off my skateboard." He pointed to the skateboard lying on its side nearby.

98

"*Dios mío*," Susie whispered to Sam, "he's a good actor."

"Is he hurt?" Sam stood by Susie's side, watching the events unfold on the driveway.

"No, he's totally faking."

"Why?"

"I think he's helping me." Susie headed to the closet door. "Watch for my mother, okay?"

Sam nodded and looked out the window. "The brat is actually helping you?" She clutched her chest. "Hell must be freezing over."

Susie nodded with a grin. She opened the closet door.

Marlee eased herself out from behind the clothes. "Is she gone?"

Susie nodded.

"I'm so sorry. Some boxes fell as soon as you shoved me in here, and I was holding them up the whole time, until—"

"It's okay, *mi vida*. It's okay." Susie stroked Marlee's face. "I'm so sorry I had to put you back in the closet." Susie grinned, hoping Marlee would chuckle at her pun, which she graciously did. Right then, Susie vowed to the universe that she would somehow convince her mother that God wouldn't strike the family down dead if her daughter loved a girl. She didn't know what would be worse—her mother's anger or God's lightning bolt. Susie shivered. Anyone who knew Isabella Maria de Fatima Torres knew the answer.

"Are you okay, sweetie?" Marlee put a protective arm around her.

"Yeah." Susie almost melted in the compassion she saw in Marlee's eyes, knowing she probably didn't deserve it.

Sam cleared her throat. "Uh, guys, I think this may be our only chance to get Marlee out of here. Your mother is heading into the house with a limping Miguel."

"Okay, let's give them two more minutes."

Marlee and Sam nodded. Sam glanced at her watch.

"Where am I gonna meet you?" Susie said with a grin. It wasn't a question of *whether she would* meet up with them but where.

"Back at Sandstoner Fields," Sam said. "I left Lisa there watching a little league girls' softball practice. I'll drive her home, okay? That way, you two can take your time doing whatever."

"Perfect, but it's going to take me a few minutes to haul the garbage out of the basement and stuff it in my trunk, so wait for me. Okay?"

They both nodded. Sam looked at her watch again and said to Marlee, "Ready?"

Marlee nodded, and she and Sam snuck toward the stairs, ready to make a run for it.

# Chapter 10

### For Real

Marlee held the plastic basket over her arm as Susie placed a gallon of milk alongside the eggs and butter.

"Is that too heavy?" Susie asked, ready to relieve Marlee of the basket.

Marlee shook her head but used her other hand to balance the weight. "C'mon, let's look around the store. I need some chips."

They strolled down the short aisles of the Stewart's convenience store side-by-side. Susie wished they could hold hands or even link arms, but she wasn't brave enough for such public displays of affection. Someday maybe, but not yet.

"You must be starving after the game," Susie said.

Marlee shrugged. "A little, but nothing a good Lay won't cure."

Susie looked at Marlee in disbelief.

Marlee smiled mischievously and reached for a bag of Lay's potato chips.

Susie laughed. "You're crazy." But there it was again. That smile. The one that promised everything would be okay. She could live her entire life waiting for that smile.

Marlee put the potato chips in the basket and looked sidelong at Susie. "I want to do this for real someday."

"Do what for real?"

"Shop. With you. For our home. For us."

Susie melted on the spot. "Me, too. Can you imagine us married in a big old house? Just us?"

"It's possible, now that gay marriages are legal in New York."

"I know. Somebody needs to tell my mother that."

Marlee smiled. Her eyes were sympathetic. "So, who's going to mow the lawn?"

"We'll take turns. Who's going to cook?"

Marlee laughed. "Uh, well, I'd like to say we'll take turns, but you'd end up with grilled cheese sandwiches and chicken noodle soup every night. That or peanut butter and jelly."

"Okay, I'll cook," Susie said firmly. "You'll want a cat, won't you?"

Marlee nodded as if that particular issue would be a deal-breaker. "You?"

"I do now."

"Good. C'mon, let's get out of here."

Susie paid for the groceries, including Marlee's potato chips and two bottles of Stewart's cream soda, one for each of them, and they headed back to the car. She put the groceries in the empty trunk. The trunk had been full when she went to the landfill, but thanks to Marlee's help, she was able to unload it all quickly. She unlocked the passenger door of her car for Marlee and held it open for her. "Thanks for helping me with that stuff at the Waste Management place."

"You mean the dump?" Marlee reached over and unlocked

Susie's door.

Susie jumped in. "Oh, c'mon. 'Waste Management' sounds so much nicer than 'dump,' but, yeah, you're right. It's just the dump."

Susie said a little prayer to the universe that her car would start, and it happily did on the first turn of the key. She didn't let on to Marlee that there might have been a chance they'd be stranded. She didn't want anything to ruin the stolen moments they were sharing. With her recent incarceration, she had gained perspective and knew that every moment she had with Marlee and with her friends was to be cherished.

"I'm sorry I have to take you back to your van."

"Me, too."

Susie leaned over and gave Marlee a quick kiss. She put the car in reverse.

Marlee pointed out the driver's side window past Susie. "Look at that lady staring at us."

Susie stepped on the brake. "Where?" Her eyes flew open wide, and she looked away quickly. "Shit," she muttered under her breath. She backed the car out of the lot as quickly as she dared, threw it into drive, and headed back onto C.R. 62. "That was Mrs. Johnson. And she saw us. She saw me kiss you. And now my mother's going to find out." Susie pounded the steering wheel. "I'm dead meat."

"Mrs. Johnson? The lady that fired you?"

Susie nodded and let out a sigh that ended with a frustrated groan. When would her life ever be her own? When could she stop worrying about who saw her where and with whom? When could she stop worrying about what other people thought?

"Hey," Marlee reached for Susie's hand and held it tight. "Someday, it'll be just you and me, and we won't have to worry about who sees us."

Susie let herself be consoled. There wasn't much she could do about it anyway. She glanced at Marlee. "I hope that's true because I can't keep going on like this. Something's gotta give somewhere."

By the time Susie pulled her car into the parking lot at Sandstoner Fields, she had calmed down and decided that she wasn't going to let Mrs. Johnson or anybody else invade her precious time with Marlee. The parking lot was half-full because of the little league softball practice in progress on the field. Susie smiled at the elementary school-aged girls playing the game she loved. She'd only been grounded for a week so far, but she severely missed playing ball with her friends.

"Hey, look," Marlee pointed, "there's something under my windshield wiper. I hope it's not a parking ticket."

They got out of Susie's car, and Marlee pulled the folded piece of paper out from under the wiper.

"What is it?" Susie regretted the question as soon as the answer came.

"It's a note from Bree." Marlee read it out loud. "She said, 'Missed you after the game. I thought we were going to hang out.'"

Susie cocked an eyebrow at Marlee.

"Hey, I never told her we'd 'hang out.' She was stalking me in the dugout before the game, so I said something like, 'I'll talk to you after the game, okay?' I said that just to get rid of her."

Susie decided to firmly believe that Marlee truly didn't want anything to do with Bree. "Look," Susie pointed to the note, "she left her phone number for you."

"And her email address, too. How lucky for me."

Susie nudged Marlee in the arm. "Look at you. You're a chick magnet."

"Shut up." Marlee nudged her in return. "You're the only chick I want. But what am I supposed to do about her?" She held up the note. "About this?" She unlocked the van's passenger door and gestured for Susie to hop in. Susie grabbed the cream sodas and potato chips and climbed in. Marlee climbed into the driver's side.

Marlee opened her soda, took a swig, and waved the note around as if still waiting for an answer.

"*Mi vida*, I don't know what you're supposed to do. She obviously likes you, but you're, uh, taken." Susie took a drink from her soda. "Mmm, you're right. Cream soda is good." She took another sip.

"Told you. So how do I let her down gently?"

"Hmm," Susie looked out the windshield at the softball field in front of her, "I don't know. We could always…"

"What?"

"We could let her know that you're with me."

"How?"

"I don't know. Let her catch us kissing or something?"

Marlee sucked her breath through her teeth. "In the van?"

"Or in the dugout after a game?"

"Yeah, yeah, yeah," Marlee agreed. "Maybe she'll get the hint and back off."

Susie nodded. "Maybe."

Marlee carefully tore Bree's note into the tiniest bits she could manage and tossed the lot into the plastic litter bag her mother kept in the van. She wiped her hands. "All gone."

"Good." Susie raised a suggestive eyebrow at Marlee. "I wish I could kiss you here."

"I know. Me, too. There are too many people and kids around."

"Yeah." Susie reached for Marlee's hand. "We can get married now in New York, but we're still too scared to let anybody see us. It's kind of stupid."

"I know, but I'm not ready to come out of the closet in front of the whole world, you know?"

Susie nodded in agreement.

Marlee leaned back in the driver's seat and pointed to the sky. "See those puffy white clouds?"

"Cumulus clouds."

"You really are a science geek, aren't you?"

"Not really. Just when it comes to rocks and earth science. I like the weather, too."

Marlee squeezed Susie's hand. It was the equivalent of a hug, one of those hugs they couldn't share in public. "Well, anyway," Marlee continued, "this was the kind of day I pictured when I had that wicked crush on you last March, and your team came to Clarksonville to play us."

"Ahh," Susie said softly. "That was the day I fell in love with you."

Marlee's cheeks turned instant crimson. "Mm hmm. But that

day wasn't like this one. That day was cold and gray. I think it even rained."

"That didn't stop us from getting together."

"Nope."

Marlee made such puppy-dog eyes at Susie that she wanted to ignore the rest of the world and swoop in and kiss her like there was no tomorrow. Instead, she cleared her throat.

"Did you know that clouds are just tiny water droplets?" Susie pointed back to the clouds. "Cumulus clouds are made when warm air rises into the atmosphere and reaches cold air. The water in the air condenses and then slowly drifts up into the atmosphere. That's how they get that cottony look. When I was growing up, *Papi* told me that clouds were created differently."

"Oh yeah? What'd he say?"

"Well," Susie continued, "he said that every day God assigned an angel to paint the sky. So, every day before *Papi* drove me to school, we'd stop to look at the sky to see what the angel had painted that morning. And every morning, we'd thank God and the angel who'd provided us with that day's canvas." Susie laughed. "Of course, some mornings in the winter, it would be pitch black, and *Papi* would scold the angel for taking the easy way out with a roller and black paint."

Marlee chuckled. "It sounds like you have a great relationship with your dad."

"Yeah." Susie grinned but then remembered. She kicked herself mentally. "*Dios*, I hope I didn't…"

"What?"

"I hope I didn't make you sad. Make you think about your own dad."

"I did think of him, but not in a sad way. He died almost six years ago, so most of the time, I can call up the good memories without losing it."

Susie reached over and hugged Marlee. "*Te quiero, mi vida.*"

"I love you, too." Marlee pulled back, squeezing Susie's hand again. "There. That's your kiss."

"Nice." Susie squeezed back. "There's yours."

They sat in silence for a moment. Susie didn't want the moment to end but knew it had to.

"Marlee, I gotta—"

"I know."

"Call me on my cell when you get home," Susie said and opened the passenger door. "*Te quiero,*" she whispered, not wanting anyone except Marlee to hear.

"Me, too." Marlee pressed two fingers to her lips and kissed them. She flicked the kiss to Susie, who scooped it out of the air with her hand and then smashed the kiss against her heart.

"Bye." Susie waved and then headed toward her car. Leaving Marlee was getting harder and harder, but she had to get home. She unlocked the car door but couldn't bring herself to get in. She turned and leaned against the door, so she could watch Marlee pull out of the parking lot.

Once the speck of Marlee's van disappeared in the distance, Susie groaned. When would they ever be alone? With a grunt, she got in the car and turned the key in the ignition. It whined and whined, but the starter didn't catch.

"C'mon," Susie said gently as if not to offend the car. She tried again, this time pumping the gas pedal a few times. The car still wouldn't start, so she smacked the steering wheel as panic rose in her stomach. "Come on," she pleaded, but to no avail. No matter how many times she tried to start the car, it stubbornly wouldn't.

She pounded the steering wheel again in frustration. She couldn't let her parents catch her at Sandstoner Fields. They'd know she went there to meet her friends, or worse, to be alone with Marlee. She thought about calling Marlee to come back, but then what? What if they couldn't get the car started? And she couldn't bother Sam. Sam was off alone with Lisa. She'd done too much for her already.

With a deep breath, she decided to call the lesser of two evils. She opened her phone and said, "*Papi*," into the receiver.

She prayed and prayed that he'd left his cell phone on. He usually did because he worked as a regional salesman for a paper product company covering the entire New York North Country and parts of Vermont. He had to be reachable at all times.

When he answered the phone, relief washed over her. Thank God she didn't have to call the home phone, or worse, her mother's cell phone.

She tried to start the car again as she talked to him, but to no avail. He didn't hesitate when she said she needed him to come get her. She cringed, waiting for the reprimand when she told him she wasn't at Stewart's or the Waste Management dump. He didn't seem to care that she was at Sandstoner Fields.

Once she hung up with her father, she got out of the car and hopped up on the hood. She watched the young softball players on the field. There was a time when she was that young and played catch with her dad in the yard. She couldn't remember the last time they'd done that. His promotion to regional manager a few years back probably had something to do with it. She was so caught up in her thoughts that she didn't hear his car pull up alongside hers.

"*Mariposita*," her father said, "are you okay?"

Susie jumped. "Yeah." She heard the frustration in her voice. "It's just annoying that she won't start." She slid off the hood and gave her father a quick hug. She loved how good looking her father was with his short dark brown hair, cut impeccably. She even liked his stylish sideburns and precise eyebrows.

She looked at the car and practically held her breath waiting for him to ask her why she was at the fields when she wasn't supposed to be. She relaxed a micron when he simply took her key and got in the driver's seat.

"When was the last time you tried to start it?"

"When I called you."

"Okay, let me try." He turned the key, and the car roared to life.

"*Papi*, how did you do that?"

"Magic." He wiggled his fingers as he stepped out of the car. "We need to get this fixed." He held the door open for her to get in. "Tomorrow I'm leaving for another road trip, but I'll be back on Saturday. How about we take this clunker to Moe's on Sunday and have him give us an estimate for a new starter?"

"Sounds good to me, *Papi*." Susie hoped he wasn't about to tell her she'd have to pay for it all by herself. She had a savings account, but it didn't have much money in it. Filling up the gas tank for trips to Clarksonville was a serious drain on her already limited resources.

"Okay, I'll follow you home." He started to head back to his car but then turned around. "If your mother asks, your car broke down at Stewart's."

"Stewart's?"

Her father's eyes became sharp laser beams directed right at her as he repeated, "Stewart's."

Oh, wow. She had an ally. "Thanks, *Papi*," she called after him.

He nodded once without turning around.

# Chapter 11
### We've Got Your Back

Sam pulled her Sebring into a parking spot at the Elmhurst Rage softball field. Susie leaped out of the passenger side and jumped onto Marlee's back. "I'm ba-ack," she singsonged in Marlee's ear.

"Yeah, and I've got the backache to prove it." Marlee hung on to Susie for a moment and then grunted. She let go, and Susie hopped down. They headed for the dugout.

Lisa leaped off the bench when she saw Susie. "Welcome back, stranger." She gave her a quick hug.

"Thanks." Susie grinned at her friends.

"Does Coach Gellar know you're here today?" Lisa pointed toward home plate, where Coach Gellar stood with the Elmhurst coach. Something on Lisa's face put Susie on alert. Maybe Coach Gellar really did hate her.

"Uh, yeah," Susie said. "I called her last night when my mother gave me the happy news. *Dios mío*, I can't believe my mother let me out a day early."

"It was your dad's doing," Sam said knowingly. "It had to be." She sat on the bench to put on her cleats.

"You're probably right." Susie's second week of incarceration

112

had been worse than the first. Not only did her mother pile on the chores, but she had been even colder, if that was possible. But Susie didn't care at that moment because she was off restrictions and free, free, free. *Aay*, except for the fact that she kind of didn't have a car. Her dad was due back from his trip later that night, and then tomorrow, they were going to bring her car to Moe's Garage to get an estimate.

Susie looked around the shabby visitors' dugout. There was no helmet rack, no water fountain, and no cubbies to put your gear in. No bat rack, either. All the bats were leaning against the fence. "This dugout sucks," she said to no one in particular.

Sam made a face. "Yeah, there's nothing to it."

Marlee and Lisa exchanged a glance, but neither said anything. It was then that Susie remembered that Marlee and Lisa went to Clarksonville High School, one of the poorest schools in the county. Their field didn't have much, just a rusty backstop and a couple of rickety old benches that didn't even fit the whole team. Forget about dugouts.

Susie grimaced at Sam, who seemed to catch her meaning.

"We're pigs," Sam whispered.

Susie nodded. The East Valley High School softball team had almost every amenity in their dugout that a team could ever want.

"Oh, hey, thanks for the ride," Susie said to Sam, desperately trying to change the subject. "I'll return the favor when my car's fixed."

"No problem," Sam said. "I've got your back."

Marlee and Lisa must have heard Sam's comment because they

turned around simultaneously.

"Me, too," Marlee said.

"Same." Lisa smiled.

"My friends are the best." Susie stood up and stretched her sore muscles. She looked at Marlee and couldn't help laughing.

"What's so funny?" Marlee asked, hand on hip.

"You two look weird in East Valley red uniforms."

Marlee looked down at her red shirt with a look of disgust on her face. "I, for one," she said with disdain, "can't wait to peel this thing off after every game."

Having impure thoughts about Marlee peeling off her shirt, Susie felt her cheeks get warm.

"Oh, you said it, sister." Lisa knocked fists with Marlee.

Susie gestured toward Marlee and Lisa and then said to Sam. "Do you see what we have to put up with?"

Sam shrugged. "I'm right there with you."

Coach Gellar walked into the dugout. She stopped and regarded Susie for a moment before saying, "Nice of you to make an appearance, Torres."

Susie had no idea how to respond, so she simply nodded.

Once the coach turned her back, Sam rolled her eyes. Susie appreciated the support, but the support earned Sam a playful smack from Lisa.

"Be nice, eh?" Lisa admonished.

"Okay." Sam stuck out her lower lip like a scolded little girl.

"Nor'easters," Coach Gellar barked, "bring it in."

Susie leaped off the bench and joined her teammates in the

loose circle forming around their coach. "Here's the starting lineup."

Susie was, but wasn't, surprised when Coach Gellar didn't call her name. She had missed two weeks, five games in all, so there was no reason to think she would be plunked back in the starting lineup. At least not right away.

After the brief team meeting, Susie and her teammates headed out to the field to run their laps, stretch, and loosen up their arms. She was allowed to take a few balls in left field during the team's pregame warmup, but not much else.

Rachel, the girl starting in left field for the Nor'easters, teased Susie after their warmups. "Nice of you to show up, slacker."

Susie laughed. Since middle school, she and Rachel had been bantering back and forth in the outfield. "I got tired of the easy life and decided to see what you bums were up to."

Rachel regarded Susie thoughtfully for a second. "You know I don't want your position, right?"

Susie nodded.

"I hope Coach Gellar comes to her senses right quick, because hon-ee, I hate left field. Centerfield is where this girl belongs." Rachel pointed to herself.

"It's kind of out of my control." Susie glanced at their coach to make her point.

Rachel followed her gaze. "Uh, yeah. She's a force of nature, ain't she?"

"Yeah." Susie nodded. "Good luck out there, and don't worry about me."

Susie watched the starting players get ready for the game and flung herself at the far end of the team bench.

Coach Gellar walked to the dugout fence. She let her gaze fall on Susie for the briefest of moments, dismissing her promptly.

"Miller," Coach Gellar called, "go coach first base."

The pain of her coach's rejection hit her hard. Susie gripped the edge of the bench until her knuckles turned white. *Betsy Miller?* Susie thought. *She passed me over to anoint Betsy Miller as the first base coach?* Betsy was the worst player on the team. She couldn't even read the coach's signs, so how in the world was she going to coach first? Susie blinked back the sting of tears.

Marlee sat next to her. "Hey."

Susie didn't look up. "What?"

"Stop that."

"What?"

"Every single person on this field," Marlee whispered, "including everybody in that Elmhurst dugout, knows that you should be in the starting lineup. Coach Gellar knows it, too."

Susie felt her throat tighten. She blinked back more tears.

"This will blow over soon," Marlee continued. "Coach Gellar likes to be in control. Of everything. I've only been on this team for three weeks, and even I know that, so you should, too."

Susie nodded.

"Just let her throw her weight around a little. Let her show you she's the boss of you, and then everything will go back to normal."

Susie rolled her eyes. "Everybody's the boss of me. My mother. My coach. When do I get to be my own boss?"

Marlee's eyes softened. "When you and I make our home together. And then you can be the boss of me, too."

Susie smiled in spite of her foul mood. They'd only been going out for three and a half months, and yet they wanted the same things. "Do you promise?"

"That I'll let you boss me around? Absolutely."

"No, dork," Susie said and smacked Marlee on the arm. "You know what I mean."

"Yes," Marlee said, her expression turning serious. "Yes, I promise." She turned toward the field. "Oops, I'm on deck." She stood up to go but turned around and wagged a finger. "No moping. This is a mope-free zone. There's no moping in softball."

Susie's fake smile became real as she watched Marlee swing the bat in the on-deck circle. Marlee's legs were so strong, probably from all that pitching. Susie felt a twinge of desire wash over her and settle deep in her belly. She reached for her water bottle and splashed cold water on her face. It didn't work. Her libido was still in high gear, and now her face was wet.

As the game wore on, it became clearer and clearer that Coach Gellar was not going to put her in the game. At the end of the sixth inning, the Nor'easters were beating Elmhurst by a score of 7-0. Marlee, Lisa, Sam, and the rest of the starters ran off the field to get ready to bat in the top of the seventh, and probably last, inning. Sitting alone at the far end of the bench, as far away from Coach Gellar as she could get, Susie had all but given up for the day.

"Torres," Coach Gellar yelled down without looking.

Susie snapped to attention and cringed as she sprinted to her coach like a trained puppy. "Yes, Coach?"

"You're pinch hitting for Tanya."

"Okay." Susie tried not to feel the slap of the words. Coach Gellar hadn't said she was going to play in the outfield. No. She was going to pinch hit and then sit back down on the bench. To further add insult to insult, Susie checked the lineup card and realized that Tanya had made the last out of the previous inning, and her batting spot probably wouldn't come up at all. *Thanks, Coach. You're an ass—*

Susie halted the expletive in her head when she caught Marlee's sympathetic smile.

"Sorry," Marlee mouthed.

Susie nodded and rolled her eyes, trying not to let her anger bubble any closer to the surface than it already had. She slinked back to the far end of the bench so she wouldn't be in the way.

Sam called a quick huddle with a few of her teammates. Susie wondered what they could possibly be talking about. After they batted, all they had to do was keep Elmhurst from scoring more than six runs. Easy for a team like the Nor'easters.

Rachel was the leadoff batter. Susie noticed her crowding the plate more than usual and wasn't surprised when she got hit by the first pitch. The Elmhurst pitcher had been throwing inside pitches the entire game to brush batters off the plate. The next batter for the Nor'easters also crowded the plate and promptly got hit by a pitch. Susie had to laugh. Her teammates had lost their minds.

Sam stepped into the batter's box with runners on first and second.

"C'mon, Sam," Susie yelled from her dark corner. This ought to be good. Sam was a good hitter. At least one run should score.

"You go, Two," Marlee yelled, using her nickname for Sam. "Hit it out there." Marlee stood up and said to Susie, "I'm on deck-deck. I gotta get ready."

It was just as well. Poor Marlee had been suffering in self-imposed incarceration in Susie's loser-of-the-day corner.

"Get a hit," Susie encouraged.

Marlee waggled her eyebrows in response, grabbed her helmet, and headed to the line of bats leaning against the fence.

"We'll take it, Two," Marlee yelled.

Susie looked up. Sam had walked to load the bases. "Ho, ho," Susie cheered under her breath. Lisa was the cleanup hitter, and that meant trouble for Elmhurst. During the last school year, Lisa had been named to the all-county batting team, so Elmhurst didn't stand a chance. Especially because there was no way the pitcher would pitch around her. Not with the bases loaded.

Susie caught the blood-thirsty gleam in Coach Gellar's eye. She obviously liked going for the kill. Marlee was right. Coach Gellar liked to be in control, and it certainly looked like the Nor'easters were just that.

Lisa could have knocked the ball out of the park for a home run but fell behind in the count and dinked a weak grounder over the second baseman's head. It didn't look like she'd swung the bat all the way around. Rachel ran home, making the score 8-0, and all the other runners advanced safely to the next base. Marlee stepped into the box as the fifth batter of the inning. Susie did the math and realized that she might actually get a chance to hit that inning as the number nine batter.

Susie stood up and gripped the chain-link fence. "C'mon, Marlee! Give 'em heck." Susie was stunned when Marlee crowded the plate. "No, no, no," Susie hissed under her breath. The last time Marlee had gotten hit by a pitch, she ended up in the hospital. "Don't do it, Marlee," Susie yelled toward home plate. It wasn't worth it.

Too late. Marlee got hit square in the back with the next pitch.

"First," the home plate umpire called and pointed toward first base.

The athletic trainer started to run toward Marlee, but Marlee waved her off and trotted to first base, unfazed by just getting hit by a fastball. Another run came in for the Nor'easters. The score was 9-0.

"Time," the Elmhurst coach called and headed toward the pitcher's circle for a conference.

Susie wished she had a camera. Sam stood on third base, Lisa on second, and Marlee on first. The bases were full of her friends.

The next Nor'easter batter got up and walked. Sam scored, giving them a 10-0 lead. Susie was officially on deck-deck and stood up to get her bat from where it stood, gathering dust against the fence. She plunked on her batting helmet and waited by the dugout gate. The Elmhurst pitcher walked the next batter, and Lisa scored, making it 11-0.

Susie walked onto the field feeling rather strange. She took her practice swings in the on-deck circle and tried to make sense of her role in the game. Pinch-hitting was new for her. Coach Gellar gave the batter at the plate the take sign, obviously wanting to milk as many walks out of the Elmhurst pitcher as she could. It worked. The batter walked, and Marlee crossed the plate for their twelfth run.

Susie high-fived Marlee as she passed by. Marlee called back over her shoulder, "Ducks on the pond, batter. Hit away."

Coach Gellar must have thought that was a good idea, too, and gave Susie the green light. Susie almost laughed when one of the Elmhurst outfielders groaned and backed up toward the fence. Her outfield teammates did the same.

"That's respect, Sus," Sam called from the dugout. "Show 'em what you've got."

Susie swallowed hard and took a practice swing. She needed to get a big hit to prove to Coach Gellar that she didn't belong on the bench. She needed to prove that she belonged back in the starting lineup.

The Elmhurst pitcher took the sign from her catcher. Susie let the outside pitch go by.

"Ball," the umpire yelled.

The next pitch hit the dirt for ball two.

Susie stepped one foot out of the box and looked at her coach for the sign. Sometimes on a 2-0 count, Coach Gellar would flash the take sign to lay off the next pitch. No such thing. Hit away. With a grin, Susie stepped back into the box and got ready. A sweet fastball came right down the middle of the plate. She swung hard, putting all her anger and frustration into it, and sent the ball rocketing toward deep left field. She sprinted toward first base, knowing she had hit at least a double, hoping she could leg out a triple. Betsy waved her on to second base. Susie sprinted and looked at her coach. Green light. Her adrenaline kicked in as she stomped on second base and headed toward third. She expected her coach to throw up a stop sign, but she didn't. Her teammates screamed for her to score, so she threw on the afterburners and rounded third toward home. Rachel stood behind the plate, yelling for her to slide. The catcher crouched down. The ball was on its way. Susie leaned back, threw her arms up, and slid desperately, hoping that home plate was somewhere underneath her.

She had no idea where the ball was but didn't need to. The umpire threw her arms out to her sides and yelled, "Safe!"

Susie's teammates stormed her from the dugout.

"In the park grand slam," Marlee yelled in her ear over their shouting teammates. "My hero."

Susie was on top of the world. Once free from her teammates, she trotted back to the dugout. She looked toward her coach, expecting some kind of smile or thumbs up, something to indicate that she was out of the doghouse. Nothing. Her coach kept her nose in the scorebook, presumably writing down the play. Susie shrugged. Whatever. She didn't live to please Coach Gellar. Still. It stung.

Susie sat down in a thump. This time she sat in the middle of the bench instead of in self-imposed exile. Every single one of her teammates congratulated her. It felt good to be part of the team again.

Marlee plopped down on one side of her. Sam and Lisa on the other. Sam looked Susie straight in the eye and said, "Like I said before, we've got your back."

Susie looked at her friends wide eyed. Why hadn't she realized it? "*Dios mío*, you guys totally set that up for me, didn't you?"

The grin on Marlee's face gave it away.

"Yes, I do," Susie said, looking up to the heavens. "I've got good friends."

She looked back down, but a particular blonde-haired spectator in the bleachers caught her eye. "Uh, oh." She pointed toward the bleachers. "Houston, we've got a problem."

Her friends turned to see where she was pointing.

Marlee gasped. "Bree." She groaned and hid her head in her hands.

Almost in unison, Susie, Sam, and Lisa said, "We've got your back."

# Chapter 12
## Two-by-Four

Plan A was to deliberately delay their exit from the dugout after their win against Elmhurst. That way, Bree would get bored waiting for them and leave. Susie tried not to laugh as Marlee moved like a robot in slow motion.

Susie snuck a peek through the dugout cinderblocks. She frowned when she saw Bree taking up residence on the bleachers.

"*Muchachas?*" Susie whispered. "Plan A has officially bombed. On to Plan B?"

Marlee, Sam, and Lisa nodded.

Sam and Lisa flanked Marlee on either side. Susie moved in behind all of them. "Got your keys, Marlee?"

Marlee nodded. The new plan was to move as a group toward Marlee's van, dive in, and drive away. They would come back later for Sam's car, once the fields were Bree-free.

"Guys," Susie said, "if Plan B doesn't work, then we go to Plan C."

"What's Plan C?" Marlee whispered over her shoulder.

"Make a run for it even if she's in the middle of a sentence."

Everyone chuckled, and Sam reached behind her to give Susie a playful smack. "Let's hope it doesn't come to that."

"Ready, everybody?" Susie asked. They all nodded. "Okay, go, go, go."

Marlee pushed the gate open, and they collectively power walked toward the van. Out of the corner of her eye, Susie saw Bree push off the bleachers and head toward them.

"Hurry," Susie urged. "She's gaining on us."

They walked quickly, weaving their way through the cars.

"Hurry, hurry," Susie urged them on. Bree was almost on them.

They reached the van, Marlee had her key ready, but then the unimaginable happened. The keys flipped out of Marlee's hand and tumbled end over end to the pavement. Everyone groaned.

Marlee scurried to pick them up and fumbled to find the right key. Susie urged her on silently.

"Nice game, Marlee," a cheerful voice said right behind them.

Susie jumped and almost laughed out of sheer panic. The four friends slowly turned around to face Bree.

"Thanks," Marlee said. "Did you, uh, have a game today?"

"Yeah, we had a home game against Mohawk." Bree looked smug. "We pounded them."

"Mercy rule?"

"Yeah, fifteen to nothing. I pitched."

Susie shot a sidelong glance at Marlee, willing her to end the conversation before it even got started. Something dawned on her. Southbridge was a hell of a long way from Elmhurst. After her game, Bree must have broken the sound barrier getting there. Where did she find time to change into her form-fitting shorts and a tight tank top? Her outfit was obviously designed to turn a certain blonde pitcher's head.

Sam exchanged a knowing glance with Susie. She must have figured it out, too.

"Oh, I'm sorry," Sam interrupted. "We haven't met. I'm Sam."

Bree looked startled, as if she hadn't realized there were other people around. "Oh, uh, I'm Bree. I pitch for Southbridge."

"I love your outfit," Sam said.

Susie clamped her lips together, trying not to laugh.

Sam took a step closer, putting herself between Marlee and Bree. She pointed to the girl's snug tank top. "Is that wickaway fabric?"

"Yeah, it's supposed to pull the perspiration away from your skin." Bree looked desperate as she tried to see past Sam.

Marlee, meanwhile, had taken that opportunity to casually unlock the sliding door of the van and toss her gear inside. Susie tossed hers next to Marlee's and then climbed in. On her way to the passenger seat, she reached over and unlocked Marlee's driver's side door. It looked like they might have to invoke Plan C after all.

Lisa, who had been standing next to Sam, said, "Where'd you get your tank? Do they have my size?" Lisa rose to her full amazon height. If that didn't make Bree back down, Susie didn't know what would.

"I got it online, I think," Bree said impatiently. With a snort, she brushed past Sam and was on Marlee in a flash. "So, uh, think you can give some pitching pointers sometime?"

Bree's cheeks turned a bright shade of crimson, and Susie almost felt sorry for the girl. Almost.

"Yeah," Marlee said in a way that Susie knew she was weakening, too. "I guess maybe I could show you some stuff the next time we play you guys."

"Tuesday," Bree said so quickly that Sam actually laughed out loud.

"Okay," Marlee gave in. She gestured toward Lisa in introduction. "I don't think you've met my catcher. This is Lisa."

"Hey," Bree said with disinterest and the barest of nods.

"Hey," Lisa mimicked. The look on her face clearly showed that Bree's lack of manners didn't amuse her.

"Lisa just got back from a hand injury, so she can't catch for us."

"That's okay. We don't need a catcher." Bree seemed undeterred in her quest to get Marlee alone. "We don't need anyone else."

"Oh." Marlee turned around to roll her eyes in frustration at Susie. Clearly, Marlee knew it was time for Plan C. She turned back toward Bree and said, "We'll just use your catcher, okay?" She looked over Bree's head and said to Lisa and Sam. "Hey, you guys? We have to get going. We don't want to be late." Marlee opened her car door and climbed into the driver's seat.

Sam's eyes grew wide in confusion. They hadn't discussed what they were doing after the game. "Ah, yes. Okay," Sam agreed. "C'mon, Lisa. We don't want to be late." They headed toward Sam's car parked a few spots down.

"Where are you guys going?" Bree's hand was now on Marlee's open door.

The look on Susie's face probably matched the look of disbelief on both Sam's and Lisa's. The girl was relentless.

127

Marlee didn't answer right away, so Susie leaned over and said, "We're going somewhere to be alone so we can make out."

Bree took a step back, clearly not knowing how to respond, but she'd let go of the door, and Marlee slammed it shut. She rolled her window down a few inches and sputtered, "Sorry, but we really have to go." She started the van.

"See ya." Bree's voice held so much disappointment that Susie almost felt rotten that they were dissing her.

Marlee yanked the gear shifter into drive and squealed her way out of the parking lot.

"*Dios mío*," Susie said with a laugh. "She's pushy."

"Dog with a bone, man." Marlee shook her head. "She's, like, crazy or something."

"Crazy in love," Susie teased.

"I know, but even though she's annoying as hell, I kind of feel bad for her." Marlee turned onto the main road.

"Me, too." Susie checked to make sure Sam and Lisa were following them. "But not really."

"I mean, like, when I fell for you, I fell pretty hard. What if you'd blown me off like that?" Marlee glanced at Susie with puppy dog eyes.

"I see what you mean, Jelly Bean." Susie thought about it for a minute. "But you were giving her all the hints she needed to know that you weren't interested."

"I need a two-by-four."

"Okay," Susie said slowly, "I'll bite. A two-by-four?"

Marlee laughed. "I never told you that story?"

Susie shook her head.

"It's a story my dad told me once."

"Yeah?"

"There are two farmers."

"Okay."

"The first farmer sells a donkey to the second farmer and says, 'This donkey is great. He'll plow all your fields. He just keeps going and going. Just say, *Hyah!* and he'll plow all day. Say, *Whoa,* and he'll stop.' The second farmer says, 'Great. I'll take him.' So the next morning, the second farmer gets the donkey ready to plow his field. He says, '*Hyah!*', but the donkey doesn't move. He says, '*Hyah!*' again, but the donkey still doesn't budge. He keeps at it for almost an hour when the first farmer comes along and asks, 'How's the plowing going?' The second farmer says, 'Plowing? This is the laziest donkey in the world. He hasn't moved an inch. I want my money back.' The first farmer says, 'Have you said, *Hyah?*' The second farmer says, 'Yes! For an hour.' The first farmer says, 'Oh, I forgot to tell you.' He picks up a two-by-four, whacks the donkey in between the eyes, and says, '*Hyah!*' The donkey takes off plowing the field, and the first farmer says, 'You just have to get his attention first.'"

Susie burst out laughing. "That's crazy. Not to mention abusive to animals." Susie laughed again as she reheard the punch line in her head.

Marlee laughed with her until they were both giggling out of control. Breathless, Marlee pulled the van down a neighborhood street and pulled over to the side. She put the van in park and, when she finally caught her breath, looked around. "I have no idea where we are."

"Me, neither. So," Susie chuckled again, "what does a two-by-four have to do with Bree?"

"Bree won't take any of our hints, so somehow we have to get her attention before we implement Plan D."

"What's Plan D?"

"I have no idea."

Susie burst out laughing again, and Marlee joined her.

Lisa and Sam appeared at the driver's side window so suddenly that both Marlee and Susie jumped, causing them to howl even louder.

"What are you guys laughing about?" Sam bugged out her eyes.

Susie caught her breath long enough to say, "*Dios mío*. It's way too long to repeat right now, but, uh, we have no idea where we are."

Sam rolled her eyes. "Well, I do. At least Bree didn't follow us, so that's a good sign."

"Thank goodness." Marlee sighed in relief but then grabbed her stomach. "Oh, man, I'm starving."

"Me, too," Sam said. "I know a good diner in Elmhurst. Let's get lunch there."

"Sounds good to me." Susie realized she was hungry, too. "We can come up with Plan D while we're there."

"Plan D?" Lisa asked.

Susie and Marlee started laughing again, and Susie said, "We, uh, haven't worked out all the details, but so far, it involves a donkey and a two-by-four."

~~~

Sam pulled the Sebring into Susie's driveway and popped the trunk so Susie could get her gear out. Sam and Susie sat for a moment talking in the dark car, the sun having set at least an hour earlier. Marlee and Lisa had already headed home to Clarksonville.

"*Dios mío*, I have so much fun with you guys," Susie said. "My stomach hurts from laughing so much."

"Oh, me, too. I'm so glad Marlee's looking for a new car tomorrow with her mom."

"That's just 'cuz you want Marlee to be able to drive Lisa here to East Valley."

"So?" Sam said with a smile. "A girl can want, can't she?"

Susie waggled her eyebrows. "Yeah, but I'm going to miss her mother's van. It's nice and roomy."

"I bet." Sam smacked the console in between them. "You don't know how many times I've wanted to rip this thing out."

Susie nodded. Every time she and Marlee were alone in her little Toyota, it had been uncomfortable and cramped. "Thanks for the ride."

"Anytime, my friend. I hope Coach starts you on Tuesday."

Susie rolled her eyes. "Riding the pine sucks." She stepped out of the car and grabbed her softball bag from the open trunk. She slammed the trunk shut and walked to the driver's side window. "If my car isn't fixed by Tuesday, can you pick me up for the game? The last thing I want to do is ask Isabella to drive me."

"I hear you," Sam said with a grin. "I'll plan on it."

131

They said their goodbyes, and Sam backed her car out of the driveway and then drove away.

Susie ran up to her room for a quick shower and then gathered her dirty laundry. Out of habit, she scooped up her keys and put them in her pocket. Heading toward the main house, she paused and patted her beloved little car on the hood.

"Tomorrow, we're gonna get you fixed, girl."

Susie whistled happily as she took off her crocs in the mudroom and headed into the house. She nodded to the Virgin Mary and then headed to the basement to dump her uniform and a few other things in the washing machine. She bounced back up the stairs thinking about the amazing afternoon she'd just spent with her friends. She couldn't help the smile that burst on her face when she thought about the alone time she'd spent with Marlee after the diner. They'd stumbled on a nicely secluded park in Elmhurst. Sam and Lisa were in Sam's car a few parking spots away, but they could have been miles away for all Susie knew.

"*Abuelita*? *Mami*? Is there any dessert left? Flan, maybe?" A girl could hope.

Her mother came into the kitchen. "*Aay*, no flan *y tu hermano* polished off the last of the *besitos de coco*. Your father won't even get any, and he should be home any minute now."

Susie stuck out her lower lip as if pouting. She wasn't overly fond of coconut kiss cookies anyway, so she really didn't mind that her brother had eaten her share. He was entitled to it ever since his academy award winning ankle sprain performance in the driveway the weekend before. Come to think of it, though, he'd kind of been milking the sprained ankle a bit too long. It might be time for him to have a miraculous recovery.

"I'll need your help for tomorrow's dinner," her mother said.

"Sure." Sunday dinner was usually a big deal in the Torres household.

"*Señora Rodriguez* is coming over."

Susie cringed. "And Robbie, too?"

"*Sí, claro.*" Her mother smiled. "*Y Roberto, también.*"

Susie groaned audibly.

"Susana, why the face? Roberto is a nice boy. He's home for a week from medical school."

Susie groaned again, but this time inwardly. "I don't like him like that, *Mami.*" Somehow, she needed to get her mother to listen to her. To do that, she'd need one of Marlee's two-by-fours.

"You need to think about your future, Susana. *Y Roberto es puertorriqueño, mmm*?" She singsonged the fact that he was Puerto Rican as if that would change Susie's mind.

"Are you, like, planning my wedding or something?" The words popped out of her mouth before she could stop them. She held her breath, hoping she hadn't just set off a landmine.

"You need to start thinking of these things early." Her mother waved a dismissive hand. "All your nonsense about geology."

Before she could stop herself, Susie blurted, "I'm going to college, *Mami*, to study geology or…something. And I might have a big wedding, but probably not in a church."

Her mother stared at her with sharp eyes. "Don't say such things." She turned her back and busied herself putting dishes away in the cupboard.

Quietly Susie said to her mother's turned back, "I won't be getting married at St. Catherine's." She looked down at the kitchen floor for a moment gathering her courage. "And I think you know why."

Her mother smacked the countertop with the palm of her hand. Susie jumped at the sound. Her mother spun around, eyes blazing. She poked the air and spat, "It's not natural." She looked like she wanted to add something else but fled the kitchen instead, leaving Susie's ears ringing with the accusation.

Her father chose that untimely moment to enter the kitchen, having just gotten home from his business trip. The master bedroom door slammed shut upstairs. He looked toward the stairs and then back at Susie with a confused expression.

"What'd I miss?"

Susie fled the kitchen, not wanting to break out crying in front of her father. She ran out of the house without stopping to put on her crocs. Not knowing what to do or where to go, she flung herself into her car. She felt vindicated when the engine roared to life. Maybe she could drive far enough away so her mother didn't have to look at her unnaturalness ever again. Maybe she'd drive to California. Maybe Christy needed a roommate.

# Chapter 13

### So Alone

Susie barely had the car out of the driveway when her tears came. She had no idea where she was going and didn't care. She had to get away. Get away from her mother, who thought she was a monster.

At that last thought, Susie banged the steering wheel. Why, oh why, had she said those things to her mother? Why couldn't she have simply shut the hell up and pretend to like Robbie? It would have been easier, but she'd have to deny her relationship with Marlee. She'd done enough of that already. That's why she hadn't shut the hell up. No way was her mother or Bree or anyone else going to take Marlee away from her. She'd almost let Christy do that. Never again.

The mere thought of losing Marlee again set her waterworks flowing even harder. Would she have to choose? Choose between Marlee and her family? The ache began deep inside her chest. The sobs started deep inside, too. When she couldn't catch her breath, she pulled the car over to the side of the road. She threw the gear shift into park and turned off the headlights so she'd be in complete darkness. She was just about to turn the car engine off but pulled her hand back in time. Thankfully the rational part of her brain had

135

asserted itself. If she turned the car off, she might not be able to get it started again.

After several long minutes, she recovered enough to take stock of where she was, a minor detail she hadn't paid the slightest attention to before. Ah, she was on C.R. 62 heading toward Clarksonville. She had unknowingly headed toward Marlee. She closed her eyes and leaned her head back on the headrest. What was she supposed to do now? Her mother's rejection had cut her heart to pieces. No one should be expected to think clearly with a shattered heart like hers.

"My own mother can't accept me," Susie said out loud to the universe. "What am I supposed to do?" She pounded the steering wheel.

Susie thought about Marlee, her sweet, tender Marlee. How could anyone hate that innocent blonde-haired, blue-eyed cutie? Susie's shoulders relaxed at the thought of Marlee's chiseled features and high-cheek bones, her oh-so-kissable lips, and the way her body moved when she pitched, so strong, so athletic. And the smile. Susie never wanted to lose the special smile that was just for her.

Susie took a deep breath and wiped her eyes on her t-shirt sleeve. Now what? Without really thinking, she turned the headlights back on and pulled the car onto the highway heading toward Clarksonville. She didn't want to drag Marlee into her mess, but she couldn't go home either, so she simply drove on without thinking.

*What if I were to just drift into the other lane? They'd all think it was an accident.* She let the car drift toward oncoming traffic, but when the wheels thunked on the raised reflectors dividing the road, she jerked the car back to her side. No, no, no. That wasn't what she wanted. She just wanted to go numb.

Mile after mile ticked by. Susie wondered if that was the way Christy had felt all those years. Alone. Nobody in her corner. Did Christy think her family would be better off without her? Susie's tears started up again, and before she could stop herself, she was sobbing so hard she was gasping for air. The hurt came from somewhere so deep inside that she felt like she was dying. She spotted a parking area ahead on the right. She pulled into it and remembered it was the same stupid parking area she'd pulled into the day she'd lost her mind in May and broken up with Marlee. She threw the car in park and turned the headlights off. This time she consciously remembered to keep the engine running.

She couldn't get her sobs under control and was disgusted with herself. She inhaled in short gasps and then exhaled in a long moan. She'd heard pregnant women on TV breathe like that when giving birth. If she hadn't been so miserable, she might have laughed at the comparison.

After an eternity, she finally caught her breath and laid her head back against the headrest, exhausted. Somehow, impossibly, she stopped crying. She closed her eyes and tried to figure out what to do.

She jumped, her eyes flying open when someone tapped on the window. She accidentally pressed the gas pedal down, causing the engine to rev. A balding middle-aged man stood right outside the door. Reality came crashing in. She was at the parking area on C.R.

62, and it was late at night. She rolled the window down two inches.

"Hey," the man said, "I'm John Smith. Are you my date?"

"What?" Susie's confusion must have been obvious.

"Sorry, I'm a little late. Are you Lola?"

"What? No!" Her heart was pounding. She hit the car locks, grateful that the doors were already locked. "Get out of here," she spat, shutting the window as fast as she could. She turned the key to start the car, forgetting that it was already running. The piercing sound of metal on metal made her wince.

The man stood his ground. "Hey, c'mon. I already paid for this."

Susie had no idea what he was talking about and threw the car into reverse. She hit the gas, not caring if she ran over his feet. Once clear of him, she shifted into drive too soon, grinding the gears. She winced but sped toward the parking lot exit.

"C'mon, c'mon." She smacked the steering wheel, waiting for a car to pass by on the highway before she could pull out. She chanced a quick look behind her, hoping he hadn't followed her on foot or something. No, thank God. He was standing in her now empty parking spot, waving his arms around in anger. Two cars away from her newly-vacated spot, a feminine arm beckoned for him. He stopped his ranting and headed toward the woman. Susie didn't wait to see what happened after that.

She pulled onto the road, her heart still pounding. She took several deep breaths to calm her heart. She had pulled into the parking area, not considering that someone might bother her there. How naïve. The parking area obviously turned into a very different place at night—a place she never ever wanted to be near again.

She reached for her cell phone to check the time but couldn't find it on the passenger seat where she usually threw it. She checked her pockets. Nothing. When it wasn't in the center console or the glove compartment or the floor, it hit her. She had left the house so fast that she didn't have her cell phone on her. Or her wallet. In fact, she had no money at all. She didn't even have shoes on.

An occasional passing car illuminated the dark road as she drove. Her heart had slowed down enough, so she could think, but *Dios*, she wished she had her cell phone. She passed a Valero gas station with a convenience mart. There were at least seven cars in the parking lot. She'd never given it much thought before but realized how lucky she was to have a safe and secure place to be at night. Her nerves jangled at the thought of that man tapping on her car window. What if he had been more aggressive? What if her car door had been unlocked?

She shuddered and tried to shake the icky feeling crawling all over her. What time was it? It had to be close to ten o'clock already. She sighed. She couldn't turn around and go home now. She couldn't face another round with her mother. Since she was already headed to Clarksonville, maybe she'd keep going and park behind D'Amico's Restaurant. Marlee worked on Sundays and would find her there. But then again, the cops might come by and ask questions. There was no other choice, really. She had to go to Marlee's. She would quietly pull into the McAllister driveway and not wake up Marlee or Marlee's mother. She could sleep in the car until morning.

Susie brightened at the thought of Marlee's smiling face when she spotted her in the driveway. Explaining her presence to Mrs. McAllister might prove challenging, but she'd think of something. She'd once told Marlee that lies come with the territory of being gay. She sighed and set her sights on Clarksonville.

Without warning, the car started making weird noises. Maybe the gear crunching had done some real damage. She looked at the dashboard controls and realized her problem immediately. How long had the damn gas light been on? She had no time to formulate a plan, because the engine went silent, and she lost power in the steering wheel. The car had enough momentum that she was able to pull the car onto the shoulder of the road.

"Aaaah!" she screamed in frustration as long as her lungs would allow and pounded the steering wheel at the same time. What was she supposed to do now? She smacked the steering wheel one last time and then folded her arms defiantly. What else could go wrong? She stared into the darkness, trying to go numb.

Several long minutes passed as she sat in denial in her dead car on the side of C.R. 62. The last thing she wanted was for some state trooper to pick her up and force her parents to come to get her. She had to get to Marlee, but how? She had no cell phone and no money to pay for a taxi. The Valero gas station—it wasn't too far back. Hopefully, it was still open. Of course, she had no shoes. She'd run out of the house so fast she hadn't put her crocs back on. Wait. Her softball gear was in the trunk. She could put her cleats on and walk in those. She was about to be excited that she'd solved one problem in her rapidly deteriorating life when she remembered that Sam had driven her to the game and her softball gear wasn't in the car. It was in her room.

"Aaaah!" she screamed into the blackness again. "What does it matter anyway?" What was she going to do at the gas station once she got there? She had no money to buy gas, and she didn't even have a gas can. She punched the dashboard this time, sparing the steering wheel, and when she did, she heard the distinct sound of coins jingling. The ashtray. She had a bunch of change in there. She tore the ashtray out of its slot and dumped the coins in her hand. She turned the overhead light on and counted. She had two dollars and fifty-two cents. She shoved the coins in her pocket. Maybe she could bribe the convenience store clerk to let her use the store phone. Or better yet, maybe the store had one of those old-fashioned payphones outside. She'd seen people use them in movies. They probably weren't too hard to use. Hopefully, it wouldn't cost more than two dollars and fifty-two cents to call Marlee's house in Clarksonville.

She doused the interior lights in case anyone got interested in her or her car and realized that her headlights were still on. She flicked them off. The darkness completely overtook her, and she blinked until her eyes adjusted. She took a deep breath, trying not to panic as she felt more alone than ever.

She pulled the key out of the ignition, and with another breath for courage, opened the car door. She stepped onto the shoulder and instantly regretted her decision not to stop for her crocs. The hard roadside gravel dug sharply into her feet. She persevered, though, and shut the car door gently, making sure it latched shut. She locked the door with her key and put the keys deep into the pocket of her shorts for safe keeping. She peered down the dark road toward Clarksonville but didn't see any kind of store or lights or anything. She decided to stick to her original plan headed back toward the gas station.

She held her chin up high and carefully placed one bare foot in front of the other.

## Chapter 14

### I Can Stay?

Susie had no idea how long she had been walking, but it seemed like an eternity when the gas station lights finally appeared in the distance. She walked faster, which was hard because her bare feet were raw and bleeding. Along the way, she tried brushing the bits of road debris from the soles of her feet now and then, but two seconds later, the crap was embedded again. She shivered in the cold night air, wearing only shorts and a thin t-shirt. She also shivered because of the unknown things in the dark. An animal had growled nearby but thankfully hadn't gotten close.

Several cars had passed by her on her long trek, but none of them stopped. A carload of obviously drunk guys slowed down and yelled obscene things at her, but, thankfully, they didn't stop. Yeah, the night was not as innocent as she had assumed. She wished she had her softball bat or a tree branch to defend herself against human and non-human night creatures.

She slowed down as she limped into the gas station. Thank God it was still open. No one was hanging out in front of the store, but she approached cautiously anyway. Ah, there were two pay phones right out front. She slinked to the one on the left, continually looking around and behind her. She didn't want to deal with more creeps like the man at the parking area or those drunk guys. She looked at the phone, unsure what to do first. There were no instructions anywhere. She snorted out a sigh. She was reasonably intelligent, so it shouldn't be that hard to figure out. She picked the phone receiver up off its hook and then pressed the cold metal buttons of Marlee's cell phone number. After only three pushes, she hung up. Marlee might have turned her cell phone off, and Susie couldn't risk wasting her money on voice mail. She wasn't sure she could walk all the way to Marlee's house at this point, especially because it felt like she had something lodged in her foot. She doubted she could even walk back to her car.

She inspected her feet one at a time. The right one was swollen and bloody from something sharp she'd stepped on just after her scare with the growling animal. Maybe the store clerk could help her out. She glanced inside but didn't spot the clerk.

She took that as a sign from the universe to call Marlee again. She reached in her pocket and pulled out a quarter. It felt oddly comforting in her hand, like it was a lifeline. She held it tightly and picked up the phone receiver again. This time she pressed the numbers for Marlee's home phone. She smiled, remembering four months earlier when she had searched the phone book for a McAllister listing. There was only one McAllister listed in Clarksonville, so she had chanced it way back then, hoping Marlee would answer. She had, and Susie prayed that she would answer now.

The phone clicked a few times, but there was no dial tone. Maybe it needed money. She slid the quarter in the slot. She heard another encouraging click, but the call still didn't connect. She slid three more quarters in, assuming it cost at least a dollar, but still got nothing. She slammed the receiver down, praying her quarters would be returned—no such luck. The coin return remained empty.

"Shit," she muttered under her breath.

"That phone's broke." An unshaven middle-aged guy wearing a stained undershirt barely containing his beer gut gestured to the phone. He had one hand on the door handle. "Use that one." He pointed to the other phone. She nodded, but he was already in the store, apparently not interested in her response, which was fine with her.

The second phone seemed even dirtier than the first, but maybe that meant it worked and more people used it. She jammed her hand in her pocket and was about to pull out the rest of her quarters when she remembered something. Her *Tío Emilio*, her mother's younger brother, would call from Brooklyn and somehow make her mother pay for it. Her mother always griped about it but paid every single time. Susie had answered the phone once when he called. What was it the operator said? Something like, "Will you accept the charges?"

She decided to try that. If that didn't work, then she'd try to bribe the store clerk to let her use the store phone with the one dollar and fifty-two cents she had left. If that didn't work…

Susie took a deep breath and picked up the phone. She punched the zero button and waited.

"Operator services," the mechanical voice said. Susie's stomach clenched as she listened to the choices. "To place a collect call, press three."

"Yes, that's it," Susie said way too enthusiastically, but she didn't care. She punched the three button, and then a live operator got on the phone. She gave the woman her information. There was silence on her end for several anxious moments, but there was no way she was going to hang up. Not when she had a live person on the other end. After what seemed like an eternity, a voice came on the line.

"Susie?" It was Mrs. McAllister.

"Yeah. Hi. I'm so sorry to call—"

"Honey," Mrs. McAllister interrupted, "are you okay? Where are you? We've been worried sick."

They'd been worried sick? Maybe she wasn't as alone as she'd thought. "I'm...I'm okay. I'm, uh, kind of stuck."

"Where are you?" Her voice sounded more worried than angry. "Do you need us to come get you?"

"Yes. I'm sorry." Susie heard her own voice catch. She desperately didn't want to start crying again. *Dios mío*, she was so tired.

"Honey," Mrs. McAllister soothed, "it's okay. We'll come get you. Where are you?"

She knew where she was but looked up at the store sign to make sure. "I'm on County Road 62 at a Valero gas station. On the East Valley side of Clarksonville." She added the last part in case there was another Valero gas station on the other side of town. "I'm sorry I woke you up."

"We haven't been to sleep."

Susie heard a voice in the background. It must be Marlee.

146

"Susie? Marlee and I are leaving now, okay? Here's Marlee."

Susie heard the phone change hands. "Are you okay? Where are you?" The panic in Marlee's voice was loud and painfully clear.

"I'm fine, *mi vida*. I ran out of gas." Susie knew her feet weren't fine, though. The longer she stood there on the concrete, the more she realized that she'd really abused them. Who knew what disgusting things she'd walked through on the road.

"Where were you going? Were you coming here?" Marlee didn't let her answer. "Sam called me over two hours ago. She and your dad have been driving around looking for you. Apparently, your family got frantic when you didn't come home. What happened?"

Susie sighed into the phone. "I don't know. I…" The man with the beer gut came out of the store, so she stopped talking. She didn't want anybody to know she was stranded. Standing there with bloody bare feet probably gave it away, but she waited.

"Susie? Are you still there?"

Susie breathed a sigh of relief when the man didn't even look at her. "Yeah, I'm here."

"Why aren't you using your cell phone?"

Susie filled her in briefly on what had happened. She left out her scare at the parking area and wasn't going to mention her bare feet but figured she should since she didn't want to get blood all over their van. "Can you, uh, bring some old towels or something?"

"Okay. Why?"

"I cut my foot." *Understatement.*

Marlee gasped. "Susie." The phone sounded muffled as Marlee said, "Mom, she cut her foot." Marlee's voice then came back loud and clear. "Stay where you are. You're only about eight or nine miles away. Are you safe where you are?"

Susie looked around. "I'll stay near the doors, so the store clerk can see me."

"Okay, my mom's ready. We'll see you in a few minutes."

"*Gracias, mi vida. Te quiero.*"

"I love you, too," Marlee said in a hushed tone. In a normal voice, she said, "I gotta go now. My mom's already in the van."

"Bye." Susie waited for Marlee to hang up first. She held the phone receiver to her ear for several long minutes pretending she was still on the phone, hoping that no one would bother her.

She couldn't hold up the pretense any longer and reluctantly hung up the filthy phone receiver. She moved closer to the doors, and no one bothered her for the most part. One middle-aged couple hesitated at the door, looking her over. Susie thought they were about to ask if they could help her, but she looked away and moved back toward the phones. The man shrugged and held the door open for the woman to enter.

After what seemed like years, the familiar white van pulled into the parking lot. The relief Susie felt made her legs wobbly, and she started to cry. Marlee was by her side in an instant. Susie leaned on her. If she wasn't so exhausted, she would have been more careful about showing affection for Marlee in front of her mother, but she didn't have the strength.

Marlee started to lead her to the van, but Susie winced. Her feet hurt so bad.

"Oh, man," Marlee said, "look at your feet. Here sit down."

"No, can we just go?" Susie didn't want to stay any longer than she had to.

"Okay, c'mon." Marlee put an arm around Susie's waist. "Put your arm over my shoulder. Mom, can you get on her other side?"

Marlee's mother was much smaller than Marlee, and Susie didn't want to hurt her, so she mainly leaned on Marlee as they helped her hobble to the van. She pulled herself up on the seat and was about to pull her feet inside when Marlee's mother stopped her.

"Honey, I know all you want to do is get out of here but let me at least look at your feet. Okay?"

Susie nodded.

"Have you been drinking or doing drugs?"

"Mom!" Marlee protested.

"It's okay," Susie said to Marlee. It was a fair question. She used to drink a lot when she hung out with Christy but not so much anymore. She shook her head and simply said, "No, I haven't."

"I had to ask."

"I know." Susie let Marlee's mother examine her feet. The look of compassion in her eyes almost sent Susie over the brink again.

"Oh, honey. You have something embedded in your foot." She stooped lower to examine Susie's foot more closely. "Ah, it's a piece of gravel. How did you walk so far with that in your foot?"

Susie shrugged.

"Marlee," her mother said, taking charge, "come on. Get in. We'll take care of her feet when we get home."

Marlee scrambled to the other side of the van and then slid into the backseat next to Susie.

Her mother slid Susie's door shut and got in the driver's side. "That piece of gravel is right there at the surface. I'm sure I can get that out, but not here." Her glance took in the busy late-night gas station. The look on her face said she must have realized how different the night was, too.

Marlee laughed, a nervous laugh, but then said, "Uh, oh. You're in trouble. Surgery in Mom's kitchen usually hurts."

Susie forced a smile because she knew Marlee was trying to cheer her up. She also caught the worried glance Marlee exchanged with her mother and knew she'd have to start talking soon.

Marlee's mother didn't ask her any questions on the way to their house, but they did stop at Susie's car to leave a note that the car ran out of gas. They also left the McAllister's home phone number taped inside the dash just in case. They'd deal with the car later.

Once she'd hobbled inside the McAllister's kitchen, leaning on Marlee's shoulder the whole way, she sat down and knew it was time to explain why she was sitting in their kitchen with banged up feet at what turned out to be midnight. The bright lights of the kitchen made her suddenly feel unworthy. She felt as low as the low-lifes she'd seen out and about that night. Mrs. McAllister must think she was the lowest of Rican trash. Susie hid her face behind her hands when she started crying again. *Dios*, she just wanted to disappear.

Marlee pulled a chair alongside Susie and rubbed her back. "It's okay, Susie. You're okay now."

"You're safe here," Marlee's mother added.

Without looking up, Susie choked, "Can I—" She cleared her throat and tried again. "Water?" was all she could get out.

Marlee's mother set a cold glass of water in front of her in a flash. Once Susie caught her breath, she lifted her head and took a sip of the water. She coughed when it didn't go down the right way but tried again, that time successfully. She was so thirsty. Marlee's mother handed her a box of tissues. Susie took one and wiped at her eyes. She took another and blew her nose.

Marlee continued to rub her back.

Susie smiled her gratitude at both Marlee and her mother. They both smiled back sympathetically. They were probably afraid Susie would break down again if they spoke.

After a while, Marlee's mom said to Susie, "Okay, honey, I have to clean up those feet."

"No, I can—"

"C'mon. Hand those feet over." Marlee's mother set her mouth firmly, but the tenderness still showed in her features.

Marlee laughed. "There's no use struggling in Mom's operating room. I'll get you a bullet to bite, okay?"

For the first time in hours, Susie laughed. Genuinely. "Okay."

Following her mother's instructions, Marlee got a bucket, some old towels, hydrogen peroxide, antibiotic ointment, and bandages. After first rinsing off Susie's feet with warm water and then washing them gently, Marlee's mother used tweezers to dig for the piece of gravel lodged in Susie's foot. White-hot pain shot through her foot, but the pain only lasted for a moment, and then it was over. Marlee's mother held up the piece of rock between the ends of the tweezers.

"It looks like an igneous rock," Susie said with a slight laugh.

Marlee laughed with her. "You really are a rockhound."

Susie nodded. "Told you."

Marlee's mother cleaned the wounds with peroxide, applied the ointment, and then wrapped Susie's feet up in gauze. Susie's feet throbbed but felt infinitely better.

Marlee's mother instructed her to keep her feet elevated. "I don't think we need to take you to the emergency room, but we'll regroup in the morning."

"I can stay here?" Susie heard the relief in her own voice.

"Of course, honey, but…"

"I know. I need to call my parents." Susie smiled inside. Marlee's mother kept calling her "honey," and it felt good.

Marlee's mother nodded. "I don't want to intrude on your personal life, but maybe I should call them."

Susie shot Marlee a look. That would be the easiest way out, but she knew she couldn't do that. The easy way out wasn't always easy. Just that morning, she wanted to be in control of her own life, so she decided that it was her responsibility to talk to her parents by herself.

"I'll call them," Susie said and then turned to Marlee. "Would you call Sam? Tell her I'm okay and that I'm staying here, and I'll talk to her in the morning."

"I'm on it. She's probably still driving around. She was going to drive all the way here, but I told her I'd call if you showed up."

"I almost made it." Susie shrugged.

Marlee smiled. "Yeah, you almost did." Susie couldn't read the expression in Marlee's eyes. Concern? Love? Both. Definitely both.

Marlee's mother pulled the cordless phone off its base. She

handed it to Susie. "I'll be in the other room if you need me."

"Thank you so much, Mrs. McAllister. I didn't mean to cause problems."

Marlee's mother put a hand up. "You're fine." She gestured toward the phone. "I think you have bigger things to worry about right now."

After Marlee's mother left the room, Susie turned toward Marlee. "I'm sorry."

"Are you okay?" Marlee caressed Susie's cheek. "Sam said you had some kind of fight with your mom."

Susie sighed and told Marlee what had happened in the kitchen back home. "My worst nightmare came true. My mother thinks I'm 'unnatural.' She thinks I'm a freak of nature."

"I don't think you're a freak of nature." Marlee leaned in and kissed Susie softly on the lips. It wasn't a passionate kiss but more of a healing one. "And if you're a freak of nature, then so am I."

"*Te quiero, mi vida.* I can't wait until we're the boss of us, and no one else is." Susie looked at the phone trying to find the courage to punch in the numbers.

Marlee pulled her cell phone out of her pocket. "Let me call Sam." She gave Susie a quick hug and tapped in Sam's number. She returned her hand to Susie's back and rubbed gently.

"Wish me luck." Susie steeled herself for round two.

# Chapter 15
### I Think She Knows

Susie pressed the phone to her ear. She held her breath when she heard her father's voice.

"Susana? Is that you?" Concern was etched in his voice.

"*Sí, Papi, soy yo.*" Susie teared up again. Marlee's hand rubbed her back.

"*Estás bien?*"

"I'm fine. I'm at Marlee's house." She wanted to say she was sorry, but she didn't quite know how.

There was a short pause and then he asked, "*Que pasó, mariposita? Tu madre está muy enojada.*"

"Oh, really?" Her gut simmered. "*Mami's* angry? Is she angry at herself or me?" *This ought to be good.* Susie squirmed in the kitchen chair. Marlee sat next to her talking quietly to Sam on her cell phone.

Her father sighed into the telephone. "You and I need to talk before you come home."

"Okay." Susie slumped in the kitchen chair. Her mother hated her.

Neither of them spoke for a while until her father said, "Are you sure you're okay?"

Susie heard the uncertainty in his voice as if he wasn't sure what to do.

"I ran out of gas, *Papi*."

"Did you call for a tow truck?"

"No, I was close to a gas station, so I called Marlee. She and her mother came to get me." Okay, so she left out a lot of details, but he didn't need to know everything.

She told him that Marlee's mother was going to take her back to the car in the morning to put some gas in and see if they could get it started. If it still wouldn't start, she'd have it towed. He told her to have the car towed to Clarksonville since it was almost there already and that he would call back in the morning to check up on her.

She hung up the phone feeling better that he wasn't running around frantically worried about her. Still, she felt rotten that she and her mother were not only miles apart, literally but also emotionally.

Susie stared at the refrigerator, not ready to join the living yet.

"Are you hungry?" Marlee asked, apparently noticing her fixation on the large appliance.

Susie smiled. "Nah. I'm just tired. And I have to go to the bathroom."

"C'mon." Marlee grabbed an arm and helped her stand up.

Susie winced as she put her full weight on her throbbing feet.

"Mom?" Marlee called. "We need you as a crutch."

Marlee's mother came in and, together, they helped Susie to the bathroom.

"Do you need help in there?" Marlee asked from the other side of the door.

"No," Susie said with a laugh. "I remember how to do this all by myself." After she had relieved her aching bladder, she realized that her mouth tasted like fertilizer. "Hey, Marlee?"

"Yeah?"

Susie smiled. Marlee was still right outside the door. "Do you have a spare toothbrush?"

"Yeah, hang on."

Susie took that opportunity to wash her face and hands. She even washed up her arms, trying to wash the evening's memories away.

"Here you go," Marlee called from the other side of the door.

Susie opened the door wide and then shuffled back. She beckoned for Marlee to come in with her. Marlee looked over her shoulder, presumably to see if her mother was watching, and then stepped in quietly and clicked the door shut behind her.

Susie opened her arms wide. She would have grabbed Marlee immediately, but it hurt too damn much to move on her feet. Marlee filled her arms willingly, and Susie kissed her once quickly and then pulled her into a tight hug. "Thank you for being my knight in shining armor tonight."

Marlee squeezed Susie hard. "You're welcome, my damsel in distress."

"I've never been anyone's damsel before."

"I've never been anyone's knight."

Susie released Marlee but didn't let her get away. She leaned in for another kiss. If she wasn't so tired, the kiss might have escalated into more, but she pulled back and stroked Marlee's cheek. "*Te quiero, mi cabellera.*"

"*Y yo te quiero tu también. Mucho.*"

Susie tried not to laugh at Marlee's butchered Spanish. "You've been practicing your Spanish."

Marlee nodded. "How else am I going to talk to my future grandmother-in-law?"

They both jumped when Marlee's mother called for Marlee.

"Be right there, Mom." She opened the bathroom door and started to leave but then darted back in to hand Susie a toothbrush, toothpaste, and a bag of clothes.

"Thanks," Susie said to Marlee's retreating back.

Marlee turned and flashed a quick grin at her. She shut the door behind her.

After Susie brushed her teeth, she changed into one of Marlee's old t-shirts and a pair of sweats. The t-shirt was a little tight across her chest, but she was too tired to care. Once she was dressed, she hobbled out of the bathroom. Marlee was waiting right outside, and ushered her toward the couch in the living room. Marlee's mother had apparently been busy because the couch was made up for Susie to sleep on.

"Thanks for letting me crash here," Susie said to Marlee's mother.

"No problem. If you need anything in the night, just yell up the stairs."

"Thanks, Mrs. M."

Marlee's mother gave Susie one of those mom smiles that said everything would be okay. "Marlee, I'm heading up. Don't stay up too late."

"Okay, Mom."

They listened as Marlee's mother made her way up the stairs. As soon as the bedroom door clicked shut, Susie slid over to make room for Marlee on the couch. Marlee snuggled in next to her, and they lay face-to-face. Susie hadn't realized how tense she had been until Marlee gave her a sympathetic smile, and the tension eased. The tension would be back in the morning, she knew, but for now, it was dissipating.

Marlee reached up and caressed Susie's face. "You can live here with me if you want," she said barely above a whisper. Her eyes were sympathetic, but there was desperation in them, too.

"Someday we'll live together, *mi vida*. Someday," Susie said.

"Promise?"

Susie nodded, and even though she didn't mean to, she yawned.

"I have to let you sleep." Marlee started to get up.

"No." Susie pulled her back down. "Just a few more minutes, okay?"

"Okay." Marlee lay back down and kissed Susie chastely on the forehead.

"Mmm, that was nice." Susie tried to keep her eyes open, but they kept closing.

"It's okay, sweetie." Marlee stroked her cheek. "Don't fight it. You're safe now."

Susie smiled. Marlee called her *sweetie* again. She let her eyes close. She vaguely remembered Marlee brushing her lips across her cheek, but then she drifted off into a dreamless sleep.

She woke the next morning slowly, not quite sure where she was. Her chest felt heavy. Was she having a heart attack? Her eyes popped open when the heavy feeling moved. She was face to face with Marlee's white calico cat.

"Hi, Patches," Susie pet the cat behind the ears. "How long have you been here?"

Patches didn't answer but simply purred, obviously enjoying the attention. Maybe having a cat wouldn't be so bad. Susie yawned and stretched her arms overhead. She flexed her swollen feet and winced. Maybe she'd have to use Marlee as a crutch for a while more. She'd figure out how bad her feet were once she stood up and put her full weight on them. Marlee's mother had been so nice letting her stay, but things might be different in the light of day. Susie decided to apologize to Marlee's mother the first opportunity she got.

"Okay, little Patches," Susie said to the still-purring cat lounging on her chest, "you have to get up, 'cuz I have to pee." The cat meowed her disapproval at getting picked up and placed on the floor. Susie was about to stand up and hobble her way to the bathroom when she heard voices in the kitchen. Even though the living room door was closed, she heard the voices loud and clear.

"Do you want more coffee?" Marlee's mother asked someone in the kitchen with her. Marlee maybe?

"No thanks, I'm going to float away as it is," an unfamiliar woman's voice said. "So, how bad do you think that fight was between Susie and her parents?"

"Just the mother, I think. When I spoke with Susie's father this morning, he seemed pretty supportive."

Alarm bells rang in Susie's brain. Marlee's mother had talked to her dad? She groaned. How much trouble was she in? What time was it?

The stranger's voice sounded grim. "Hmm. That's terrible. How can a mother reject her child?"

"I don't know."

There was silence in the kitchen, and Susie wondered if she should make her presence known by loudly heading to the bathroom. She changed her mind when Marlee's mother spoke again.

"Marlee was devastated when Bill died. I think a little of her died that day, too. Oh, she always had friends, played softball, got good grades, and, if you didn't know her, she seemed fine. But there was always a somber mood about her, you know? Like a dark cloud hanging over her head."

"I've seen it."

"But, Joan, then she started talking about her friend Susie. Susie this, Susie that. And she started doing things with her all the time. Best friends, I told myself, even though she already had a best friend in Jeri, you know?"

The woman named Joan must have nodded because Marlee's mother continued. "But this was more. Suddenly my baby was all lit up. Inside and out. She was smiling all the time and humming and taking the stairs two at a time. The happy, carefree little girl I knew before her father died had come back." Marlee's mother's voice cracked with emotion. Susie got choked up listening. "There could only be one explanation for it."

"She's in love," Joan said.

"Yes." Marlee's mother cleared her throat. "It took me by surprise, I have to tell you, but if my baby's back, I don't care."

"Oh, Marge, Marlee's got a good head on her shoulders."

"I know. Her, uh, her friend—"

"It's hard to say the word 'girlfriend,' isn't it?"

"Yes. Okay, I'll say it. Girlfriend. Marlee's girlfriend, Susie, is a wonderful young woman. Polite, funny, intelligent." She laughed. "She wants to be a geologist."

"Nice."

"And she's attractive, too. If she were a boy, she'd be exactly what Bill and I always wanted for Marlee."

"Are you okay with the fact that Marlee's in love with a girl?"

"Actually, I think I *am* okay with it. It freaks me out that I'm *not* upset. I should be upset, right?"

"I don't think it's a requirement, but Paulie and I don't have kids, so I'm no judge."

Their conversation turned, and Joan teased Marlee's mother about finding a new love of her own one day. Susie definitely didn't want to hear about Marlee's mother's love life, so she yawned loudly and coughed a couple of times. She was trying to stand up on her still-swollen feet when there was a knock on the door.

"Susie?" Marlee's mother called. "Are you all right?"

"Yes." Susie laughed. "I'm trying to stand up, but it's not working out too well."

"May I come in?"

"Sure."

Marlee's mother opened the door and walked into the room. An older woman with gray hair pulled back into a ponytail was right behind her.

"Susie, this is my good friend Joan."

"Nice to meet you," Susie said.

Joan walked over and shook Susie's hand. "I hear you had a rough night."

Susie rolled her eyes and laughed. "You could say that."

Joan smiled at her. "You probably need to use the facilities?"

Susie nodded and tried to stand up again.

"Hang on, youngin'." Joan scurried out of the room. She came back in with a beat-up silver wheelchair. "It doesn't look like much, but she's got a lot of good miles left in her." She patted the back of the chair. "C'mon, hop in."

Susie decided it was pointless to protest, so she shifted her weight on the couch and threw herself in the chair without putting too much pressure on her feet.

"Now, youngin', once you're done primping, I'm going to have a proper look at those feet, okay?"

Susie nodded but looked up questioningly at Marlee's mother.

"This is Dr. Joan Aldwell. She's our family pediatrician as well as my good friend."

Dr. Aldwell nodded once. "Go on. Get yer wheels movin', kid." She pointed toward the bathroom.

Susie did as she was told and only had a little bit of trouble navigating the turn into the hallway. She had to leave the wheelchair outside the bathroom since it was too big to fit in the doorway. Once she was done 'primping,' she plopped back into the chair and wheeled herself to the kitchen where everyone had gathered. Marlee was up, pulling out two bowls for cereal.

The smile that lit Marlee's face melted Susie's heart. How nice it was to get up in the morning and not only have Marlee there but making breakfast for her as well. Marlee's mother and her friend Joan noticed Marlee's smile. Susie was sure of it because they exchanged a knowing look. If Susie hadn't overheard their conversation, she might have been worried about them seeing the affection she and Marlee shared. Marlee had been freaking out in her quiet Marlee way about coming out to her mother, but now Susie knew it would be okay. Susie had to find a way to reassure her that all hell wouldn't break loose like it had at her house.

After a quick breakfast of Kellogg's corn flakes, Dr. Aldwell examined Susie's feet.

"Whoever cleaned you up last night did an excellent job." Dr. Aldwell smiled approvingly at Marlee's mother. "I'm going to clean out this open wound again, put this salve on it," she held up a tube of antibiotic cream, "and then I'll rebandage both of your feet. Do you know when you last had a tetanus shot?"

Susie shook her head.

"Okay, that's a question we'll need answered from your folks. You'll need another if it's been too long. Who knows what you stepped on in your journey." She took one last look at Susie's feet. "Your dogs are still pretty swollen, kid, so I think it's the chair for you for a couple of days, and softball's probably out for at least a week."

Susie tried her best not to react to the "no softball" rule. "Thank you so much, Dr. Aldwell."

"Call me Joan. And you're welcome, kid. Marge'll get the chair back to me eventually. It's a spare one we have in the office."

Susie thanked her again but didn't call her Joan. It seemed too disrespectful. "How much do I owe you for helping me?"

Dr. Aldwell smiled and exchanged a glance with Marlee's mother. "You're fine. I don't charge family."

Susie sat up taller in the wheelchair. Family. Yes, that would be nice. She wanted to be part of Marlee's family. Someday.

"All right, ladies. I have a medical practice to run and must head out the door." Dr. Aldwell turned toward Marlee's mother. "I'll come by later to check up on our patient. If I don't like the looks of those feet, I'll prescribe some antibiotics. Actually, let me just go ahead and do that now." She pulled out her prescription pad and scribbled on it. She handed the prescription to Marlee's mother.

Marlee's mother walked her friend out to the driveway and to her car.

Once they were gone, Marlee took that opportunity to steal a kiss from Susie. "Ha. Looks like I have you hostage. Maybe you can look at cars with me today. Think my mom will let me get a van?" Marlee blushed and then grinned mischievously. "I kind of like us in that van."

"I do, too." Susie waggled her eyebrows suggestively. "But I think I have to deal with my own dead car today."

"Actually, my mom said that your dad was on his way to get

your car this morning." Marlee glanced at the kitchen clock. "In fact, he probably already met Paulie with the tow truck by now."

"Dr. Aldwell's husband?"

Marlee cocked her head. "Yeah, how'd you know?"

Susie realized her mistake too late. "Oh, uh, Dr. Aldwell said something to your mom about him before." Not exactly a lie, but she didn't want Marlee to know that she'd listened in on her mother's private conversation. "So, is my dad coming here?"

"Yes," Marlee's mother said from the other side of the screen door. She opened it and walked back into the kitchen. "I told him you'd call once you were up."

"Okay." Susie smiled at Marlee's mother. "Mrs. McAllister?" She paused, trying to gather up her strength. "I'm astronomically sorry to drag you and Marlee into my family drama. My mother just—" Susie's throat choked up with emotion, and she couldn't finish. Not that she had any idea how she was going to finish the sentence. She willed herself not to cry again.

The silence hung thick and awkward in the McAllister kitchen until Marlee's mother said, "It's all right, honey. She'll come around. It might take her some time, but moms usually come around eventually."

Susie nodded and attempted a smile that she didn't quite feel.

"Girls," Marlee's mother said, "I'll be upstairs if you need me."

Marlee waited until her mother had gone up the stairs. "I think my mom is onto us. I think she knows exactly what your fight with your mom was about."

Susie nodded. "I think you're right. Maybe it's time you came out to her."

"I don't know. When you tried it with yours, it didn't go so well." Marlee gestured at the wheelchair.

"Maybe we should tell her together." Susie shrugged. "Power in numbers, maybe? I get the feeling she already knows. And, hey, she wouldn't beat up an invalid, would she?" She gestured to the wheelchair.

Marlee laughed. "No, but *I'm* not in a wheelchair."

Susie leaned forward for a kiss, but the phone rang, and Marlee pulled away.

"I'll get it," Marlee called to her mother. To Susie, she said, "Maybe that's Sam or Lisa." She picked up the phone. "Hello?" Marlee waited for a moment. "Is anybody there? Okay, well, I can't hear you, so I'm hanging up now." She placed the phone gently in its cradle and headed back to Susie at the table.

Marlee was the one who leaned forward, this time demanding a kiss, but a knock on the screen door interrupted them. Susie's father stood on the other side.

## Chapter 16

### Fight or Flight

"*¡Papi!*" Susie tried to stand up, but her hand slipped on the arm of the wheelchair, and she fell back down.

"Oh, no, you don't." Marlee snapped her fingers. "Stay right where you are." She opened the screen door for Susie's father. "C'mon in, Mr. Torres. I'm Marlee."

"¡ "Nice to meet you." He entered the kitchen, and Susie could tell by his posture that he didn't feel entirely comfortable. "Thanks for taking care of *mi mariposita*."

"Any time." Marlee gestured for him to sit in the chair she had just vacated and then turned to Susie. "My mom and I'll be upstairs, okay? Yell if you need anything."

Susie nodded, grateful for the care that Marlee and her mother were giving her, both physically and emotionally.

Susie's father stood a few feet away, taking her in. Her wheelchair, her bandaged feet. In a rush, he pulled her into a hug and held on a long time. Susie held on, too. He wiped at his eyes when he pulled back and sat down hard in the chair.

He pointed toward the screen door. "Did you see today's canvas?"

"No." Susie looked out at the vibrant blue but cloudless sky and smiled. "A roller."

"Sky blue paint." They both chuckled, and Susie relaxed a little.

Her father's smile was sad, though. "*Estás bien, mi princesa?*"

"I'm fine, *Papi. La señora McAllister tiene una amiga que es una doctora.*" Susie told him how Dr. Aldwell checked out her feet. She also told him she had to stay in the wheelchair for at least another day but left out the part about not playing softball for a week.

He looked at her feet for a long time. "Your car was almost six miles from that gas station. I tracked the mileage. Did you walk it?"

Susie looked down at her hands on the table and nodded.

"In the dark?"

She looked up at him again, this time with tears in her eyes.

"With no shoes." It wasn't a question.

Susie nodded once.

He pressed his lips together, obviously trying to keep his emotions under control. Susie teared up, ashamed that she may have made her father angry.

He took a deep breath. "This is my fault. If I'd just gotten your car fixed at the first sign of trouble—"

"*Papi,* this isn't your fault. It's mine. I didn't know what to do or where to go, so I took off. I didn't check the gas gauge or anything." Everything came out in a rush. "I didn't even know where I was going."

"Why didn't you tell me what happened? You didn't have to run away."

"I didn't want to hurt you, too."

"Me?" The look of shock on his face surprised Susie. "You were worried about hurting me?" He sighed. "Your mother goes to extremes sometimes."

"Sometimes?"

Her father shrugged and then nodded. "She'll come around, *mariposita*. I think this is that 'Elect Joe Wilson' thing all over again. We just have to wait for that switch to flip in her brain. *¿Comprende?*"

"I understand, *Papi*. But what if it doesn't flip? What if it doesn't flip in my lifetime?"

He looked skyward for a moment as if trying to figure out what he wanted to say next. "Throughout every walk of life, there will be people who, for whatever reason, won't like who you are or what you do. Sometimes it makes no sense, but the important thing to remember is that the loss is theirs." He pointed at her. "You can't let other people's opinions of you stop you from being who you are."

Susie nodded and looked down. It was amazing how they could have an entire conversation about her liking girls without saying any of the actual words like *queer* or *gay* or *lesbian*. She looked back up at her father. "Does *Mami* hate me?"

"No, she's just confused, I think." He sighed. "All of this is new for her, and I don't think she's thought it through yet. She doesn't realize how happy you are." He glanced up the stairs where Marlee had gone. He sat back in the chair. "When we first came to New York from Puerto Rico, we moved to Brooklyn. Your *Tío Emilio* had moved there first and found a Puerto Rican neighborhood. We thought it would be a good place to start our family. Lots of opportunities for schools. Such a big state." He smiled at the memory. "But then we realized soon enough that not everybody was fond of our kind moving in. People shouted nasty things at your mother and me, calling us wetbacks, and other derogatory names."

"Isn't 'wetback' an insult for Mexicans?"

Her father nodded. "See? They couldn't even get their insults right."

Susie smiled but frowned inside, thinking about the abuse her parents and *Tio Emilio* must have taken.

"The last straw, though," her father continued, "was when a couple of white teenagers threw a beer bottle at your mother."

"Did it hit her? Was she okay?" Susie had never heard that story.

"It did hit her. She had a big bruise on her cheek near her eye." He touched his own cheek. "She was more shaken up than anything, but it was then we decided to move and start our family somewhere else. My supervisor in Brooklyn arranged for me to transfer up here, so within a month, we were in the North Country starting all over again. We'd done it before, so we knew we could do it again."

"Were things better for you here?"

"Well," he shrugged, "yes and no. We felt a little like aliens up here, but we vowed that we weren't going to let anything deter us from our goals again. We weren't harming anyone and had a right to be here as much as anybody else. Of course, we made sure you kids spoke mainly English, so you wouldn't have the troubles that we did. Other than that, we decided to be ourselves and be proud of who we were."

Susie traced the wood grain pattern on the kitchen table, trying to digest what her father was saying. She looked up at him. "So, I should be proud of who I am?"

He nodded. "I will always be proud of you, *mi mariposita*. No matter who or what you are." His smile was reassuring.

Susie's heart filled. She always liked the way her father's eyes twinkled when he smiled. "*Gracias, Papi.*"

"You may have a tough road ahead, but you have to be true to who you are. *Mami* doesn't hate you, but you have to be strong and stand up for yourself."

The way he looked at her made her remember that her biggest battle still lay at home. "I'll try, *Papi*. I'll try."

"That's all any of us can do." He gave her another hug and said, "Marlee seems like a very nice girl." He winked at her and changed the subject. "So, let's talk about your car."

"Is it okay?"

"Mrs. McAllister's doctor friend and her husband own a repair shop and," he pulled a business card out of his pocket, "Aldwell's Auto Repair will be replacing the starter for a helluva lot cheaper than Moe's ever would have. My daughter's got good connections here in Clarksonville."

"I didn't even know it." She laughed. "When will my car be done?"

"It'll take about a week, so I guess you'll have to bum rides for a while."

Susie looked back down at the table, trying to organize her thoughts. She needed time to think. Time to figure out how to handle her mother. She almost lost her nerve when she looked back up and took in her father's concerned expression. She forged ahead anyway. "*Papi*, I think I need to stay away for a few more days. I'd like to stay here." She looked back down at the table.

She had no idea what he was thinking and wouldn't have been surprised if he insisted she come home with him. She held her breath, waiting for him to respond.

"I don't blame you," he said after what seemed like a year. "I'll figure out something to tell your mother, but…"

"What?" She remembered to breathe again.

"You have to come home eventually."

"I know, *Papi*. I think *Mami* and I both need time to regroup."

"We all do." He stood up and gave her another hug. "My little girl is all grown up, I think."

Susie smiled. "Tell *Mami* that."

He grunted. "I need to get back home."

"You should meet Mrs. McAllister first."

"Okay."

"Marlee?" Susie called toward the stairs.

"Yeah?" came the quick response from the top of the stairs.

"My dad's leaving and wants to meet your mom."

"Okay."

After a minute, both Marlee and her mother came down the stairs into the kitchen. Susie did the introductions, and her father thanked Marlee's mother several times for taking care of his baby. Marlee's mother assured him that it would be perfectly all right for Susie to stay a few more days.

As he was leaving, Susie's father and Marlee's mother

exchanged a glance that made Susie understand that they knew the road ahead might be tough for both of their daughters.

Susie felt a little empty while she listened to his car back out of the driveway and pull onto the main road. She listened until she couldn't hear the rumble of his car anymore. Marlee and her mother hovered in the kitchen but respected her silence. Marlee's mother flashed her a reassuring smile.

The kitchen door burst open five minutes later, and Susie knew she'd be okay when Sam, Lisa, and Jeri flew in. They were on her in a flash.

Sam hugged her. "What the hell, Sus? What happened to you?" She gestured at the wheelchair and then threw her hands in the air in a frustrated gesture.

Susie knew Sam was pissed at her, so she tried to downplay things. "What're you talking about?" Susie smiled. "I've never been better."

"Seriously." Sam laid a hand on her arm. "What happened?"

With Lisa's help, Marlee dragged some kitchen chairs in a semi-circle around Susie. Once everyone was situated, and Marlee made sure her mother was upstairs and out of earshot, Susie relayed the sordid details of the fight with her mother.

"And then I just left. I got in the car and drove around for hours."

"Fight or flight," Jeri said. "You chose flight."

Susie nodded. Like a coward, she had chosen to run away rather than stay and stand up for herself.

Marlee picked up the thread of the story and told them about

Susie's long walk without shoes to the gas station. "I started crying when I saw her bloody feet."

"You did?" Susie's heart clenched. "I didn't see."

"Susie, your feet were so bad, and you looked so defeated that I couldn't let you see me crying, too. You were upset enough as it was."

Susie drank in Marlee's concern and compassion and knew she was lucky to have her.

"Dork, just come to my house next time," Sam said. "Okay?"

Susie nodded but vowed there would never be a next time.

An awkward silence grew around the five friends until Lisa said, "I'm glad you're okay now."

"Thanks."

"We all are," Jeri said.

Marlee, apparently sensing that the mood needed lightening, blurted out, "Hey, you guys, my mom's giving me the van."

All heads whipped toward her. "What do you mean?" Susie asked.

"My mom asked me if I'd be okay keeping the van. Joan, that's Susie's personal doctor, by the way, offered to sell my mom her old Cadillac. Cheap."

"Ooh," Jeri said, "The McAllisters are loaded now, are they? Did you win the lottery or something?"

"I wish." Marlee snorted. "No, my mom says that a Cadillac will look more professional for carting around real estate clients."

Susie leaned in closer to the center of the table. Everyone else did, too. "So, let me make sure I heard you right. The van is all ours?"

Marlee exaggerated her nods and shot Susie a smoldering look.

"Nice." Susie sat back.

"Can we borrow it?" Sam folded her hands in prayer. "Please?"

"Hell no," Susie said. "Get your own van."

"Hey, guys, no fighting," Marlee said.

The phone rang. "Who could it be? You're all here." They all laughed as Marlee jumped up to answer it. "Hello?" She waited a moment and said, "Hello? I can't hear you, and I'm going to hang up now." She cradled the phone gently. "That's so weird. It sounded like there was someone on the other end, but they didn't say anything." She shrugged.

"I bet that was Bree," Lisa said.

All heads turned toward Lisa.

"Why do you think it was Bree?" Marlee asked.

"Well, once upon a time, I blew up Sam's phone when she wasn't taking my calls."

Sam hung her head. "One of my not-so-mature moves."

"Nor mine." Lisa grinned. "But I bet she just wants to hear your voice."

Jeri tapped the table. "You guys, this Bree situation is getting kind of serious. You need to get this under control."

Marlee shrugged. "I guess it's time to seriously plan Plan D."

"Plan D?" Jeri looked confused. "What happened to Plans A, B, and C?"

Lisa pushed Jeri on the arm. "You really need to get out more."

"Obviously," Jeri said with a laugh.

Marlee filled Jeri in on Bree's unwanted attention and their failed Plans A, B, and C.

Jeri said with a slow shake of her head. "You've got yourself a real-life stalker."

"No kidding." Marlee tapped the table a few times. "Okay, guys, c'mon. Plan D. Throw out ideas."

"Let's try to scare her off somehow," Sam said. "Let's make Marlee less desirable to Bree somehow."

"Ooh," Lisa said, "Marlee, you can eat lots of onions and garlic and have really bad breath. Ooh, and don't shower. That way, you'll stink, too."

Marlee frowned and stuck out her lower lip. Susie wanted to hold her tight but settled for patting her hand since the wheelchair restricted her movements.

"Or wait," Sam said. "We could tell Bree that Marlee's pregnant."

"Yeah," Lisa agreed, "with Susie's baby."

Susie and Jeri burst out laughing.

Marlee grinned but looked confused at the same time. "Why do I have to be the one who's pregnant?"

Sam cocked her head to one side, "Because you're the one with the stalker."

"Oh, man," Marlee shook her head. "Can we please think of something else?"

"You could be stupid or boring," Jeri suggested. "Like tell her a story that goes on and on and on—"

"Oh, like one of your stories, maybe?" Marlee teased.

"I resemble that remark," Jeri said with a laugh.

Sam looked at Marlee with a serious expression. "You could tell her you're straight."

"Lie?" Marlee frowned.

Susie looked at Marlee. "It comes with the territory. You know that."

"I know, but—" Marlee glanced up the stairs. "I hate the lying part."

"We all do," Sam said.

Lisa cleared her throat and turned toward Susie. "Will you be able to play on Tuesday?"

Susie shrugged. She wanted to play because she had already missed two weeks of the season, and if she missed any more, Coach Gellar would kill her. She had to play. Feet, or no feet, she had no choice.

"Uh, oh," Sam said. "Susie, you've got that same look in your eye that someone else had recently." She shot an amused but accusing glance at Lisa.

"I know. I know," Lisa said and held up her healed hand. "She watched me stubbornly play four games with a broken hand."

"Which was really dumb," Sam made a face at Lisa, "but I understood why. They were playing for a state championship."

"Clarksonville!" Jeri cheered. Marlee and Lisa joined her in a chant of "State champs! State champs! State champs!"

Susie rolled her eyes for their benefit and then looked at Sam. "*Dios mío*, one little state championship, and they get all smug."

"Yeah, really." Sam rested her head on her chin, looking bored.

Susie made a show of yawning big.

Once the impromptu celebration ended, Marlee said, "Seriously, Susie, this is just a summer game. It's not worth it."

"I know." Susie shrugged again, but if Coach Gellar granted her the honor of putting her in the game, then she would have to play.

"Hey, guys," Marlee pleaded, "I'll work on her later."

Lisa burst out laughing. "I'm sure you will."

Susie laughed along with everyone else, but Marlee stuck out her lower lip again. "C'mon, guys. We have two days to come up with Plan D."

# Chapter 17

## Una Cabróna

Susie sat in the passenger seat of Marlee's van at Sandstoner Fields. They were waiting for Sam to bring Susie's uniform and gear. Her friends weren't happy with her insistence on playing in the game, but she convinced them it would be okay and that her feet had started to heal. Marlee even made her do ten jumping jacks in the kitchen to prove she was okay. Susie did it, but she wanted to scream every time she landed on her raw feet. Somehow, she kept a grin on her face throughout the torturous trial.

The three days Susie spent at Marlee's had calmed her nerves somewhat. Whenever Marlee's mother left the house to go to her office or to show a property, they had the whole place to themselves. They imagined that it was their house, and they had started their life together. Marlee fixed breakfast every day, and the one night they were on their own for dinner, Susie made *arroz con pollo* with fried plantains for dessert. She made sure there were enough leftovers for Marlee's mother to have when she got home. That had been a big hit, and Susie couldn't help thinking she'd scored some major points with Marlee's mom that evening.

The worst times were when Marlee had to go to D'Amico's to work. On Monday, Susie called Christy to give her the 411 on her latest drama, but it seemed as if Christy just wanted to talk about her own problems. It was then that Susie realized Christy had never been there for her over the years. Christy always leaned on her, but they rarely talked about Susie's stuff. After Susie hung up, she understood that Christy just wasn't capable of being there for her.

Other than the one phone call to Christy, Susie tried to distract herself by watching television, but more often than not, she simply turned it off and slept or played with Patches. The best times were when Marlee was home and lay down with her on the couch. Susie wasn't up for much more than cuddling, and Marlee seemed okay with that. Susie hoped Marlee had been serious about one day living together because she wanted that, too. More than ever.

Sitting in the van holding hands with Marlee at the field, Susie tried to hang on to the sweet memories but couldn't help the feeling of dread hanging over her. Would Coach Gellar completely ignore her again? And, even worse, would her mother start another shouting match when she got home after the game? She hadn't seen her mother in three days, after all, and had even missed the special Sunday dinner with Robbie and his mother.

Marlee touched her arm. "Are you okay? You're a million miles away."

"I'm okay." Susie plastered a smile on her face knowing it didn't reach her eyes. "I just hope my feet will hold up." She attempted a laugh, but it sounded false even to her own ears.

"At least the swelling's gone."

"Yeah," Susie agreed, but the swelling wasn't completely gone, and her cuts hadn't healed yet. Not that she told Marlee, but every step hurt like hell. Maybe the swelling had been masking some of the pain. She really wasn't sure how she was going to cope if a miracle happened, and Coach Gellar put her in the game.

"There's Sam and Lisa." Marlee pointed to Sam's Sebring.

Sam parked her car next to the van. She and Lisa got out and pulled their gear and Susie's out of the trunk.

"Here you go." Sam handed Susie her softball gear and a Price Chopper bag with Susie's uniform inside.

Susie nodded her thanks. "Did you see Isabella when you went by my house?"

"Nope," Sam shook her head. "Your grandmother had everything ready when we pulled up. I think she even ironed your shirt."

Susie laughed and pulled out her uniform jersey. "She did. Check this out." She held up her shirt. There was a crisp crease running down each sleeve. "Thanks for running over there for me. I was too chicken."

"Hey," Sam shrugged, "I don't blame you. You were avoiding World War III."

Susie nodded and then hopped into the van to get changed.

"C'mon," Sam turned toward Lisa. "Let's give Ms. Torres some privacy."

Lisa shouldered her catcher's gear. "We'll see you guys in the dugout." They headed toward the field.

Susie slid the van's side door closed and then changed into her uniform. She slipped on her cleats and almost cried out at how tight they felt. Yeah, her feet were still a little swollen. She loosened the laces, and that helped ease the pain.

Taking a deep breath for courage, she stepped out of the van onto the pavement. Her feet protested when she put her full weight on them, but there was nothing she could do about it for over two hours.

"Ready?" Susie grabbed the handle of her softball bag.

"Are you sure?" Marlee's blue eyes searched Susie's brown ones.

Susie softened at the concern she saw reflected in Marlee's face. "I'll be fine. C'mon, let's kick some Southbridge boo-tay."

They headed toward the field, but Marlee stopped and scanned the quickly filling parking lot. "Jeri said she was coming to the game today."

"She just wants to watch Plan D in operation, I think." Susie frowned.

"I know you don't like Plan D, but Sam thinks it's the only way."

"Plan D sucks," Susie growled.

They stepped onto the field, and Marlee groaned. "Speaking of Southbridge stalkers." She pointed toward the Southbridge side of the field with her chin. Bree stood on the outfield grass, stretching with some of her teammates. As if sensing that Marlee was watching her, Bree looked up and waved. Marlee plastered a cheesy smile on her face and waved back. "Plan D better work. I can't take much more of this."

"Me, neither." Susie tossed her bag on the bench and took out her glove and batting gloves. She pulled her bat out of the sleeve compartment of the bag and hung it on the rack. She plunked her batting helmet into the cubby with her name on it.

Her Nor'easter teammates headed onto the field in dribs and drabs to stretch and warm up their arms. It felt so good to get back out on the field with them. Susie had mixed feelings about whether or not she wanted Coach Gellar to put her in the game. Her head said, "Yes," but her feet said, "Hell, no!"

"Circle up, Nor'easters," Coach Gellar called from where she stood just outside the dugout.

Susie's stomach knotted up as she waited for the starting lineup.

"Okay, girls. We're the home team, so we'll be in the field first. Here's today's lineup and batting order. Jacobs in center, Payton at second, Torres in left, Brown catching, McAllister pitching…"

It was a miracle. She was starting. Coach Gellar must have thought that Susie had learned her lesson, whatever lesson that was supposed to be. Maybe her rocky boat was smoothing out. Susie scoffed at the thought. Yeah, right. And maybe Susie's mother would welcome her home with open arms, too.

After both teams took their pre-game warmups, the home plate umpire called for the Nor'easters to take the field. Just before running out, Marlee whispered to Susie, "Take yourself out of the game if it gets too bad."

Susie frowned.

"Susie, c'mon," Marlee pleaded. "Fake a different injury if you have to, okay? It's not worth it."

Susie couldn't resist Marlee's pleading expression. "I will. I promise." And she meant it. She took off running for left field. Her feet hurt, but surprisingly, they didn't protest as much as she thought they would.

She found her spot in left field and threw her glove to the ground. She took off her hat and pulled the hairband off of her hair. With both hands, she pulled her hair back into a tight ponytail and then twisted the band back on. She placed her ponytail on her head and plunked her hat back on. The familiar ritual helped Susie feel grounded. The smell of the freshly cut grass mixed with the distinctive smell of the infield dirt made her feel like she was alive. As always, her troubles faded when the umpire said, "Play ball."

Through the first six innings, the game remained scoreless. The Nor'easters had plenty of base runners and plenty of opportunities to score, but Bree seemed to have developed a few more pitches and held them scoreless. On the plus side, Marlee had pretty much single-handedly kept the Southbridge Bombers scoreless, too.

Susie ran back onto the field as the Nor'easters took the field at the top of the seventh inning. "Go get 'em, Tiger," she said as she sprinted past Marlee in the pitcher's circle.

"I'll do my best," Marlee called after her.

Susie's feet had swollen up again major big time, but since it helped mask the pain, that was fine with her.

Susie found her favorite spot in left field and punched her glove, ready to hold the Southbridge team scoreless yet again. The first batter of the inning flew out to right field, but then the next batter reached first safely when Abby, the Nor'easter's shortstop, made a rare fielding error. The third batter of the inning got on base with a clean base hit up the middle. Marlee must have been rattled because she walked the fourth to load the bases. Susie groaned and smacked her glove. Bree was up with the bases loaded and only one out. All she needed to do was punch a single through the infield or hit a sacrifice fly ball, and the Southbridge team would score a go-ahead run. Susie crouched low. The last thing she wanted was for Bree to be the hero for her team. That would be like adding salt to the Bree wound.

"C'mon, pitcher," Susie shouted to Marlee from left field, "fire it in there." *Don't let Bree be the hero.*

Marlee put her hands together and fired the pitch. The pitch hung over the plate, and Bree launched a rocket down the left-field line.

Susie sprinted toward the sharply hit line drive and made a split-second decision to dive for it. She took two more steps, pushed off with her right foot, and leaped toward the screaming liner. She stretched her glove arm out as far as it would go. The ball thunked into her glove, and she squeezed it tight, bracing for impact at the same time. She hit the ground with a grunt but held on to the ball. Her teammates' cheers gave her the strength to scramble to her feet. The runner was scrambling back to third base, probably thinking the ball would drop in for a hit. Susie rifled the ball to third a split second before the runner got back.

"Out!" the umpire yelled.

Susie leaped in celebration. A move she regretted as soon as her swollen feet landed back on earth. She didn't care. She had just taken a hero moment away from Bree. She trotted back toward the Nor'easters' dugout. On the way, she leaped over the ball lying in the pitcher's circle. *The ball's back in your court, Bree.*

Susie opened the dugout gate and high-fived her teammates.

Coach Gellar walked past her on the way to the third-base coach's box. "Looked like you had lead in your feet there, Torres. My granny could have gotten to that ball faster." She left the dugout, not waiting for Susie's response.

Susie clamped her lips shut and closed her eyes, afraid her Puerto Rican temper would flare up. She felt a hand on her back.

"Breathe," Marlee said.

Susie opened her eyes and blinked back angry tears. Why did her coach have to be *una cabróna*? She didn't know how much more of her coach's sarcasm she could take.

"C'mon," Marlee said. "You're on deck."

Susie put her helmet on, grabbed her batting gloves and bat, and headed to the on-deck circle. She put her batting gloves on and took several practice swings imagining herself hitting the ball solidly.

Up at the plate, Sam fouled off pitch after pitch until she finally walked to give the Nor'easters a base runner with no outs. Susie stepped up to the plate, determined to get a hit, and put Bree in her place once and for all. She dug her back foot into the batter's box and took her stance, waiting for the pitch.

Bree took the sign from her catcher. Susie zeroed in on Bree's hip, where the ball would be released. Bree went into her windup. The ball was on its way, heading right for Susie's knees. She jumped back but couldn't move fast enough. The ball zinged into her calf.

Susie bit back the pain and headed toward first base. What she really wanted to do was storm the circle and sock Bree in the mouth with her fist. That way, Bree's pain would match her own. Instead, she calmly trotted toward first and waved back the athletic trainer who had come running out of the dugout to see if she was okay.

"Way to take one for the team," Jeri called from the bleachers.

Susie took a deep bow toward Jeri, wondering how long she'd been there.

"Hey," Betsy, the first base coach, said, "are you okay?"

"Yup." Susie tried to ignore the throbbing pain in her calf. There was no way she'd look down at it now. No way she'd give Bree the satisfaction.

"Are you sure? 'Cuz I think she hit you on purpose."

"Oh, really? Why do you think that?" *Because I think that, too.*

"The catcher did this." Betsy held her thumb to the side and then flicked her wrist up. "Does that mean anything?"

Susie tried not to laugh. "No, it just means to pitch inside." Which it didn't, but Betsy didn't know that apparently. The thumb flick was the international bean-ball sign. Susie counted herself lucky that Bree hadn't actually aimed for her head.

With Sam on second base and Susie on first, Lisa stepped into the batter's box with no outs. Marlee swung a bat in the on-deck circle. Susie laughed to herself, wondering how Bree was going to pitch to Lisa with Marlee standing so close. After four pitches, it became apparent that Bree couldn't concentrate because she walked Lisa to load the bases with no outs. Marlee stepped into the batter's box and dug in. All they needed was one run, and they would win the game.

"C'mon, Marlee," Susie called from second base. *Be the hero.*

Bree wound up and threw a beautiful fastball on the inside corner. She had obviously been practicing. The second pitch, a curveball, nicked the outside corner for strike two. Marlee stepped out of the box, clearly unhappy with the umpire's call. Susie kind of agreed with her because the call could have gone either way. Susie watched the signs from Coach Gellar. She wanted Marlee to hit away.

Bree took the signal from her catcher. A change up headed toward the plate. Marlee must have mistimed it because the ball trickled toward Bree in the circle. Sam ran toward home, Susie toward third, and Lisa toward second. Bree tossed the ball to her catcher, easily getting Sam out at home. The catcher then pivoted and shot the ball to first base.

"Out," the field umpire yelled, calling Marlee out at first.

"Shit," Susie muttered, standing on third. She slapped her thigh. It was a nice double play by the Southbridge team, but now, instead of bases loaded and no outs, they had two outs, and Abby was up. Abby had struck out every time at bat so far that day. If Susie didn't score, they'd be forced into extra innings. Susie was desperate to get the game finished because her feet were throbbing. She needed to get some ice on them and her calf.

"Okay, Torres," Coach Gellar said from the third base coach's box. "You're the winning run. You're not forced, so don't be the hero trying to score."

Susie nodded. That's all her coach was going to get from her from now on. Nods. Susie felt the hard glare from her coach's eyes from behind the dark glasses she wore. Apparently, a diving catch to save at least two runs wasn't enough to get her out of the doghouse. *Dios*, it wasn't her fault her mother grounded her for two weeks.

Well, maybe it was. She shook the thoughts out of her head as Abby stepped into the batter's box.

Susie wasn't sure, but it looked like Bree had puffed up like a peacock. Susie decided right then standing on third base that her soul purpose in life would be to wipe that smug smile off Bree's face.

Bree took the sign from her catcher and put her hands together. Susie rocked back on the base when Bree started her wind up. Susie exploded off the base as the ball exploded out of Bree's hand. Susie stopped her lead when Abby swung and missed the rise ball. The catcher leaped up, holding the ball high, ready to throw to third. Susie trotted back to the base. Susie was sure Bree would throw the rise ball again.

Susie exploded off the base again, and sure enough, another rise ball was on its way toward the plate. Susie's heart leaped into her throat when the ball sailed over the catcher's head. She turned on the speed and raced toward home. Bree sprinted to cover the plate while her catcher ran to the backstop to track down the ball.

It was going to be close. Susie threw her arms back and started her slide. Bree crouched low, waiting for the toss from her catcher. She caught the ball and threw herself on top of Susie.

Susie couldn't hear the umpire's call over her shouting teammates, so she had no idea if she had been called safe or out. All she knew was that Bree still lay on top of her with the ball in her glove, even though the play was long over.

"Get off me." Susie shoved Bree and sat up.

Bree stood up and dropped the ball in Susie's lap. "What's your problem? You just won the game." She turned her back and headed toward the Southbridge bench. She ripped the glove off her hand and flung it at the dugout fence, almost hitting a teammate.

Susie didn't have time to see what happened next because her teammates piled on top of her at home plate, and she found herself at the bottom of a dog pile.

Susie extricated herself from the pile and followed her teammates to the dugout, not expecting much from Coach Gellar, except maybe a smile. She didn't even get that.

Coach Gellar stepped in front of Susie blocking her way. "That was a pretty risky move, Torres. You got lucky this time." She turned and walked away, leaving Susie staring after her in disbelief.

# Chapter 18
### The Devil

Susie, Sam, Lisa, and Jeri plopped themselves on the highest row of the bleachers. On the field below, the Mohawk All-Stars were taking on the Grasse River Tomahawks in the second game of the evening. Susie plunked her swollen feet on the bleacher in front of her and started to untie her cleats.

"Wait." Sam put a hand on Susie's.

"Why?"

Sam nodded toward Coach Gellar on the field, talking to the Mohawk coach. "You don't want her to see your funky feet."

"*Aay*, good idea."

Susie waited until their coach got in her car and drove away. "Gosh, wasn't it so nice of her to tell me that my diving catch to save the game was awesome?" Susie's voice dripped with sarcasm. "Oh, and scoring the winning run? She was so grateful. How nice of her to say."

"Not," Sam added.

"And how nice of her to ask if I was hurt after Bree hit me with that pitch." Susie turned her foot out to expose the darkening lump on her inner calf.

"Geez." Lisa sucked air through her teeth. "That looks bad." She turned toward Sam. "Do you have the—"

"Yup." Sam reached into her softball bag and pulled out a plastic ice pack.

"Where did you get that?" Susie asked.

Sam grinned as she smashed the ice pack on the bleachers to mix the chemicals inside. "Not me. Your girlfriend." She pointed toward the warmup pitching area behind left field, where Marlee was working with Bree. "She helped herself to Coach Gellar's first aid kit." Sam reached in her bag and pulled out gauze pads, alcohol wipes, antibiotic ointment, athletic tape, latex gloves, and an ace bandage.

Susie's heart swelled. "Marlee got all this stuff for me?"

"Yeah," Jeri said with a grin. "Your sweet innocent Marlee turned to a life of crime just for you."

Susie turned to watch Marlee work with Bree in the pitching area. She sighed. "I don't know what sucks more. Coach Gellar riding my ass or that." She pointed to Plan D in operation.

"Sus," Sam applied the ice pack to Susie's bruised calf, "I know you hate this. Hold that for a second." Susie held the ice pack in place while Sam wrapped an ace bandage around it. "We all agreed on Sunday that we would let it play out."

"Yeah, but they don't even have a catcher." Susie gestured helplessly toward Bree, standing way too close to Marlee. Marlee held a softball up and must have been demonstrating a grip or something, but Susie seriously doubted that Bree was studying the softball. "No, I don't like Plan D at all." She grunted and distracted herself by untying her cleats. She pulled them off one at a time. If feet could sigh, hers did. She stretched her feet and tried desperately to relax. It wasn't working.

"Okay, let's review," Sam said. "Plan A failed because Bree couldn't take a hint and waited forever for us to come out of the dugout. Plan B failed because Bree couldn't take a hint and caught up to us at Marlee's van. Plan C failed because even though we totally left her standing in the parking lot in mid-sentence, she still couldn't take a hint."

Jeri laughed. "This chick definitely can't read social cues."

"No kidding." Susie rolled her eyes.

Jeri turned to Lisa. "If you and Marlee had just stayed in Clarksonville and played in the Nichol Park League with me, none of this would have happened."

"Yeah," Lisa laughed, "I'm not sure how Marlee and I got brainwashed to play on an East Valley traveling team in the first place." She shuddered as if she had eaten something sour.

"Oh, c'mon," Sam said. "You know you love us."

"I do," Lisa gushed.

Jeri scowled playfully. "So tell me more about this Bree character. All I know at this point is that she's certifiable."

Susie laughed. "Marlee says we need to hit Bree with a two-by-four."

Jeri's face brightened. "Ah, I know that one. The donkey story. The two-by-four to get her attention, right?"

"Exactly," Sam said. "Plan D was designed because Bree is like a dog with a bone and won't give up. So, we're giving her what she wants. She's going to get so sick of Marlee that she's going to be the one that runs away."

"Tell me again why this whole reverse psychology thing is a good idea?" Susie bugged her eyes out at her friends.

"I'll tell you why," Lisa chimed in. "I've seen her type. Bree is all about the hunt. Once she feels she has Marlee's attention, she'll get bored and lose interest." Lisa exchanged a glance with Sam. "Hopefully."

"*Aay*, it's that 'hopefully' that scares the crap out of me. I'm just supposed to sit up here and watch Bree hang all over Marlee?" Susie threw her hands up in a helpless gesture.

"Actually," Jeri said, "I think Plan D might work. If we let Bree get what she wants, then she's got nothing else to want."

"While I sit here and watch the devil make a play for my girlfriend." Frustrated, Susie reached down to yank one of her socks off.

"Stop, stop, stop." Lisa grabbed Susie's hand. "You're gonna rip your skin off."

"Listen," Sam said. "We're right here if Marlee can't handle things."

"It's not Marlee I'm worried about."

Sam nodded. "I know," she said softly. She gestured toward the ice pack covering Susie's bruise. "It's obvious what kind of person Bree is."

Lisa put her hand on Susie's sock. "May I?"

"Sure, whatever." Susie leaned back to give Lisa room.

"Your right foot's a mess," Lisa said. "You've bled through the gauze and your sock, too." She put on a pair of latex gloves and slowly peeled off Susie's bloody sweat-soaked sock. She held it up and made a face. "I think we'll just throw this out, okay?"

Susie nodded but was barely paying attention until Lisa unwrapped the bloody gauze.

"Does that hurt?" Lisa stopped unwrapping.

"No," Susie said in a high-pitched voice, trying to be tough in front of her friends.

Sam laughed. "By 'no,' she means 'yes.'"

Lisa narrowed her eyes at Susie. "Trying to be a tough guy, eh? You don't have to be invincible in front of us."

"Yeah," Jeri said, "I personally know all East Valley players are sniveling weenies."

"Oh, nice, Jeri," Sam pretended to be hurt. "We'll see whoever eats at D'Amico's again." She folded her arms and looked away.

Susie grimaced at Lisa and reached down to look at the gauze that had adhered to her feet. "It does hurt, kind of."

Lisa ever-so-slowly separated foot from gauze, and when she was done with both feet, she said, "This'll feel so much better once we get you cleaned up." She flashed Susie a smile which Susie couldn't help but return. Sam was lucky to have found Lisa.

"You should be a doctor," Susie said. "You have a great bleacher-side manner."

"Thanks." Lisa exchanged a glance with Sam.

"Actually," Sam said, "Lisa wants to be a paramedic."

"Cool," Susie said. "By all means, practice on me."

"Okay, here we go." As she cleaned up Susie's feet, Lisa talked about constantly applying first aid to her three younger siblings. She uncapped the tube of antibiotic ointment but hesitated. "You know what? I think we should let your feet air out a little bit. I'll put this stuff on and bandage you up right before we leave."

Susie nodded. The warm summer evening air felt good on her feet. "And this way, I can't run over to kill Bree, right?"

"There's that, too." Lisa laughed and patted Susie on her good calf. "Try to chill out and relax, okay?"

"Pfft. Easier said than done."

"I know." Lisa smiled again and sat back against the bleachers.

Susie's own smile faded when she glanced toward Marlee and Bree. Marlee was laughing at something Bree had said. Marlee wasn't supposed to be enjoying Plan D.

Two fingers snapped in front of Susie's face. "Stop that." Sam pointed to the Mohawk/Grasse River game being played on the field in front of them. "Just watch the game. We play Mohawk on Thursday and Grasse River on Saturday, so take notes or something."

Saturday. Susie's heart lightened. Maybe after the Grasse River game, she and Marlee could find a place to be alone. But for now, she had at least an hour of Plan D to suffer through.

~~~

Marlee pulled the van into Susie's driveway and put the car in park. "Stop worrying, okay?"

"I know," Susie said, "but you and Bree were over there for two whole hours. It killed me watching her come on to you."

196

"I know." Marlee shivered. "She gave me the creeps, man. I mean, hanging out alone with her tonight was disturbing."

"What do you mean, Jelly Bean?" Susie hoped the playful nickname would at least make Marlee smile.

"Well, Jelly Bent," Marlee flashed a quick grin but then got serious again, "it's hard to describe. It was like I wasn't even there. Like she had me captive, and that's all she wanted. She didn't really listen to what I told her about pitching or anything. I think Lisa was right. It was all about the conquest."

"Lisa would know, right? Because of her ex-girlfriend?"

"Tara? Yeah, her part-time stalker." Marlee looked toward the front door at Susie's house. "I wish I could come in with you to make sure you're okay."

Susie smiled. "Why don't you?"

"Don't kid, because I will. I mean, you haven't seen your mother for three days. You know, since—" Marlee gestured at Susie's feet.

"Actually, for once, I'm not kidding. I think it's time I introduced you to my mother. You've met everybody else, right?"

Marlee nodded but flashed Susie a concerned look. "Okay, I'll go in, but how *out* are we going to be?"

"One step at a time. I'm going to introduce you as my friend."

"Okay, I'll follow your lead." Marlee took a deep breath. "Ready?" She put a hand on the door handle.

Susie's stomach had been quivering ever since they'd headed home, but as soon as Marlee's hand went to the door, it went totally topsy turvy.

"Are you okay?" Marlee placed her hand on Susie's arm.

Susie let out a sigh. "I'm okay—my dad's home. You're here. I'll be okay." She reached for the door handle. "Let's do this." She opened the door and gingerly put her weight on her aching feet. She met Marlee in front of the car, and they headed toward the house.

Susie opened the door to the mudroom and shook the crocs off her feet. She desperately wanted to keep them on but didn't want to risk giving her mother anything more to fuss about. Marlee took her sneakers off as well, and they headed inside.

The blare from competing televisions assaulted Susie's ears. She followed the sounds of a baseball game and beckoned for Marlee to follow her into the kitchen.

"Hi, *Papi*," Susie leaned down to hug her father. "You remember Marlee?"

Susie's father nodded to Marlee. "It's nice to see you again."

"Nice to see you, too."

Susie motioned toward Miguel, who was intent on watching the game. "Miguel," she waved a hand in his face, "say hi to Marlee."

He glanced at Marlee for a second and said, "Hi." His attention went right back to the small television on the kitchen counter.

"Hey, how's your ankle doing?" Marlee asked him.

Miguel tried to hide his smile as he said, "Good. It's better now." Susie couldn't help the grin on her face. He and Marlee were going to get academy awards for their performances.

"That's cool." Marlee looked at the television. "Who's playing?"

"Your favorite team," Susie said.

Miguel narrowed his eyes and looked at Marlee. "Don't tell me you're a Braves fan."

"No way," Marlee said with disdain. "Let's go, Mets. All the way."

Susie's father laughed. "Not this year." He pointed to the screen. "We're losing in the bottom of the ninth. Again."

"Figures." Marlee laughed. "That's why they call us diehard fans. We stay with them through thick and thin. Even though it's usually thin."

Susie's heart warmed as Marlee chatted with her brother and father. Would her mother ever warm up to Marlee the way they obviously had?

"C'mon," Susie smacked Marlee gently in the arm, "let's go."

"Good luck," Susie's dad called after them.

Susie grinned at her father, and then she and Marlee headed toward the television blaring in the living room. Susie's stomach knotted itself even tighter. Her *abuelita* and mother sat on the couch watching some sort of reality show.

"*Abuelita? Mami?*" Susie said. "Marlee came in to say hi."

Susie's *abuelita* stood up, shuffled over to Marlee, and gave her a big hug. "Nice to see you, Marlee."

Marlee pulled out of the hug. "*Gracias, Abuelita. ¿Cómo estás?*"

"I am good. You Spanish so good."

"*Gracias.*" Marlee smiled. "*Usted Ingles es muy bueno, también.*" Marlee grimaced, probably knowing she hadn't quite gotten the Spanish right.

Susie's *abuelita* grinned and headed back toward the couch. After she sat back down, all of the air seemed to get sucked out of the room.

"*Mami*, this is my friend Marlee." Susie swallowed hard against the lump in her throat.

The molten glare that Susie's mother sent her could have melted granite. "I'm glad to see that you're okay." It was the first time her mother had seen her since she fled the house three days before. Her mother's expression changed from fire to dispassion as she faced Marlee. "I've heard a lot about you."

Marlee smiled. "It's nice to meet you, Mrs. Torres."

Susie's mother didn't respond but turned back to face Susie. The angry glare was back. Her mother was obviously less than pleased with Marlee's presence in her house.

The awkward silence grew louder than the television show.

Susie grabbed Marlee's shirt sleeve. "Okay, I'm going to walk Marlee out." She pulled Marlee with her and tried not to run.

"Come right back in here after she leaves," her mother said in clipped tones.

Susie couldn't get her crocs on fast enough when they got to the mudroom. "Hurry, hurry," she pleaded to Marlee.

"I'm going as fast as I can. Believe me, I want out of here, too."

Once Marlee finally got her sneakers back on, Susie practically shoved her out the door. Marlee unlocked the van, scrambled into the driver's seat, and slammed the door shut. She whipped on her seatbelt, started the engine, and rolled down the window.

"I'm sorry, sorry, sorry." Susie put her forehead on the windowsill in misery. "Do you see why I didn't want you to meet her? She hates me. She hates you." Susie picked her head up and looked at Marlee through a haze of tears. "She hates *us*."

Marlee leaned out the window and rubbed Susie's arm. "Man, oh, man. Your mom really has a problem with this."

"Understatement."

"I had this fantasy that I'd walk in, and your mom would see how wonderfully charming I was like you were with my mom, and everything would be all right."

Susie attempted a smile. "I'm sorry my mother was so rude to you."

"No, she wasn't that rude. Not really. I think she wasn't expecting me to waltz right into her house unannounced. Me—the devil who corrupted her daughter."

Susie softened her expression. "You're not the devil, and you didn't corrupt me. If anything, I corrupted you."

Marlee flashed Susie a mischievous smile. "I do remember somebody dragging me behind a shed and, uh, compromising my reputation."

"Mmm, such a nice reputation it was." Susie grinned back but then sighed. "I hate to say it, but I think you'd better leave now. I have to go back in and face the music."

"I'm not leaving you."

"I'll be okay, really."

Marlee narrowed her eyes. "I'm going to drive to that Stewart's, the one where that lady saw us. What was her name?"

"My former employer?" Susie said icily.

Marlee nodded.

"Mrs. Johnson."

"Right. That Stewart's where Mrs. Johnson saw us kissing. I'm going to wait there until you call me and tell me what happened."

Susie paused for a moment wanting to tell Marlee to go home, but something made her reconsider. "Okay."

"Good, and if you don't call me within an hour, I'm coming back." Marlee caressed Susie's cheek.

Susie leaned in the van for a quick kiss. She was done caring who saw them. She backed up to watch Marlee's van head out of the driveway and down the street. Once the van was completely out of sight, she took a deep breath and looked up at the star-filled night, trying to find the strength to go back inside.

# Chapter 19

### Enemy Number One

Susie trudged back into the house but purposely left her crocs on for two reasons—her sore feet were swelling up big time, and more importantly, she wanted to be ready if she needed to make another speedy exit. The baseball game in the kitchen was apparently over, but her father and brother were watching the post-game commentary. The reality show in the living room continued to play and seemed to be reaching a pivotal moment. As much as Susie wanted to hide in the kitchen with her father and brother, she headed to the living room to face her mother.

Without making eye contact, Susie sat on the couch next to her *abuelita* and watched some poor woman trying to eat a bowl of worms on the television screen. Susie might have taken more of an interest in the show, but the air in the room was thick with tension. Every time she tried to calm her shaky nerves, they flared up even worse. She tried to take a couple of deep, calming breaths but was afraid she would start hyperventilating, so she settled on watching the woman fail in her worm-eating attempt.

After a painful ten minutes, both on and off the screen, the show was finally over. Susie's *abuelita* reached for the remote control and changed the channel to Univision for some kind of nighttime drama. Susie didn't have time to figure out what the show was about because her mother stood up, took Susie in with a long glare, and said, "Follow me." She walked out of the living room, past the kitchen, and up the stairs to the second floor. Susie followed behind like a prisoner being led to the gallows.

Her mother opened the door to the master bedroom and let Susie enter first. After closing the door, she gestured for Susie to sit on the bed.

Her mother paced back and forth silently in front of the closed door but then stopped in front of Susie. "How could you do this to me?"

"Do what?" Susie knew her mother was talking about bringing Marlee over but wanted to hear her mother say it.

"That girl. How could you bring her kind in here?"

"What *kind* is that, *Mami*?" She wanted to remind her mother that a few short weeks before, she'd wanted to meet Marlee. Susie had to be careful, though. She never knew what would send her mother completely over the edge.

"You know what *kind* I mean. It's disgusting."

*Say the word, Mami, just say it.*

Her mother began pacing again. Susie exhaled, not realizing she'd been holding her breath. The shakiness of it surprised her.

"Do you—Are you like her?" Her mother stopped moving and leaned against the closed door.

This was the moment Susie had been dreading ever since ninth grade when she realized she seriously liked girls—this moment right now when she would have to tell her mother. Her stomach clenched as she tried to figure out how to answer. She blinked back tears, took a deep breath, and nodded once.

Her mother smashed the bedroom door with the back of her fist. Susie jumped at the violence of it. She wanted to stand and run but couldn't. Her mother blocked the only exit.

Two short strides were all it took for the slap to sting Susie's face. Susie put a hand over her cheek. At first, she looked at her mother in shock, but her mother's piercing glare forced her to look away.

"How dare you!" her mother roared.

Susie hid her tears behind both hands. She never expected her mother to get this hysterical.

Her mother began pacing again. "I can't even go to work without people staring at me. They say, 'There she is, the mother of a lesbian.'" She pounded the door again. "They whisper behind my back when they think I can't hear them. 'Her daughter likes girls,' and then they laugh at me." Her mother stopped pacing and glared at Susie. "*Aay, Santo.* Do you know what that's like? To have shame? No, because they don't say it to you. They say it to me." She began pacing again.

Susie cowered, wondering why her mother thought she was such a monster.

"What did I do wrong?" her mother demanded. "Why did you turn out this way?"

"*Mami,* there's nothing wrong with me." Susie wiped at her eyes, determined to get back in control. Her mother didn't answer but went to the window to look out. Susie had a clear escape route but didn't take it. Somewhere inside, she knew that she and her mother had to have this out. "I'm sorry your work friends are giving you a hard time because of me."

Her mother continued to stare out the window. "I walked in on Mrs. Johnson and the other supervisor in the break room the other day. They didn't see me, but Mrs. Johnson was saying, 'I don't know why I ever let that dyke in my house. Can you believe I left her alone with my children all day?'"

"You can't catch it." Susie wasn't trying to be flippant. She was just confused.

"Don't take this lightly, young lady. *Una lesbiana, sola con las niñas. ¡Aay, Dios mío, sálvame!*"

Susie translated her mother's sentence out loud. "A lesbian, alone with little girls. God save me." In a flash, she realized what her mother was implying. She stood up so fast that her mother seemed startled. Susie bit back her disgust as she picked her words carefully. "Is that what you think? That I'm a child molester?" Anger made her voice shake. "Just because I like Marlee doesn't mean I hurt children. I have never hurt baby Emma or Bethany. I never touched them in any wrong or disgusting way. Why did you let her say those things about me, *Mami*?" Her mother looked a little lost, but Susie kept talking, the anger in her voice clear. "I can't believe you would ever think that of me. *Dios mío, Mami*, what kind of monster do you think I am?"

Her mother glared at her, but when Susie held her head high in defiance, her mother steeled her chin, eyes glistening with tears. "I don't know. What kind of monster *are* you?"

"*Mami*—" Susie groaned, not sure what to say next. She softened the tone in her voice and said, "I'm not a bad person. I'm still me. I just love somebody. I would never hurt anyone. Not on purpose. I didn't mean to cause you stress at work, but, c'mon, Mrs. Johnson is a bigot. You said it yourself."

Her mother's eyes grew wide. "Don't disrespect her. She's my boss."

"But you'll let her disrespect me? I'm your daughter. Your family!" Susie's voice rose in anger. "What about *my* feelings? What about *my* reputation? I've done nothing wrong, *Mami*. Nothing. You said once Mrs. Johnson treated me bad because of our darker skin. She probably treats you the same way at work. She does, doesn't she?"

Her mother avoided Susie's eyes.

Susie clapped her hands together once. "I knew it. You couldn't stand up to her, so you made me take that babysitting job, even though you knew she was treating me as badly as she treats you. Do you know how hard I worked for her? For those kids? I did the jobs of a whole crew of people. I cleaned, cooked, did yard work, and cared for her children. And for all that, I got paid shit."

"Don't you curse at me."

"I'm not cursing at you." Susie's voice got softer. "I'm trying to make you see something—"

"I see plenty." Her mother's voice boomed. "I see that my daughter has turned into some *thing* I don't know."

The door to the master bedroom creaked opened, and Susie's father stood in the doorway. Susie thanked the universe for letting him have the courage to come up the stairs.

Susie narrowed her eyes at her mother. "And you've turned into somebody I don't know, either."

"Don't you dare be disrespectful to me," her mother roared.

"Isabella, that's enough!" her father bellowed. Her mother shot him an angry glare and then turned her back. He turned to Susie. "Go to your room. I'll be there in a few minutes." When Susie hesitated, he said quietly, "Just go."

Susie groaned, feeling like she and her mother had just gotten started, but she obeyed her father and fled the house as fast as her swollen feet would take her. She barely noticed her brother looking petrified in the doorway of the kitchen as she flew by. She cursed the universe that her car wasn't there because she had shoes on and her cell phone in her pocket this time. She pulled the cell phone out to call Marlee. She wanted Marlee to swoop in and rescue her from the madness but then thought better of it and snapped it shut.

She opened the outside door to the garage and headed up the stairs. She'd stay long enough to hear what her father had to say. He was the one, after all, who said she should stick up for herself. He was the one who said she needed to stop running. When she got in her room, she locked the door behind her. She needed to feel safe because there wasn't much of that going on in her life lately.

She flopped onto the floor of her bedroom and did a hundred crunches so she wouldn't have time to think. She was about to turn over and do pushups when she heard her father coming up the stairs. She leaped to her feet and unlocked the door just as he knocked on it. She threw her arms around him.

He hugged her back and then held her out at arms' length. "Are you okay, *mariposita*?"

Susie shrugged and then sat on the bed. Her father sat in the desk chair and spun it around to face her.

"*Mami* hates me."

"She doesn't hate you."

Susie grunted. "Did you hear any of that?" She pointed toward the main house.

"I did. I was standing outside the door for a long time. Your mother is upset that things aren't going the way she planned for you."

"What did she plan for me?" Susie hugged her pillow.

"She always talked about a big wedding. A handsome son-in-law. *Nietos preciosos.*"

Susie blushed. "We can have a big wedding. Okay, maybe not at St. Catherine's, but we can still have a wedding. And, *Papi*, I can have children. *Mami* can have precious grandchildren." *It may be Marlee having them, though,* she thought but didn't dare say it out loud. "I didn't choose this for myself, you know. It chose me."

He nodded. "I just want you to be happy. Believe it or not, your mother does, too."

"That's kind of hard to believe. She thinks I'm a child molester."

"I'm sure she doesn't really think that."

Susie shrugged. "I've known about myself for over three years. I didn't tell anyone until last year. And I didn't fall in love until I met—" her voice caught in her throat. Her lower lip quivered as she remembered the bad things her mother had said about Marlee.

"I know, *Princesa*. I thought something wonderful had happened to you. You've been floating on a cloud lately."

"I have?" She hadn't hid it as well as she thought.

"*Tu abuela* saw it, too."

"I know."

"It's not exactly what either your mother or I had envisioned for your future, but I, for one, think Marlee is sweet. And her mother seems nice, too. I'm sorry you didn't trust me earlier to tell me."

Susie felt her cheeks get warm. "I can't believe I'm having this conversation with you right now."

"Me, too. For years I thought I'd be using one of your softball bats to chase the boys away."

"See? I saved you all that trouble."

He looked at her for a long moment. "Just be careful. I know they passed the marriage equality law in New York, but the world truly isn't that enlightened yet. I know I told you to stand up for yourself and not to cower to anyone, and I still mean that, but don't go looking for trouble. Don't flaunt it where you don't need to."

"It sucks that I can't be myself all the time. Marlee and I know we have to hide sometimes. How did *Mami* figure out about me?"

"Mrs. Johnson told her."

"She did?"

He nodded. "When she called to fire you that day."

"Oh, nice."

"I, however, figured it out on my own." He seemed pleased with himself. "Other people will, too. Just figure out who your real friends are."

Susie nodded. "Thanks, *Papi*. But what are we going to do about *Mami*? Because right now, she feels like enemy number one. I don't want to run anymore." Before he could respond, she blurted, "I am officially asserting my right to stay. She can throw me out of the house in December when I turn eighteen, but for now, I'm staying." She sat up and placed both feet flat on the floor.

"As long as I am breathing, you will always be welcomed in my house." He laughed softly. "Or in the garage."

She laughed with him. "Thanks, *Papi*. My feet can't take much more running."

He frowned for her benefit. "How are they?"

"Fine. I played tonight, and they didn't fall off."

"Good." He stood up. "Your mother doesn't know about your feet yet. I think I'll give her all the details when I go back inside. It'll give her some insight into what you've been going through. If we give it some time, maybe we can flip that switch of hers and get her on your side."

"I hope so because once that switch flips, we can go back to the way things were. I hope we can, anyway." It was reassuring to have her father in her corner. "I hope *Mami* can accept me."

Her father nodded. "I think she will, but she has to think it through some more. And, as we both know, it has to be her idea." He headed for the door. "Wish me luck."

"Good luck."

He put a hand on the door jamb and turned to face her. "Call me anytime things get too much for you. If I'm on a business trip, go to Sam's or back to Marlee's. Somehow, we'll work this out, okay?"

Susie nodded. "I love you, *Papi*. Thanks for being on my side."

He smiled. "Goodnight, *mariposita*."

"'Night."

He headed down the stairs, and she locked the door behind him. She pulled her cell phone out and said, "Marlee," into the voice dial.

"Are you okay?" Marlee answered in a rush.

"I've been better, but my father's in my camp, so I think I'll be okay. You can go home."

"Are you sure? I've imagined all kinds of things over here."

"I'm sure. I'll be okay." Susie flopped onto the bed and hugged her pillow with her free arm. "Are you still at the Stewart's?"

"Yeah. I'm drinking a cream soda right now."

"You are?"

"Yup. Wishing I could share it with you. Hey, remember what I told you last time we were at Stewart's? When we were shopping?"

Susie couldn't help the smile that crept up her face. "That you want to play house with me for real someday?"

"I mean it."

"Me, too, but we have one giant hurdle."

"What's that?"

"Enemy number one. Isabella Maria de Fatima Torres."

## Chapter 20

### Take No Prisoners

Susie sat in the bleachers lacing up her cleats. Marlee sat to her left and Sam and Lisa to her right. They were playing in the late eight o'clock game against Grasse River that evening, so they waited for Bree's Southbridge team to finish beating the Northwood Sharks. Northwood didn't have a home field, so they played all their home games at Sandstoner Fields in East Valley. Bree was pitching and, so far, throwing a one-hitter. She struck out a Northwood batter to end the bottom of the sixth inning.

"Marlee," Susie said with a laugh, "you've gotta stop teaching that girl how to pitch."

Marlee leaned in, so all her friends could hear. "I didn't. She's been striking those people out with her screwball, and I never showed her that pitch."

"Speaking of screwballs, P." Sam twirled a finger near her ear and pointed toward Bree.

Marlee smiled but then looked back at the field. "I think Bree has a private pitching coach or something. She didn't need me at all."

Lisa agreed. "There's no way she's gotten that much better with just the couple of things you showed her two days ago."

"She obviously wants to impress you," Sam said. "To make you think your personal tutelage helped her improve."

"Speaking of personal tutelage," Lisa teased, "has she called you?"

"Or texted or emailed?" Sam added with a laugh.

"She calls me on my home phone." Marlee leaned down to unzip her softball bag. "I never gave her my email or cell phone number. She asked me for them on Tuesday, but I couldn't do it. I mean, I know I'm supposed to be giving her so much attention that she chokes, but it's creeping me out, guys. I'm not digging Plan D."

Susie's grin faded. "Me, neither."

"Bree's been strangely quiet tonight." Lisa's expression was serious.

"Yeah," Sam said, "she hasn't once run by us or said anything to you."

"The calm before the storm?" Susie suggested with a shrug.

"Maybe." Marlee pulled her cleats out of her bag. "She was supposed to be history by now, wasn't she? I spent all that time with her on Tuesday, but she called me three times yesterday and four today. She wants me to go somewhere with her tonight. Alone."

"Hell no." Susie glanced at Bree swinging a bat in the on-deck circle. "Not while I'm still breathing." She lowered her voice. "Guys, it's time for Plan E."

"I don't care what we do." Marlee rolled her eyes. "I just want everything to go back to normal."

Sam leaned toward Susie, her hand on her chin. "Okay, mastermind. Spill it. What's Plan E?"

"It's like I've been saying. Giving in to what she wanted didn't feel right. I say we shouldn't give her any attention. Marlee, especially. None."

"Just cut Plan D off right now?" Marlee's face was lined with confusion. "As much as I'd like to, she thinks we're pals now."

"That's too bad," Susie said. "I'm sure she'll be hanging around after the game waiting for you, so all you have to do is go up to her and say something like, 'I don't want you to call me anymore.'"

Marlee sighed. "Do I have to?" She finished tying her cleats and reached back into her softball bag. The sudden look of surprise on her face made Susie curious.

Marlee looked mortified as she pulled out a small stuffed bear with a handwritten note attached. She looked at Susie. "This isn't your handwriting. Is this from you?" A look of confusion passed over her face.

Susie shook her head. Sam and Lisa leaned in closer. "Is it from Bree?" Lisa wondered out loud.

Marlee shivered and tossed the bear onto the bleacher in front of her. "I think it is. The handwriting looks like hers from the note she left on my windshield. When the hell did she sneak that in my bag? Man, this whole thing creeps me out."

"Do you want me to read it?" Susie asked. When Marlee nodded, she reached down and opened the note. She kept her voice low, barely above a whisper. "It says, 'Where have you been all my life? Ever since I saw your picture in the newspaper, I've loved you.'"

Marlee put a hand over her mouth, her expression clearly showing how upset she was. "Oh, God. I don't want to hear any more. Read the rest to yourself and let me know if I need to run." She looked away.

Susie read over the letter silently, with Sam and Lisa reading over her shoulder. Bree's note outlined her imagined life with Marlee, which included sailing around the world, so they could be alone together forever. Susie shuddered. The girl was crazy. When they finished reading, Susie tucked the note in her softball bag. She put an arm around Marlee. "Let's just say that I don't think this girl is sane. She didn't threaten to hurt you or anything like that, but her grasp on reality is a bit shaky. Do you guys agree?"

Sam and Lisa nodded.

Lisa looked at Marlee. "Plan E right away, okay?"

Marlee didn't answer. She looked like she was in shock.

"Marlee?" Susie squeezed her shoulder with the arm still wrapped around her. "Plan E, okay?"

Marlee nodded but looked shaken.

"We should never have tried Plan D." Sam frowned. "I'm sorry I bullied you into it."

"I had no idea such crazy people were out there." Marlee ran her fingers through her hair.

Susie wanted to run her own fingers through Marlee's short hair, to comfort her, but her arm around Marlee's shoulder was pushing it already. She remembered where they were and, after giving Marlee another reassuring squeeze on the shoulder, pulled her arm back. She remembered her father's advice. Don't look for trouble.

Sam nudged Susie in the leg. "So, how are the feet?" Bless Sam for changing the subject.

"Believe it or not, my mother cleaned and redressed them yesterday. It was kind of our first step toward a cease-fire. She said my feet are practically healed. Oh, and Lisa?"

"Yeah?"

"My mother said that you and Marlee's mom did a great job cleaning up my feet."

Lisa beamed and sat up taller. "Cool."

Sam smiled at Lisa, and then they leaned into each other. It looked like Sam and Lisa had their own private way of hugging in public, too.

Sam looked back at Susie, "And, the calf bruise?"

"Good." Susie plunked her foot on the bleacher in front of her and turned her gloriously bruised calf for all to see.

"Nice." Lisa touched the bruise. "The swelling is way down."

"Isabella's touch."

Lisa raised her eyebrows in question.

"My mother."

"She's a nurse, right?"

Susie nodded.

"So, how is public enemy number one?" Sam asked.

"Well," Susie wasn't quite sure where to begin, "she's talking to me, but it's more like 'pass the milk,' or 'set the table.' We're at a standstill. I don't talk about it, and she doesn't ask."

"Don't ask. Don't tell," Marlee said with a sigh. "I know your father and grandmother are cool, but your mother? I still feel bad that I set her off like that just by breathing in her house, you know?"

"Ooh, what happened?" Sam leaned in close. "Did you, like, kiss Susie right in front of her mother?"

"No," Susie whacked Sam on the bicep.

"Hey." Sam rubbed her arm.

"You deserved that," Susie said to Sam. "Marlee didn't do anything but be her cute sweet, charming self."

"Oh, gag me." Sam groaned and got another whack from Susie for her commentary.

"Tomorrow," Susie raised her eyebrows, "my mother and I are going shopping. I am so not looking forward to being held captive in the car to and from Walmart."

Sam hooted. "We'll all be praying for you."

Marlee and Lisa laughed. Susie rolled her eyes.

"I don't know," Marlee said. "The way your mom flipped out makes me not want to come out to anybody. You know?"

"Once bitten, twice shy," Lisa agreed. "My mom knows, but I still haven't come out to my dad yet. I mean, my bio-dad knows, but not my real dad."

"Neither of my parents knows," Sam added. "And I'm not sure they ever will."

Susie cringed at the hurt look that passed over Lisa's face. She'd seen that same look in Marlee's eyes just a few short weeks before.

"I'm not out to my mom yet," Marlee said with a defeated tone. "I'm kind of scared to."

Susie patted Marlee's leg. "You know what?"

"What?"

"I think it'll be okay."

"Really? Why do you think that?"

"Your mom's cool." Of course, Susie didn't let on that Marlee's mother already knew.

"But how do you do it? Like, what do you say?" Marlee leaned closer to her friends. "I mean seriously. Lisa, how did you come out to your mom?"

"My mom came out to me, actually." Lisa laughed. "I mean, she dragged it right out of me. Remember when Sam and I were, you know," her cheeks turned bright red, "having our little misunderstanding?"

Marlee nodded.

"Well, she wanted to know why I was so down in the dumps, and she asked if I liked Sam. *Really* liked Sam." Lisa grinned. "William, my bio-dad? He just knew. His sister's gay, so he knew the signs, I guess."

Susie smiled at Lisa and then turned to Marlee. "You could wait for your mom to ask you, but if the opportunity presents itself, I say go for it. Honestly, it's better to tell her before someone else does. Like the way stupid Mrs. Johnson told my mother."

"That was just wrong." Sam shook her head. "It wasn't any of her business."

Susie whacked Sam on the arm for the third time that night. "When are you gonna come out to your own parents, *muchacha loca*?"

"Never."

"Denial anybody?" Susie stood up, and Sam whacked her. "Hey." Susie rubbed her arm.

"I'm just getting even." Sam leaped up and bounded down the bleachers toward their home dugout. Bree's team had just beaten Northwood by a score of 9-0 and held on to Bree's one-hitter.

"Maybe you're right." Marlee reluctantly put the bear back in her bag. "Maybe I'll tell my mom, but I don't know when or how or where or what." She stood up and grabbed on to Susie's elbow.

"You'll figure it out when the time comes." Even though Susie's feet were pretty much healed, she let Marlee help her navigate the bleacher steps. Everybody needed a little extra coddling now and then. "And what are you going to do after the game?" Susie cocked an eyebrow.

"I know. I know." Marlee took a deep breath. "Plan E. Take no prisoners."

Susie smiled, hoping that Marlee would have the *cojones* to stand up to Bree once their game was done.

They reached the dugout gate, but Bree blocked the way. They couldn't get on the field unless she moved. It looked like Plan E was going to be implemented sooner than expected.

"Miss me?" Bree flashed Marlee a toothy smile.

*Stay strong, Marlee,* Susie willed.

Marlee didn't say anything but simply opened her bag and pulled out the bear. "I can't accept this."

"Oh, but he's so cute." Bree opened the gate to let them in.

Marlee stepped onto the field, and Susie stood tall and strong by her side. "I can't take this from you," Marlee repeated and held the bear out, but Bree still didn't take it. "I don't think it's a good idea for us to, uh, hang out anymore, either."

"What?" The hurt expression on Bree's face made Susie feel bad, but only for a split microsecond.

*Dios mío, don't back down now, Marlee,* Susie encouraged silently. *You can do this.*

After a few nerve-wracking moments, Marlee said, "We can't hang out, and you can't call me anymore, either."

"Why not?" The tears in Bree's eyes were almost pitiable. "When did you stop liking me?" Her shoulders drooped.

"I never liked you." Marlee turned to head toward the dugout. "Just leave me alone, okay?" She dropped the bear on the ground and walked away.

Susie hustled alongside her. "*Perfecta, mi vida.* Well done," Susie whispered in Marlee's ear. She wanted to look back at Bree but didn't dare.

Marlee let out the biggest sigh Susie had ever heard when they got in the dugout.

"That sucked." Marlee shook her head.

"Unfortunately, I don't think it's over." Sam pointed to the bleachers. Bree had settled down on the first row near the Nor'easters' on-deck circle.

Susie didn't know whose groan was louder, hers or Marlee's.

"Nor'easters," Coach Gellar barked, "bring it in."

Susie and her friends hustled to the team circle for the starting lineup. Susie sighed in relief. She was starting in left field again. Maybe her time in Coach's doghouse had ended.

The game against the Grasse River Tomahawks was relatively uneventful. Coach Gellar took Marlee out of the game after the third inning when it became clear that the Nor'easters were going to win by the mercy rule, which they did by a score of 15-0.

Susie fell in line behind Marlee as they high-fived the Grasse River team after the game. They had been keeping tabs on Bree as the game went on, and, sure enough, she still sat in the first row watching Marlee's every move.

"She's still here," Susie whispered in between, saying, "Good game," to the Grasse River players.

"I know," Marlee said over her shoulder. "What do we do?"

They headed toward the dugout, and Susie positioned herself between Marlee and Bree. "Just don't look at her. Don't even acknowledge her."

"Easier said than done, man," Marlee mumbled.

They ducked into the dugout, glad to be out of sight.

"If she says anything to you, ignore her if you can." Susie tried to plaster a confident expression on her face, even though she shook inside. "If you can't, then try not to get upset. Stay cool and calm, be respectful, but tell her again that you don't want anything to do with her."

Marlee bit her bottom lip. "You make it sound so easy."

They put their gear away, slung their bags over their shoulders, and slithered toward the exit. Sam and Lisa joined them, and Susie filled them in on their exit strategy.

Susie positioned herself in the front. Sam and Lisa flanked Marlee, one on each side. "Okay, let's go." Susie opened the dugout gate, and they headed toward Marlee's van.

Bree leaped up off the bleachers when she saw them and hurried over. "I know you didn't mean what you said. Did you, Marlee?"

Susie kept walking; the others followed. Marlee didn't say a word. Bree kept pace.

"C'mon, after all we've shared already? That's just the tip of the iceberg." Bree's voice sounded confident.

Susie walked on and weaved her way through the cars. Bree followed them. She called, "I know you like me, too. Why can't you just say it?"

Marlee whirled around to face Bree. Sam and Lisa jumped, startled, but recovered enough to make a human wall between them. Susie turned and grabbed Marlee's arm just in case.

"I don't like you," Marlee said with a shaky voice. "I don't want anything more to do with you." She turned and ran toward her van.

How Bree broke through the Sam/Lisa wall, Susie didn't know, but she didn't have time to think about it. She just reacted and grabbed Bree by the shoulder and pushed her back against a parked car. She leaned down close to her face. "The girl said she doesn't like you," Susie hissed. "Take a hint and leave her alone."

Bree didn't even seem to notice that Susie had her pinned. Her head turned as she looked for Marlee.

Susie wasn't sure what to do. She had expected some kind of reaction from Bree but got none. She shook the girl by the shoulders and leaned even closer. "Do you hear me?" she growled.

Bree turned her head back around and shot Susie a bored look. "How can I not hear you?" she said calmly. "You're shouting in my face. And you have bad breath, too."

Disarmed, Susie gave her one last push and backed away. "Just get the hell out of here, *idiota*." She, Sam, and Lisa blocked the way toward Marlee.

Bree stood up and made a show of brushing herself off. "What's it to you, anyway?" She pointed toward Marlee, sitting in the driver's seat of her van, the engine running. "She can think for herself, you know."

"Everything okay here?" Susie jumped at the sound of Coach Gellar's voice.

Susie continued to glare at Bree. It was several long seconds before she answered. "Some people are more bull-headed than donkeys around here."

"Whatever." Bree turned and walked away from them.

Coach Gellar cocked her head as if trying to figure out what had just happened. "Okay, then. It seems like you have it well in hand. I'll see you all on Saturday."

Susie breathed a sigh of relief as their coach turned away. She, Sam, and Lisa ran to Marlee in the van.

Marlee opened the side door for them to jump in. Her eyes were red-rimmed. She wiped at them and said to Susie, "What happened to the 'stay cool and calm' part of the plan?"

"What else was I supposed to do? I didn't have a two-by-four."

# Chapter 21

### Was it Something I Did?

Susie got out of bed and stretched her arms to the ceiling. Her team had gotten up to bat so many times against the struggling Grasse River team the night before that Susie was a little stiff and weary. Thinking about her impending shopping trip with her mother made her even more tired, and she was tempted to go back to bed.

After changing into a pair of hip hugger khaki shorts and a Taylor Swift concert t-shirt, she threw on her crocs and was about to head down the stairs to the main house when her cell phone rang. She pulled it out of her back pocket and threw herself on the bed once she saw who it was.

"*Hola, mi vida.*"

"Hi, yourself," came Marlee's sultry reply.

"What are you up to this fine morning?"

"I'm trying to find a giant two-by-four."

"To hit Bree with?"

"Yeah." Marlee grunted. "Like you did last night. My hero."

Susie felt her cheeks warm at Marlee's praise. "I don't know how we're going to get that girl's attention. Maybe we should call the cops or something. I'm sure Sam's family knows the chief-of-police in East Valley."

"I don't know." Marlee sounded defeated. "Maybe I should tell my mom at least."

"Maybe." Susie got off the bed to open a window. Her room had gotten rather stuffy and warm. "But you should probably have that other talk first."

"Don't remind me." Marlee groaned. "Speaking of moms. Good luck on your shopping extravaganza this morning."

"*Aay*, don't remind me." Susie laughed and added, "It'll be okay. How much damage can she do to me at Walmart?"

"Hey, don't kid around like that."

"Sorry." Neither of them spoke for a moment, but then Susie said, "I miss you."

"Me, too," Marlee said. "I'll see you tomorrow, though. Ask your parents if you can come home with me after the game. Your car is supposed to be done tomorrow morning, right?"

"Yeah."

"And we haven't been alone, you know, in a long time."

"I know." Susie smiled at the thought of being alone with Marlee at Lake Birch or just anywhere.

"Mmm," Susie murmured. "I think I'll steal my mother's car right now and come get you."

"Can't. Have to work. D'Amico's calls."

Susie groaned for Marlee's benefit. "Duty calls here, too. Off to shop with Isabella and try to stay sane in the process." She laughed. "I'll ask my dad about going home with you after the game tomorrow."

"Cool."

Susie didn't want to be the first one to hang up the phone, and apparently neither did Marlee, so they exchanged several rounds of "No, you hang up first" before deciding to hang up at the same time.

Susie bounded down the stairs to the driveway. The early August heat wave assaulted her. No wonder her room had been so stifling. The muggy days of August usually only lasted for about two weeks, and then the typical North Country summer of mild days and cool evenings came back until the fall chill set in.

Susie headed across the hot driveway and opened the door to the mudroom. Losing her nerve, she plopped on the bench wanting to gather herself before facing her mother. She mourned the closeness she and her mother used to have, hoping one day they could get it back. Maybe they would once the whole mess blew over. If it ever did.

Susie kicked at her brother's sneakers lying in a heap. With all the drama going on, she hadn't had time to look for a job. She wanted a real one, one she could keep during the school year. Of course, wherever she worked, they'd totally have to understand about softball in the spring. Thinking about softball perked her up, so she flipped her crocs off and felt ready to take on her mother.

"*Mami*?" Susie called when she got into the main house. "Are you ready to take Walmart by storm?"

"Be right down," her mother called from her bedroom. Her voice was almost cheery. Susie's father had gone into the office for the day, and her *abuelita* sat on the living room couch watching a mid-morning talk show.

"Have a good day, *Abuelita*." Susie gave her a hug. She looked up toward the master bedroom. "Wish me luck."

"*Sí, sí*." Her *abuelita* smiled at her. "Be honesty with you *mamá*."

Susie held back her smile. She loved her *abuelita*'s attempts to speak English. "I'll try."

After receiving a reassuring hug from her *abuelita*, Susie headed to the kitchen to search for a piece of fruit. Miguel sat at the table eating a bowl of cereal.

"What's up, *hombrecito*?" Susie headed toward the fruit on the counter.

"Nothing." Miguel kept his eyes riveted on the magazine in front of him.

"Your life sounds really exciting," she said playfully.

Her brother's magazine page was opened to a picture of some tattooed guy holding a skateboard. Susie rolled her eyes. She hadn't caught him smoking again, so hopefully, those days were over, but she hoped he wasn't thinking about tattoos next. She grabbed a banana from the wooden banana tree. The morning mail was sitting on the counter, so she absently sorted through it. She was surprised when she found an envelope addressed to her from Clarksonville Community College. Maybe they were recruiting her to play softball. She laughed and tucked the envelope in her back pocket to open later. There was no way she was going to a community college. She was going to SUNY Brockport to study geology or earth science.

Susie turned back around to face her brother. "You want anything from Wally-world?"

Miguel looked up without smiling. "She's making you go, isn't she?"

Susie nodded. "I guess she wants some mother-daughter bonding time."

"I'm glad I'm not you."

"*Aay*, it'll be fine. I'm not worried." She was, in fact, just the opposite. "If I don't come back, you can have my weight bench." When he still didn't smile, she sat at the table next to him. "I was just kidding."

"You didn't come home last time."

"I was at Marlee's. I was okay."

He looked away for a second and wiped his eyes.

"I promise," Susie said, trying to reassure him. "I was okay."

"What about your feet? I saw *Mami* cleaning them. What happened to you?"

Susie wasn't sure how much her thirteen-year-old brother would understand. As she tried to figure out what to say, she heard her mother's quick footsteps on the stairs. "Don't worry. I'll be back to bug you. Never fear." She stood up from the table.

"Promise?"

"Promise what?" her mother asked as she set her purse on the kitchen table.

"I promised to get him a pack of baseball cards." She turned back toward him and winked. "What Mets player are you still missing?"

"David Wright."

"Ooh, a must for any collection." Bless the kid for playing along.

229

"Ready, *Mami*?" Susie tried to stay cheerful even though the shopping trip would probably be as icy as things at home had been.

Susie's mother scooped her purse off the table. "Let's go."

Susie followed her mother out of the kitchen but turned around and mouthed to her brother, "I promise."

He nodded back to her.

Susie usually drove if she and her mother went anywhere, but her mother got in the driver's seat. Susie hesitated for a second and then went to the passenger side without question.

"Your feet," her mother said. "You should rest them when you can."

"Okay." Susie strapped on her seatbelt. At least her mother wasn't ignoring everything in her life.

Susie turned on the air conditioner and cranked it high. She breathed a sigh of relief when the cool air flowed from the vents. It was always hit or miss whether the air conditioner would work after not being used for an entire year, but this year they were lucky.

Susie's mother pulled the car out of the driveway in silence, and they headed up their street toward the main road. Earlier that week, when her mother suggested the shopping trip, Susie decided to let her mother run the show, including starting all conversations.

They hadn't quite made it out to C.R. 62 when her mother cleared her throat and said, "It's nice having a day off."

Ahh, small talk. Susie could handle that. "How did you ever get Mrs. Johnson to give you a day off?"

"I lose my sick days if I don't take them."

"And you never take them."

"I decided that maybe it's time to check in with my family every now and then. And besides," Susie's mother flashed an evil grin at her, "maybe high and mighty Mrs. Johnson needs to get off her ass and work for a change."

Susie was shocked to hear her mother talk about her boss that way. Usually, her mother took great pains to keep disparaging words about her boss from flying off into the universe.

"Let's see if she can keep up with all the work I do," her mother continued. "*Dios mío*, all she does is sit on her butt in the break room eating donuts." Her mother laughed. "Donuts that *I* bring in."

Susie shook her head, not quite knowing how to tread on such dangerous territory. "How about all the things I did for her? Cooking, laundry, cleaning, kids, yard work. Forget it."

Her mother got strangely quiet, and Susie kicked herself for mentioning her babysitting job at Mrs. Johnson's. She and her mother had once been able to talk about things. Why couldn't they talk now? Was it only because her mother knew she liked girls? No, not girls, Susie thought with a smile. Just one girl.

They rode in silence down C.R. 62 for a while in the heavy Friday morning traffic. Susie wondered where in the world everyone was going at ten-thirty in the morning. They stopped for a red light at the post office, and her mother glanced at her. "Was it something I did?"

"What do you mean?" Susie pushed a lock of hair behind her ear as her nerves jangled.

"Was it something I did that turned you *lesbiana*? Did I not do enough girly things with you? Should I have made you wear more dresses?"

"I wear dresses. Not all the time, but sometimes."

"Softball? Maybe you shouldn't be playing that softball."

"*Mami*," Susie said more sharply than she intended. "I love softball. I want to play in college. Maybe I can get a scholarship." There was no way she was going to let her mother take that away from her. She'd move out, sleep in her car somewhere, and be homeless before she'd give that up.

"I don't know what I did wrong."

"Why does it have to be about you, *Mami*? You didn't do anything wrong, and neither did I. It's about me. I love her." *Dios mío, I can't believe I just said that to my own mother.*

"Marlee."

"Yes." Susie looked down at her hands in her lap. She couldn't help the smile on her face.

The silence that overtook them was so thick that Susie wanted to open the car window and stick her head out. She thought better of it, though, deciding that the air conditioning that went with the silence was preferable.

Her mother pulled the car into the Walmart lot and parked in a spot underneath a shady tree far away from the store entrance. "In Puerto Rico, the best parking spots were always the ones in the shade." She flashed a smile and then added, "I will always love you, *mi hija*, but I'm struggling to understand this. You're such a pretty girl." She reached over and stroked Susie's dark auburn hair, the natural version of her own. She pulled her hand back and then smiled. "Lots of boys would like you."

"*Mami*, I don't like boys that way."

"Do you hate men? Your father? Your brother?"

"I don't hate men. I just don't want to date them, okay?" She tried to keep the irritation out of her voice, but it was getting hard.

"Do you want to be a man then? Wear men's clothes? Does she?"

Susie groaned. "No, I don't want to be a guy. Neither does Marlee. We're both happy with who we are." Susie wondered where her mother had come up with these ideas.

"Will you get a crew cut? Ride a motorcycle? Get fat and ugly?"

"Now you're getting insulting. Is that what you think gay women are? Fat, ugly, motorcycle riding women with crew cuts who hate men but want to be them?" This time the anger showed in her voice.

"But you can get a boyfriend, Susana. Roberto likes you. You don't have to pair up with another girl. I don't understand." She shook her head and looked straight ahead.

It was as if being with a man was the only option her mother could see for her. Susie tried to make sense of where her mother was coming from.

"Do you think I'll live a lonely and miserable life if I don't have a man?"

"Who will take care of you?"

Her mother still didn't get it. "Marlee will take care of me. My friends. My family. And, *Mami*, I'll take care of myself, too."

Susie could almost see the smoke rising from her mother's head as she tried to make sense of Susie's answer.

"Won't you be lonely, *mi hija*?" Her mother's voice softened.

Susie took her cue from her mother and relaxed her own tense shoulders. As gently as she could, Susie said, "I won't be lonely because I won't be alone. I want to be with Marlee forever. I want to live in a house with her and have a cat and maybe kids." Her mother raised an eyebrow, but Susie rolled on. "We want to be each other's life partners or whatever you call it." She didn't dare say the words 'wife' or 'marriage,' even though marriage equality had become legal in New York. That might send her mother into a tailspin.

"You're both too young to be making such big decisions."

"I know, but that's how we feel about each other. I want to wait until after college at least." Could it be that her mother had actually heard what she said? Could it be that her mother had allowed herself to consider the possibility that she and Marlee could get married?

"How can two girls support each other? How can you make a family?" Her mother sighed.

"Lots of les—, uh, lots of women couples have done it." Susie blew out a sigh. She had been about to say the word 'lesbian' to her mother. Susie wasn't comfortable with the word herself and knew her mother wouldn't be too keen on it either.

Her mother looked at her for a long time, the invisible smoke still streaming from her head. She turned the car off, threw her keys into her purse, and said, "C'mon, I need some shopping therapy."

"Okay," Susie took off her seatbelt, "let's go." She fell in step with her mother and threw out the best olive branch she could think of. "Hey, *Mami*, didn't you say sundresses were on sale?"

## Chapter 22

### Hell Has Officially Frozen Over

On Saturday morning, Susie stood in the mudroom and opened the screen door to the house. "Sam's here. I'm going to my game."

Her father called back from the kitchen, "Do you have the check?"

"Yeah, in my bag." Good luck or divine intervention had been on her side when her parents gave her permission to ride back to Clarksonville with Marlee after the game. She had been all prepared to make her case about picking up her car from Aldwell's Auto Repair, so they wouldn't have to slog all the way out there, but her father gave her the okay right away. Her mother even told her to have fun. Maybe her mother's switch was flipping over. Susie could only hope, but she wasn't going to hold her breath.

Susie's father popped out of the kitchen. "If the bill is anything different than Mr. Aldwell told me over the phone, you call me right away."

"I will, *Papi*. I gotta go, okay?"

"Have a good game."

Susie smiled. "I'll try."

She shut the screen door to the house and got in the passenger side of Sam's Sebring convertible. "Top down. Nice."

"It's, like, ninety degrees." Sam chuckled. "I have the air-conditioner on, too." She pulled the car out of the driveway and headed for Sandstoner Fields.

"Thanks for being my taxi. Again." Susie hated relying on Sam for rides, but it was better than asking her parents.

"Any time. So, you're going home with Marlee after the game?"

Susie's cheesy grin answered Sam's question.

"Ah," Sam said. "Lisa and I are going out to the yacht again."

"Your parents don't mind you using the yacht?"

Sam laughed. "My dad thinks it's great that I've finally shown an interest in it, but we don't take it out. We just, uh…"

Susie laughed. "Yeah, I get it."

"Hey, there's, like, no other place Lisa and I can go to be alone, you know?"

"Tell me about it. Lake Birch in Clarksonville is nice, but, c'mon, there's no real privacy there."

Sam nodded. "Have you, uh…" She hesitated for a second. "Okay, you don't have to answer this, but have you guys, you know, like, gone all the way?"

"Sam!" Susie hit her friend on the arm. "What kind of question is that?"

Sam's face turned bright red. "Sorry. I said you didn't have to answer."

"No."

Sam looked over. "'No' what? 'No' you don't want to answer, or 'No' you guys haven't."

"No, we haven't. How about you?" It was kind of weird talking to Sam about things so intimate, especially since they had gone out once upon a time.

"Nah. We haven't found a place private enough yet."

"Yeah, us, too. I want it to be special, but how is the back of a van at Lake Birch, where anybody can walk by and see us, special?"

"I know. My parents' yacht is cool, but it's docked in a slip with boats on either side surrounded by a hundred others. Anybody could walk by and hear, you know, things." Sam's cheeks turned an even brighter shade of red. "I'm working on something, though."

"Oh, yeah?"

Sam nodded and pulled the car into the Sandstoner Field's parking lot. She pulled into a space and then hit the button to put the top up.

"Hello?" Susie waved a hand in Sam's face. "What is it you're working on?"

"The lake house." Sam waggled her eyebrows.

Susie must have had a confused look on her face because Sam laughed and added, "Labor Day weekend. You and Marlee. Me and Lisa. I don't think my parents are planning on using it, so I've been hinting around about taking some friends up to Lake Bonaparte before senior year starts."

"*Dios mío*, that would be *fantástico*, Sam."

"Don't say a word to Marlee or Lisa, yet 'cuz I don't know if I can pull this off."

"Okay. What about Helene?"

"I'll be eighteen in January," Sam said. "Do I really need nanny supervision?"

"Nope." Susie laughed. "C'mon, let's get out there. Coach Gellar's pacing already."

Just as Susie opened the car door, her phone dinged. She had a text message. She smiled when she saw it was from Marlee.

MARLEE: I told my mom this morning.

MARLEE: Ack!!

SUSIE: Good for you! I can't wait to hear the details! What's ur ETA?

MARLEE: 10 min

SUSIE: See you in 10. I love you.

MARLEE: I love you toooooooo!

Susie grinned and then stashed her phone in her pocket. As promised, Marlee and Lisa pulled up to the fields in Marlee's van about ten minutes later. Susie gave each of them a quick hug, and after they put their cleats on, they all went out to left field to stretch. Susie plopped down on the newly mowed grass and inhaled the sweet smell. "*Aay*, I love summer."

Marlee sat down next to her and started stretching. "Me, too."

"Same," Lisa and Sam said together and laughed. Lisa added, "I can't believe we've only got two weeks left of softball. I feel like I just got here. How am I supposed to get my hand in shape?" She held up her recently fractured hand that had taken weeks to heal.

"Oh, I know," Sam commiserated. "And school will be here before we know it."

Susie groaned. "*Dios mío*, don't remind us." She looked from Lisa to Marlee. "You guys should transfer to East Valley."

Marlee's jaw dropped open. "Uh, that would be no. You guys should transfer to Clarksonville." Lisa nodded in agreement.

"I would if I could, *mi vida*. In a heartbeat." Susie glanced at Coach Gellar. "C'mon, you guys, we have to at least pretend to be stretching." She put the soles of her feet together and pulled them in for a butterfly stretch. The others stretched, too. "So, tell us," Susie said to Marlee. "What happened this morning?"

"Oh, man. You told me to wait for a good opportunity, and this morning, Mom was making pancakes, and she turned around and said, 'Daddy would have liked Susie.'"

Susie's mouth dropped open. "*Aay*, see? I told you she knew."

"I think she did." Marlee nodded in agreement.

Sam stretched her arm behind her head. "Then what?"

"Well, then after I debated in my head for a couple of seconds on what to say, I said, 'I like her, too. A lot.' Then my mom smiled at me. You know that kind of smile moms have that tell you they knew all along?"

Lisa laughed. "Yeah, I've seen that look from my mom. The one that reminds you how wise they are and that they know and see all? Yeah, been there."

"So, then she says," Marlee continued, "'I'm happy for you.'" Marlee's cheeks turned bright red as she relayed more details. She added, "She seems cool about it, but she did ask me one thing, though."

"What's that?" Susie asked.

"She wanted to know if I was sure."

The look Marlee threw Susie almost knocked the breath out of her.

"And?" Susie drank in Marlee's blue eyes, not able to look away.

"I told her I was sure."

"Hey, break it up, you two." Sam nudged Susie with her foot. "Here comes Coach."

Susie began stretching in earnest as their coach walked up.

"McAllister? Brown?" Coach Gellar pointed to the pitching area. "Go warm up."

"Okay." Marlee leaped to her feet. She and Lisa scurried back to the dugout for their gear.

Coach Gellar briefly glanced at Sam but then looked directly at Susie and said, "Torres, I hope you've snapped out of your funk because these teams are gunning for us. We're undefeated, and it needs to stay that way."

Susie nodded as if she knew what the hell her coach was talking about, which she didn't.

"I'm glad we understand each other." Coach Gellar's face never gave the barest hint of a smile or friendly overture. She turned on her heels and headed back to the dugout.

Sam stood up and whispered, "What the hell was that?"

"*¡Maldita sea!*" Susie shook her head. "I have no freakin' idea." She leaped to her feet, and they ran their warmup laps around the field.

When the umpire called for the home team to take the field, Susie sprinted out to left. She threw her glove on the ground and whipped off her hat. She redid her ponytail and tucked it under her hat, and put her glove on her hand. Even though Coach Gellar seemed to be giving her shit for some reason, no one could bother her in left field. This was her own personal territory for seven whole half-innings.

"C'mon, Marlee," Susie called. "Fire it in there."

Just as Marlee was getting ready to throw her first pitch, Susie's eye was drawn to the stands. "*Mierda*," she spat. Bree had settled herself on the first row of the bleachers on the Nor'easters' side of the field.

After getting two quick strikes on the first Mohawk batter of the game, Marlee struck her out on the third pitch. Marlee made quick work of the following two batters as well, striking them both out to end the top half of the first inning. Susie sprinted toward the Nor'easters' dugout. She felt so proud of Marlee. She wished they could play their senior year together on the same high school team. "*Aay*," she muttered under her breath as she reached the dugout gate, "maybe in college." She and Marlee had only talked about college in vague terms before. Christy had been right when she said that Susie was going, going, gone over Marlee, and Susie couldn't imagine only seeing Marlee on vacations from school.

Susie patted Marlee on the back. "Nice pitching."

"Thanks. Nice, uh, standing around in the outfield getting a tan." Marlee flashed Susie a big toothy grin.

"I'm gonna let that one go." Susie wagged her finger and then pulled her batting helmet out of her cubby. "For now."

Marlee did her best to look scared, but it kind of ruined the effect when she started laughing.

Rachel, the Nor'easters' lead-off batter, hit a single down the left field line to reach first base. Sam stepped into the batter's box, and Susie headed for the on-deck circle. Unfortunately, the on-deck circle was right in front of Bree. Bree stood up and hooked her fingers through the chain-link fence.

Doing her best to ignore the pestilence from Southbridge standing five or six feet behind her, Susie shouted, "C'mon, Sam, get a hit."

"This ain't over, you know," Bree hissed.

Susie ignored the comment and took her practice swings.

"She knows I'm better for her than you."

Anger boiled in Susie's gut. She almost wished the fence wasn't in between them because she'd use her bat as a two-by-four and take a swing that would knock Bree all the way back to Southbridge.

"Not in your wildest dreams, sister," Susie growled at Bree. She turned in time to see Sam bunt her way on base safely.

Susie got ready in the batter's box and took a deep breath focusing on the Mohawk pitcher. Not much speed, but she hit corners well. Susie let one pitch go by for a strike to get an idea of what she was looking at. The next pitch came in low, but Susie sent it soaring into left field for a line-drive single to load the bases.

Standing on first base, she was shocked to see her parents, *abuelita*, and brother making their way onto the bleachers. She had no idea why they were there on a sweltering Saturday morning. Not that she minded, but they hadn't said a word about going to the game. Thankfully they sat on the visitors' side and wouldn't be able to hear any of the crap coming out of Bree's mouth.

Lisa got up to bat next and hit a triple on the first pitch that scored all three base runners. Susie was a little winded by the time she sprinted all the way from first to home. Once her feet fully healed, she'd have to get in more cardio workouts.

After scoring, Susie turned and waved to her family. They enthusiastically waved back. Susie pointed to the hat that her *abuelita* had on. It was one of Susie's old East Valley softball hats. Her *abuelita* whipped it off her head and waved it in the air, chanting, "Go East Valley" several times. Everyone in the bleachers laughed. Susie scurried back to the dugout. Bree said something as she ran by, but Susie couldn't quite make out the words. Not that she wanted to.

Susie took a long sip of water from the water fountain. When she looked up to see how Marlee was doing up at bat, she caught Coach Gellar's fierce scowl. Apparently, Susie shouldn't have been waving to her family.

Susie, used to being in the doghouse, didn't have time to worry about Coach Gellar because Marlee hit a double into the left-center field gap sending Lisa home. The Nor'easters were now up by a score of 4-0 with no outs in the bottom of the first inning.

The game continued in that fashion, and the Mohawk team who

had been "gunning for them," according to Coach Gellar, simply crumbled. The Nor'easters won easily by a mercy-rule score of 12-0.

After the landslide win, Susie packed up her gear. She said to Marlee. "Did you see Isabella in the stands?"

Marlee nodded slowly, her eyes wide with fear. "Your mother petrifies me."

Sam and Lisa laughed.

Susie bumped Marlee with her hip. "Act natural."

"How? She freaked out the last time she saw me. I'll just wait here." Marlee plopped down on the dugout bench and clutched her bag tightly to her chest.

"C'mon, *galena*." Susie clucked like a chicken. "I'd wait in here with you, but Isabella can out-wait anybody. "

"You can't stay in here, anyway," Lisa added.

"Why not?" Marlee stuck out her lower lip.

"Bree's team is waiting for this dugout."

Marlee stood up so fast that Susie, Sam, and Lisa laughed.

"Let's get this over with." Marlee led the way out of the dugout.

Coach Gellar fell in line behind Susie and Marlee as they exited the dugout. Sam and Lisa were stuck behind their coach as they all headed toward the bleachers.

"Another fine pitching performance, McAllister," Coach Gellar said. "Any way I can get you to transfer to East Valley?"

Marlee flashed Coach Gellar a look that said hell would have to freeze over first.

"Okay, okay, McAllister. Just don't tell Dottie I asked. She'll have my head for trying to steal her New York State MVP pitcher."

"Okay, Coach. I won't."

With their attention diverted to their coach, Susie didn't realize that Bree was right in front of them. As they passed each other, Bree slammed her shoulder into Susie's. Susie, not expecting the contact, stumbled backward into her coach. By the time she realized what had happened, Bree had walked on and was out of reach.

"Sorry, Coach." Susie stood her ground and glared after Bree. "Some people don't have any manners."

"How long has this been going on?" Coach Gellar asked, a hand on her hip.

When Marlee didn't answer, Susie said, "A couple of weeks."

"Are you still handling it?" Coach Gellar cocked an eyebrow.

Susie shrugged. "Yeah, for now."

Coach Gellar narrowed her eyes at Susie. "Tell me the moment it gets out of hand."

Susie was paralyzed under the glare of her coach's piercing eyes.

"You hear me, Torres?" Her coach's question almost sounded like a threat.

Susie nodded. "Yes, Coach."

Coach Gellar reached around Susie and stuck her hand out in greeting. "Mr. Torres."

Susie's father shook Coach Gellar's hand. "Nice to see you, Coach."

Susie almost gagged at her coach's sickening sweet change in personality.

"Mrs. Torres." Coach Gellar didn't offer her hand but smiled sweetly at Susie's mother. Susie's mother nodded and smiled back.

"Ah," Coach Gellar continued, "Grandmacita and baby Torres, too." She ruffled Miguel's hair as if he were five years old. "It's so nice to see the whole Torres family out at the fields on such a fine sweltering day." She fanned herself.

Everyone, except Susie, laughed. Susie had never realized what a two-faced person her coach was.

Susie's father hugged Susie and said, "We figured we'd come out to see our all-star play."

"Ah, yes," Coach Gellar beamed at Susie. "She's a keeper, that one."

Marlee whispered, "I think so, too."

Coach Gellar excused herself and headed toward the parking lot. Susie wondered how her coach was able to fool everyone into thinking she was a nice person. But then again, up until a few weeks before, Susie had thought her coach was cool, too, just like everybody else. Not so much anymore. Susie was just beginning to realize that her coach was as human and imperfect as the rest of them.

Sam gave everybody, except Miguel, a hug in greeting. She bumped fists with him instead. He was, after all, a teenager now and way too cool for hugs. Sam then introduced Lisa to Susie's entire family.

Susie couldn't delay anymore. "*Mami, Papi*, you remember Marlee?" Susie gestured to Marlee, who had been hanging back. Susie caught the look on her father's face and knew that she wasn't the only one waiting to see how her mother reacted.

Susie's mother nodded. "It's nice to see you again, Marlee."

"It's nice to see you again, too." Marlee played it so cool that Susie wondered if she had imagined her pre-Isabella nerves.

Susie's *abuelita* squeezed Marlee in an overlong hug. Susie almost got jealous when the hug Marlee got was almost twice as long as the one she had gotten.

"Hey, Miguel." Marlee pointed to Susie's brother. "I have something for you."

"Me?" Miguel smiled.

Marlee nodded and unzipped the outer pocket of her softball bag. She reached in and pulled out a stack of baseball cards. "These are for you." She handed him the cards.

"No way," he said, thumbing through them. "Look, Susie." He held out a card for her to see.

"David Wright. Very cool."

"What do you say?" Susie's mother said to Miguel.

"Oh, sorry. Thanks, Marlee."

"You're welcome," Marlee said.

Susie beamed at how bright pink Marlee's cheeks had gotten.

"Marlee?" Susie's mother began. "Would you like to come to dinner at our house next Saturday? After your game?"

Susie almost choked.

"Uh, sure. That would be nice," Marlee said.

"Please invite your mother, too. It would be nice to meet her."

"Umm, okay. I will. Thanks for inviting us. Is there anything we can bring?"

"Just bring yourselves."

Susie felt kind of numb all over, as if what was happening in front of her was some weird alternate reality that she'd wake up from any second. She snuck a peek at her father, and he smiled reassuringly at her. Yep, her mother's internal switch was moving.

They said their goodbyes to her family, and the four friends headed to the parking lot in a dazed silence.

Sam broke the stillness. "What just happened?"

Susie didn't miss a beat. "Hell has officially frozen over."

# Chapter 23

### Hunger

Susie groaned as they passed the Valero gas station on the way to Aldwell's Auto Repair shop.

Marlee glanced at her from the driver's seat. "Are you okay?"

"Yep," Susie said, tight-lipped. "I'm glad you and your mom came to get me that night. I don't think my feet could have carried me much further."

"No, I don't think they could have."

"I'd like to erase that whole night from my memory."

Marlee shot Susie a sympathetic smile and said, "But here's what I don't understand."

"What's that?"

"Why in the world did your mom invite me to dinner on Saturday?"

Susie laughed. "I have no idea. I don't know what's happening. Maybe my dad talked some sense into her."

"Maybe."

"And maybe she's changed her mind about me. About us."

"That would be nice. By the time dinner's over, your mom will be planning our wedding."

Susie's eyebrows shot up. "*Aay, mi vida,* you have the best imagination. That's why I love you."

"And I love you, too." Marlee reached for Susie's hand.

As they passed the spot where Susie's car had run out of gas, Susie refused to think of the bad things that could have happened to her on that awful night. From there on out, she decided to find something positive in every negative. And that included things like Coach Gellar riding her ass, Bree stalking Marlee, and her mother hating her.

"No, no," Marlee said as she turned into the parking lot of the Aldwell's Auto Repair Shop. "No thinking."

Susie was about to protest but decided against it. "You know me too well, *mi vida*."

Susie got out of the van and paid for the repairs. She was ecstatic when her car started up on the first twist of the key. She followed Marlee the three or four miles to her house.

Marlee parked her van in front of the garage, and Susie pulled her car in beside it. Marlee's mother's new Cadillac wasn't in the driveway, which was expected because she was showing a commercial property in Northwood. Marlee hopped out of the van and lifted up the back tailgate. Susie grabbed her softball bag, dumped it in her trunk, and then pulled out a bag of clothes she would put on after showering. They headed into the house. Patches raced toward them and rubbed against Susie's legs.

"Oh, man," Marlee said. "I think I've lost my cat."

Susie grinned at Marlee and reached down to pet the cat. "What can I say? All the McAllister women love me."

"Hmm," Marlee stepped closer, "I think you're right." Marlee called out, "Mom, are you home?" When she got no answer, she pushed Susie back against the refrigerator. "I had to be sure." Marlee put both her hands beside Susie's head, effectively pinning her.

The last time Susie had been at Marlee's house, she had so many things on her mind that their alone time had been more about making the hurt go away than anything else. This time, though, Susie was hungry. Hungry to feel Marlee's body pressed up against hers. She pulled Marlee to her, and after sending steamy silent messages with her eyes, kissed Marlee like she'd been starving.

They were both out of breath when they broke apart.

Marlee looked dazed. "Wait 'til I get you alone."

"Aren't we alone now?"

Marlee grinned and pointed to Patches on the kitchen table, watching them. "No."

Susie laughed.

"Actually," Marlee continued, "I have a new place for us."

"Not Lake Birch?"

Marlee shook her head. "Much more private than Lake Birch."

"Ooh, where are we going?"

"Nope. Showers first, then I'll show you."

Susie let herself be ushered up the stairs to the bathroom, where she got out of her uniform, showered, and then changed into shorts and a button-up shirt. She'd specifically chosen a shirt that buttoned up the front in the hopes that at some point, Marlee would unbutton it. Thinking about that spurred Susie into dressing faster.

"Hey," Susie called down the stairs, "I'm done. I'm just putting on my shoes."

"Okay," Marlee called up. "You have to come down and make sure the chicken doesn't burn."

"Chicken?" Just as she said the word, the wonderful aroma of fried chicken wafted up the stairs. Susie slid her sandals on, shoved her dirty uniform into her bag, and headed down the stairs. "You made fried chicken?"

"Oh, sure, because I'm that good a cook." Marlee rolled her eyes. "I bought a box of fried chicken at Price Chopper last night, and I'm reheating the pieces in the oven. We're going on a picnic."

"No way."

"Yes, way." Marlee headed up the stairs. "Don't let them burn, okay?"

"Hurry, I'm starving." *In more ways than one,* mi vida. *In more ways than one.*

Susie checked the oven. The fried chicken covered an entire cookie sheet and seemed to be fine, so she ran out to her car to throw the bag of dirty clothes in the trunk. She breathed in the sultry summer air and, before heading back inside, took in the patchy blue skies and the acres and acres of meadow surrounding the house. Marlee had told her once that they owned about thirty acres of what used to be farmland. Susie loved living in upstate New York. She had been to Brooklyn a few times to visit her *Tío Emilio* and his family, but she had hated all the concrete and the fast pace. She'd take the North Country every time.

With a start, she realized she was supposed to be watching the chicken in the oven and sprinted back into the house. Her heart was pounding when she looked in. Phew. All was well, but the chicken looked done, so she turned the oven off.

Marlee bounded down the steps, her hair still wet. "Mmm, that smells good, doesn't it?"

Susie nodded. "What can I do to help?"

"You can get the blanket and picnic basket from the top shelf in the hall closet."

Susie pulled them down as requested. "This basket looks like it belongs in one of those old Yogi Bear cartoons." She set it on the kitchen table.

"Oh, I know. It belonged to my mom's mom. My mom inherited it when she died. That was before I was born."

As they packed the basket with all the fixings they needed for lunch, Susie realized that there were a lot of things she didn't know about Marlee. Did Marlee have grandparents still living? Aunts and Uncles? Susie had a bunch of cousins, some in Brooklyn and some in Puerto Rico. Did Marlee have cousins?

"We're all set," Marlee declared, picnic basket in hand. "Ready?"

"I'm starving. Where are we going?" Susie held the blanket draped over one arm.

"Follow me." Marlee grabbed her keys off the kitchen table and locked the door behind them. They headed toward the van, and Susie thought they were going to get in, but Marlee walked right past it.

"We're not taking the van?"

Marlee shook her head. "Nope, we're going for a picnic in the McAllister back thirty."

"No way." Susie followed Marlee into the meadow behind the garage. "Oh, this is so cool."

There was the tiniest of paths carved out of the wilds. The path wasn't wide enough for them to walk side-by-side, so Susie followed behind. Some of the wild grasses were almost waist high. Purple and white and yellow wildflowers were everywhere. She quietly picked a handful of the purple asters and tied them into a bouquet with a stalk of wild grass.

They walked on for another five minutes or so in relative quiet. The silence was only broken when Marlee pointed out a butterfly or bird.

Susie looked back to get her bearings. The garage and house were far off in the distance. "You do know where you're going, right?"

"Yeah," Marlee said. "I have my own private hideout back here. I made this path right after my dad died, so I'd have a place to cry, and my mom wouldn't hear me. I even used to come out here in the snow."

Susie's heart squeezed tight. "And you're sharing it with me? Your very own private hideout?"

Marlee nodded. "It'll be *our* private place now. Of course, it'll suck if it starts to rain." She pointed to the dark-bottomed cumulus clouds moving in overhead.

Susie, remembering that she vowed to find the positive in every negative, said, "But we'll be with each other, so it won't matter."

Marlee stopped on the path so quickly that Susie almost bumped into her. Marlee whipped around. "That's why I love you.

Even if it rains, everything's going to be perfect because you're here."

Marlee stroked Susie's cheek and started to spin back around, but Susie grabbed her arm and handed her the flowers.

"See?" Marlee said. "You're perfect." Marlee hugged the flowers to her chest as they continued their trek to the private hideout. "We're almost there. Now, don't get too excited about it. It's just a flattened-out piece of land." Marlee entered a small clearing in the middle of the acres and acres of meadow. "I've been coming out here for the past week and pulling out the tall stuff and stomping down the rest."

The secret hideout was a small worn-down area about ten feet around. Susie was struck by how far away from the house it was, as if Marlee had wanted to make sure no one would ever find her out there. Susie tossed the blanket on the ground and pulled Marlee into a tight hug. "I'm sorry you had to come out here to cry after, you know, your dad passed."

Marlee was quiet for a moment. "And I'm sorry your mom has been so, umm, difficult. But you know what?"

"What?" Susie pulled her head back a little so she could see her sexy girlfriend's face.

"It's natural."

"What's natural?" Susie loved how Marlee's eyes sparkled when she was excited about something.

"Us."

"What d'ya mean, jellybean?"

"I used Jeri's computer and did some research. This National

Geographic website said that most species of animals have same-sex, uh, relations."

"Really? Which ones?"

"Most of them. I read about queer dolphins, penguins, sheep, seagulls, ducks, pigeons, vultures." She looked skyward as if looking there for more animals to name. "Oh, yeah. Swans, horses, dogs, cats."

"Cats? You mean Patches might be gay?"

Marlee chuckled. "Yeah, the furry wonder might be a lesbian."

Susie laughed.

"There are way more. Most monkey species, which we're supposedly evolved from, have sex for fun, and some of it is queer sex. There's even this one monkey species called the Bonobo, and the females have sex with each other all the time, more sex than the males."

"That's weird."

"And giraffes, too." Marlee's voice turned to a whisper. "I read that male giraffes have anal intercourse."

Susie grimaced. "They do?"

"Yeah, and so do bison."

"How come we've never heard about this before?"

"The article said it was kind of controversial and that most researchers didn't want to open up a can of worms or something."

Susie shrugged. "That makes sense, I guess."

"So, you see?" Marlee smiled. "You and me?" Marlee twirled Susie in a circle. "We're natural." She pulled Susie into a closer hug, and they stood that way for a few quiet moments until Marlee slid her hands in Susie's back pockets. "What's this in your pocket?"

Susie heard the crinkle of paper but had no idea what it was. She'd only worn the shorts for her short trip to Walmart the day before. Maybe it was a receipt. She reached in her back pocket and pulled it out. "Oh, I forgot. It came from Clarksonville County Community College."

Marlee spread the blanket on the beaten-down grass and sat down. "What's it say?" She pulled out two paper plates from the basket.

Susie plopped down on the soft blanket hip to hip with Marlee. "I don't know. Let's see." The tall grasses made it seem like they were in their own cocoon, away from prying eyes. Not that there were people anywhere near, but still, it was comforting. Susie opened the envelope and read the first paragraph to herself.

Marlee handed Susie a paper plate filled with chicken and potato salad. She slid a fork onto Susie's plate and a napkin into her lap.

"Thanks." Susie picked up the fork, but before stabbing the potato salad, said, "It's from the Science Department at the college. It says something about offering a paid internship to high achieving high school students who want to study Earth Science in college." In addition to the letter, there was an application form.

"Oh, cool. Did you apply for that?"

Susie shook her head. "I have no idea how they got my name and address." She reread the letter. "It sounds like the best job ever. Can you imagine the things I'd learn? Before college? And get paid, too? *Dios mio*, it's my lucky day."

"Will you have to go to Clarksonville College? Is that part of the deal?"

"It doesn't say. I guess I'll have to check their website or call somebody there. I have butterflies in my stomach. This is incredible."

"It sounds amazing, but to be honest, I think those butterflies are hunger pangs." Marlee gestured toward Susie's food. "C'mon, let's eat."

Susie put the letter back in her pocket and dug into the picnic food heartily. Since the subject of colleges had been brought up, she decided to pursue it.

"What are your plans for college?" Susie picked up a forkful of potato salad so she wouldn't have to make eye contact.

When Marlee didn't answer right away, Susie looked up.

"I've been avoiding that topic," Marlee said, "but I guess we have to talk about it sometime, don't we?"

Susie nodded, her stomach knotting up. Maybe Marlee didn't want them to go to the same college together.

"I want to study physics or engineering," Marlee said. "I want to learn more about, like, quantum mechanics or maybe electromagnetism. I guess I want to be a science nerd like you." She bugged out her eyes. "Anyway, my math teacher from last year wants me to apply to Cornell, but to be honest, I don't think my mom and I can afford that."

"I know what you mean, Jellybean." Susie desperately wanted to suggest that they apply to the same colleges in the fall but didn't want to sound too needy.

"How do you feel about, um…." Marlee hesitated.

"About what?"

"How do you feel about going to the same college? I mean, we don't have to, if you don't want—"

"I want." Susie blurted as her stomach unknotted. *Dios mío,* why had she been so insecure with Marlee? They'd weathered the Bree and Isabella storms together, wasn't that proof enough that Marlee wanted her to stick around? "You won't get sick of me?"

Marlee put her plate down and pulled Susie into a tight hug. "Not a chance. I can't be away from you for four years. No frickin' way."

Susie's eyes welled up. "Let's do it. Well, if my mother even lets me go to college, that is."

Marlee pulled back from the hug, but Susie averted her eyes, pretending to watch a red-winged blackbird in the meadow around them. When Marlee went back to her chicken, Susie quickly wiped her eyes with the napkin.

After they ate and put their food and trash back in the picnic basket, Marlee pulled out a box of chocolate chip cookies.

"Cookies, my sweet?" Marlee opened the lid and held them out to Susie.

Susie shook her head slowly. The only sweet thing she wanted was Marlee. She'd waited long enough. Susie took the box, closed the lid, and put the cookies back in the basket without saying a word. She put both hands on Marlee's shoulders and pushed her down on the blanket. Marlee didn't protest.

Susie, leaning on one elbow, kissed Marlee softly. Marlee had other ideas, though, and pulled Susie on top of her. Susie let her weight fall gently but kept herself propped up on one hand so that she wouldn't crush her girlfriend. Marlee pulled her tighter and wiggled just enough so that Susie's thigh nestled in between her own. She then turned her head, inviting Susie to kiss her on the neck. Susie obliged and trailed kisses from Marlee's neck across her collar bone to the other side.

Marlee's quiet moans encouraged Susie to move further down. She pulled the collar of Marlee's t-shirt as low as possible and kissed as much of Marlee's chest as she could reach. What she really wanted to do was rip Marlee's shirt right off her but didn't dare. She had to go at Marlee's pace.

Marlee hugged Susie tightly with both arms and then, with one swift movement, flipped Susie onto her back. Susie giggled at the suddenness of it, and Marlee smiled, but the smiles soon faded as Marlee ran her fingers over every square inch of Susie's shirt.

Susie was squirming. She needed Marlee's touch on actual skin. Marlee seemed shy about moving forward, so Susie guided Marlee's hand to the top button, giving her permission. Marlee took the hint and undid the button. She kissed the skin underneath. Button after button came undone, kiss after kiss trailed after until Susie felt the warm August breeze on her bare stomach. Marlee sighed and kissed her way across Susie's stomach and then lower, from hip to hip, following the path of Susie's hip-hugger shorts. Warm tingles flared into life throughout Susie's body.

Susie tugged at Marlee's t-shirt, demanding equal time. The t-shirt soon landed somewhere on the other side of the picnic basket.

Susie couldn't help the moan that escaped her lips when Marlee lay on top, their skin pressed together. More, she wanted more of Marlee. She couldn't help it. She wanted to go slow for Marlee's sake, but she was on fire. The good meal, the warm breeze, the hideout in the meadow, all of it was perfect, so perfect that Susie sat them both up and took her unbuttoned shirt off the rest of the way. She then reached behind her back and undid the clasp to her bra. Marlee bit her lower lip, watching. Susie shrugged out of her bra and felt her face flush as she freed herself. She reached behind Marlee's back and undid the clasp. Marlee pulled her bra off the rest of the way. Susie sighed. Marlee was so pretty. She pulled Marlee back on top, and her body sang when Marlee's silky smooth skin touched her own.

"*Dios mío*, you feel so good," Susie murmured, letting her head fall back as a rush of heat shot through her.

"So do you." Marlee said, her breathing labored.

Marlee leaned to one side and explored Susie's breasts with her fingers. Her mouth soon replaced the fingers. Susie arched up into the touch and melted, her ache building past the point of no return. She grabbed Marlee's hand and guided it lower. Susie's moan came from deep inside as Marlee worked to satisfy Susie's throbbing hunger.

# Chapter 24
### It's About Damn Time

Susie pulled her car into the parking lot at the Southbridge softball field. She and Sam leaped out of the car, grabbed their gear, and ran toward Marlee and Lisa, who were sitting on the bumper of Marlee's van. Sam put a finger to her lips. She wanted to jump out and scare Lisa, so Susie went on ahead.

"*Hola, mi vida.*" Susie couldn't help the huge grin creeping up her face. It was Tuesday evening, and she hadn't seen Marlee since their amazing picnic in their new hideout on Saturday. Living so far away sucked. Big time.

The hug Susie gave Marlee was quick, even though she desperately wanted far more.

"How's it going, Lisa?"

"I'm good. Where's Sam?"

Susie shrugged, trying to hide a grin. Sam was sneaking up alongside the van.

Sam popped out, startling them all. She gave Lisa an overlong hug. Watching them, Susie remembered the incredible afternoon she'd spent with Marlee in their new hideout. Marlee must have been thinking the same thing because she scalded Susie with a look.

Sam tore herself away from Lisa. "What's shaking, Marlee?" She backed away a few steps. "Oh, God. You two need to take cold showers."

"Hey," Susie protested, "I could say the same thing about you guys."

The grin on Lisa's face told Susie she was right. Unfortunately, they had a softball game and Bree to deal with first.

They shouldered their gear and headed toward the immaculate visitors' dugout on the Southbridge field.

"Oh, hey," Susie said to Sam. "I filled out that application." Susie and Marlee didn't know for sure but figured Sam was the one who had arranged for the Earth Science internship at the College. Sam's family had given the college a considerable donation, and the science building wasn't called the Payton Science Center for nothing.

Sam looked confused. "What application?"

"Internship? Clarksonville Community College?" Susie figured Sam was trying to play it cool.

"Sus, I don't know what you're talking about." Sam looked completely baffled.

Susie could tell that Sam didn't know anything about it, so she explained the letter she had gotten from the college. "If it wasn't you, then who was it?"

Sam shrugged. Susie wondered if her Earth Science teacher from school had recommended her. That must be it.

They set their gear down and got ready for the game. Several of their teammates were already stretching.

"Geez, Bree looks awful." Lisa pointed toward the Southbridge home dugout. "Plan E must be working, eh?" They all turned to look.

"*Dios mío*, she looks like *mierda*," Susie said. Bree's hair was greasy like she hadn't washed it in a few days, and there were dark circles under her eyes as if she hadn't slept, either.

"Yeah," Marlee agreed. "She looks, like, wild or something."

Their conversation was cut off when Coach Gellar called them together to read the starting lineup. She gave them a pep talk about staying focused on the win. "Southbridge lost to us last Tuesday," Coach Gellar said. "That's their only loss." She looked each player in the eye as if telepathically transmitting how important the game was.

Coach Gellar's laser beam eyes stopped on Susie. "Torres, keep your head out of the stars tonight."

Susie knew her face betrayed the shock she felt. Would Coach Gellar ever give her a break?

When Coach Gellar dismissed the team, Susie wanted to punch the cinder block wall but didn't. She couldn't. She refused to let her coach know how irritated she was.

Marlee patted her on the back. "C'mon, let's go stretch."

"Okay." Susie followed Marlee out of the dugout but then had an idea. If Coach Gellar was going to single her out all the time, then she would work to get her entire team's support behind her.

"Hey, Nor'easters," Susie called to her teammates. "Bring it in here." They gathered around her in right field. "Let's stretch as a team." Christy had always been the one to call the team together to stretch during the school season, but Christy wasn't there anymore.

Looking like a unified team might scare the Southbridge team, too, so that was a double bonus.

"Good idea," Sam said and helped organize the Nor'easter players into a tight circle.

Susie led the stretching and then suggested they run their laps together as a unit. She noticed Coach Gellar watching her as she finished her first lap around the field. Susie couldn't tell if she was scowling or not. Probably. Coach Gellar hated when anybody else took control or did something that wasn't her idea. *Good*, Susie thought, *at least now you can hate me for a real reason.*

The Nor'easters got up to bat in the top of the first inning, and Susie was surprised that Bree wasn't pitching. Instead, Bree sat alone at the end of their team bench, chewing on the ends of her hair.

Susie always thought Bree was Southbridge's best pitcher, but their new pitcher had a wicked rise ball that caught them all off-balance. Susie managed to foul off a few pitches but ended up striking out. She wanted to slam her bat down and curse but decided she wouldn't give Coach Gellar something else to fuss about. She hustled back to the dugout and put her bat and helmet away as calmly as she could. She grabbed her glove and sprinted to left field.

"C'mon, Marlee," Susie called once she got set in left field. "Pick me up."

Susie was relieved that Marlee had also brought her A-game, and the first three Southbridge batters went down quickly.

Susie hustled back into the dugout and cheered when Lisa stepped into the batter's box. Unfortunately, the cheering was short-lived because Lisa sat back down in three quick pitches, becoming another victim of the rise ball.

"C'mon, Nor'easters," Susie encouraged. "We can do this." Despite Susie's encouragement, Marlee also struck out, and they weren't able to get a single runner on base that inning. The Nor'easters trudged back onto the field.

Bree stepped up to the plate in the bottom of the second inning. Apparently, she was the designated hitter for their pitcher. It looked like Marlee was trying to pitch around her, and Bree ended up walking. Luckily, Marlee fought hard with the next three batters, and Bree never got past first base.

Over the next four innings, a few isolated batters on both teams got on base, including Susie and Lisa, but neither team was able to convert their base runners into runs. At the end of six complete innings, the game remained scoreless when the Nor'easters came to bat in the top of the seventh. If neither team scored, they would head into extra innings. That was the last thing Susie wanted because she was dying to be alone with Marlee.

Sam put her batting gloves and helmet on and then dug in at home plate. Susie warmed up in the on-deck circle. "C'mon, Sam. Get on base. I'll get you over." If Sam could score, they would have the go-ahead run.

The umpire signaled for the Southbridge pitcher to start the inning. Sam slapped at the first pitch and sent it past the pitcher. The second baseman fielded the ball on the run, but Sam was too fast and beat out the throw.

Susie headed toward the plate and looked for the signs. Coach Gellar wanted her to bunt on the first pitch no matter where it was because Sam was going to take off for second base. Any other time, Susie would have been mad that Coach Gellar didn't want her to hit away, but Susie put her ego aside. Susie hid a smile as she saw the left fielder back up a few yards. That was respect for her bat. At least other people knew she could hit.

The Southbridge pitcher put her hands together and took the signal from the catcher. Susie waited until the last second to pull her bat down for the bunt. She couldn't spare a look at Sam but hoped she'd gotten a good jump toward second. The ball glanced off the bottom of her bat and hit the ground in front of home plate. Susie threw her bat down and hustled toward first base. The catcher fielded the ball and threw Susie out.

"Yeah," Susie yelled and clapped her hands. Even though she had made the first out of the inning, Sam was standing safely on second base, and Lisa was up to bat with Marlee on deck.

"Nice sacrifice," Marlee said as Susie walked by.

"Thanks. Now it's up to you guys to get Sam in." Susie opened the dugout gate and pulled each of her teammates off the bench to stand at the dugout fence. "C'mon, you guys. It's do or die right here. Cheer as loud as you can."

Susie took a spot against the fence in the middle of her teammates. She noticed Coach Gellar glaring at her again. *Sorry, Coach,* Susie thought sarcastically, *you're not here to tell these lost sheep what to do, so I'm doing it.*

Susie knew she'd probably get reamed out after the game, but she didn't care. There was no way she wanted Bree's team to win. It seemed symbolic somehow.

Lisa apparently had the green light to hit away and sent a long fly ball to right field. Although the right fielder caught it easily, Sam tagged up on second base and sprinted toward third. The right fielder had a great arm and threw the ball to the base on one hop. Sam slid, but a cloud of dust covered the play, so Susie couldn't tell if Sam was safe or out.

"Safe!" The umpire threw her arms out to the side.

"Yeah!" Susie yelled while she and her teammates rattled the dugout fence.

Lisa made her way back to the dugout, and before she could get her helmet off, Susie pounded it. "Way to go, Lisa."

Lisa yanked her helmet off and looked dizzy. "Thanks. I think."

Lisa joined Susie at the fence. "I hope she scores." Lisa sighed. "I can't handle extra innings tonight."

"Me neither." Susie rolled her eyes. She turned back toward the game. Marlee had stepped up to bat. "C'mon, *mi*—" Susie clamped her mouth shut. She had been about to yell, "*mi vida.*" She cleared her throat and tried again. "C'mon, Marlee. Get her in."

Marlee dug her heels into the batter's box. She took the first pitch for ball one. The second pitch came in at her knees for the first strike. Marlee stepped out of the box and looked to Coach Gellar for the signs.

"It's got to be hit-away, eh?" Lisa said. "What else could she do? There's two outs."

Susie nodded in agreement. Marlee had no choice but to try to hit the ball.

The next pitch was a rise ball, and Marlee swung but missed for the second strike.

"*Dios mío,* she's gonna strike out on that stupid rise ball."

"Yeah, but Marlee's a pitcher and knows she'll throw the rise again." Lisa's voice sounded hopeful.

"I hope you're right."

The Southbridge pitcher put her hands together and went into her wind up. Marlee, looking determined, swung her bat and connected with the predicted rise ball.

"Yeah," Susie yelled and watched the soft line drive land in the outfield just over the shortstop's head.

Sam scored the first run of the game, and Marlee was safe at first. Unfortunately for the Nor'easters, the next batter popped up to the first baseman, and Sam's run was the only one they got.

The Nor'easters seemed energized, though, and every player, including Marlee and Lisa, ran out to their positions on the field. Marlee struck out the first batter. Bree was the second batter of the inning and stepped into the box, never taking her eyes off Marlee.

Marlee turned to look at Susie as if trying to find the courage to pitch to the girl that creeped her out. Susie pumped a fist in the air for encouragement. Marlee nodded and got ready for the pitch. Lisa squatted down and gave Marlee the sign. Marlee must have put the pitch in the fat part of the plate because Bree sent a sizzling line drive right back up the middle. Susie's heart leaped to her throat, but Marlee jumped out of the way in time. The ball bounced its way to Rachel in center field. Bree ran to first base and stopped, a smug grin plastered on her face. Susie shook her head. Somehow, she'd find a way to wipe that smile off Bree's mug.

As the next Southbridge batter stepped into the batter's box, the entire Southbridge team pounded on the dugout fence and cheered. Susie had never heard their team get so loud.

"C'mon, Nor'easters," Susie yelled to her teammates, "we can do this." She pounded her glove and crouched in her ready position. There was no way a ball was going to get past her. Especially not with Coach Gellar watching her every move.

Marlee threw the pitch. The batter swung hard and hit a sharp ground ball to Abby at shortstop. Susie ran in to back up the play, but Abby fielded the ball cleanly and tossed it to Sam, covering second base. Bree slid in hard, but Sam managed to throw the ball to first base in time to snag the double play ending the game.

Susie leaped in the air and sprinted toward Marlee. They had just beaten the Southbridge Bombers by a score of 1-0, but more importantly, they had beaten Bree.

Susie stopped dead in her tracks when she heard the scuffle at second base. Bree had knocked Sam over with her slide, and they were still scrambling to get untangled.

"Who do you think you are, Payton?" Bree sat up first. "Rich fucking bitch." She pulled back a fist and then punched Sam square in the face. Sam howled in pain and fell backward.

"Oh, hell no." Susie ran toward them.

Bree hit Sam again, but this time Sam had her arms up in front of her face. Marlee started to follow Susie, but Susie yelled, "No! Go to the dugout." She was relieved when Marlee didn't argue and headed in the other direction.

Susie reached down and pulled Bree off her friend. She dragged

Bree several feet away and then positioned herself between them.

Lisa barreled her way toward Sam, but Susie didn't try to stop her.

Bree got to her feet slowly with both fists clenched. She looked like she wasn't done hitting things. "C'mon, Rican. You want a piece of me?"

Bree lunged forward and took a swing, but Susie leaped out of the way. She put both hands up defensively and said, "Back off, Bree," as calmly as she could. Out of the corner of her eye, she noticed that Lisa had Sam on her feet, and they were heading toward the dugout.

Susie's Nor'easter teammates streamed toward them. Susie shot them a glance, afraid to take her eyes off the crazy chick in front of her. "Get back, you guys. Help Lisa get Sam to the trainer." When they didn't move fast enough for her, she barked, "Now!" in her best Coach Gellar imitation.

The Southbridge players stood behind Bree, looking like they really didn't want to be involved but had to support their crazy teammate. Susie was completely outnumbered but hoped the kickboxing class she took the year before would pay off.

Bree's eyes looked wild, making Susie pray she was doing the right thing. Bree took a step toward her, but Susie stood her ground. *C'mon, crazy bitch. Give me one more excuse to beat the crap out of you.*

Bree moved to within arms' length. Susie wasn't worried, though. A tall beefy woman was sneaking up behind Bree, hopefully getting ready to grab her. Just as Bree pulled back to throw a punch, the woman's strong arm came up from behind and pulled Bree away.

Bree squealed in frustration. The tall black woman looked like a police detective or something. She held Bree's arm behind her. The woman said, "Third strike, Bree. You know what happens now."

Bree struggled for a while but then let herself be strong-armed off the field. Susie headed toward the dugout, but Coach Gellar blocked her path.

"Way to go, Torres."

Susie wasn't sure if Coach Gellar was being her usual sarcastic self or not. "She's crazy." Susie watched Bree get handcuffed by the woman who'd led her off the field. "What's going on?"

"I did a little digging, and it seems that this isn't the first time Bree has developed an unrequited crush on somebody."

"That woman said something about a third strike." Susie watched Bree get put in the backseat of what looked like an unmarked police car.

"Apparently, Bree was on probation," Coach Gellar said. "She'd been let out of juvenile detention hall for good behavior. Go figure." Coach Gellar shrugged. "Let's just say she won't be around for quite some time."

Susie sighed. The girl really was loony.

"I'm proud of you, you know," Coach Gellar said.

Susie almost fainted on the spot. Coach Gellar never gave out direct praise. Praise, if it ever came, was always in the form of a backhanded compliment.

"Why are you proud of me?"

"Taking charge of this team tonight and sticking up for Sam and the rest of your teammates just now. You were ready to take on that whole Southbridge team by yourself." Coach Gellar chuckled. "I've been waiting a long time to see some leadership from you, Torres. I'd almost given up." A rare smile crept up Coach Gellar's face. "I'm breaking tradition for the spring season and appointing two captains. You and Sam will be co-captains."

"Really?" Susie knew her eyes had grown big. "Thanks, Coach." Susie was chomping at the bit to get back in the dugout to see how Sam was doing. The athletic trainer who was working on her would probably be able to tell if Sam's nose was broken. Susie hoped not. Sam's parents would never let her play softball again.

"Go on." Coach Gellar pointed toward the dugout. As Susie took off running, she heard her coach mumble, "It's about damn time."

# Chapter 25
## For Years and Years and Years

Saturday morning's game came and went quickly. Susie sat on the visitors' team bench and took off her cleats and socks. She let her feet air out for a moment and then threw on her crocs.

Sam grinned. "We took the bite right out of those Cobras. Didn't we?"

"The three of us did." Susie twirled her finger to include herself, Marlee, and Lisa. "You just sat here riding the pine looking pitiful with a swollen black eye."

Sam stuck her tongue out at Susie.

"And that completes the picture," Susie said with a laugh. "You're just lucky Bree didn't break your nose."

"Yeah, I know." Sam smiled, looking pitiful as she did so. "My mother didn't want me anywhere near the fields today, but Helene convinced her I would be okay as long as I didn't play."

"Helene's cool," Susie said, and Lisa nodded in agreement.

Sam groaned. "I wish I could have played. You guys were hitting machines, and I missed out. You got at least three hits apiece, right?" She opened the gate to the Milford Cobras visitors' dugout, and they headed toward the parking lot.

Marlee gestured to Susie and Lisa. "These two were in a home run derby or something."

"Geez," Lisa said with a roll of her eyes, "you can't hit three homers without everybody buggin' you about it."

"Susie hit two," Sam said.

"I know," Lisa said with a laugh, "that's why I had to hit a third one."

"Show off." Susie gave Lisa a friendly shove. "C'mon, you guys have to administer last rites before Marlee and I head back to my house."

Sam put a hand on her hip and gave Susie the look, which was still quite effective despite the black eye. Susie knew what that look meant because she'd told Sam about her new outlook on life. She'd slipped up and forgotten that she was trying to stay positive.

"Oh, wait," Susie amended. "What I meant to say was this. Please wish us a good time when Marlee comes over for a lovely dinner with my parents."

Sam grinned. "Better." She turned toward Marlee. "And how do you feel about all of this?"

Marlee took a deep breath. "Okay, I guess. I mean, I'm nervous and all, but my mom will be there, so it'll be cool."

"I'm scared shitless." Susie leaped away from Sam's backhand. "You missed."

Before they went their separate ways, Susie hugged Sam and whispered in her ear, "Any progress on getting the lake house for Labor Day weekend?"

Sam pulled out of the hug with a frown. She shook her head. "I'm going to ask my father again in a couple of days, but so far, he's not cool about four girls staying there alone."

Susie groaned inside. Too bad. It had been a good idea.

They said their goodbyes, and Sam and Lisa made their way toward Sam's car. Susie headed to the passenger side of the van and called back to them. "Have fun on the yacht."

Sam and Lisa both turned around with wicked grins on their faces. They were lucky that Sam's family owned a yacht where they could go to be alone. *Aay*, Susie hoped she and Marlee would get some time alone together after dinner. They didn't have access to a yacht, but Marlee's van had lots of room.

Marlee drove the van back toward East Valley, and the conversation was pretty limited to the game they'd just won. That is until Marlee blurted, "I don't know if I can do this."

Susie jumped. She took a second to gather her composure before answering. "You can do this. I'll be right there with you."

"But your mother—"

"—is making *pollo agridulce* for dinner, and we're both going to love it." Susie grinned at Marlee in an attempt to keep her calm and steady, although she felt completely the opposite herself.

"What's *pollo agridulce*? Some kind of chicken?"

Susie was glad Marlee was letting herself be distracted. "Sweet and sour chicken."

"That's Chinese food."

"They don't have a monopoly on sweet and sour chicken, you know. My mother makes it way better than any Chinese place anyway."

They distracted each other by talking about the menu, which included Susie's description of the orgasmic delights of flan. Susie's nerves shot to full attention, though, when Marlee pulled onto Susie's street. They were both relieved to see that Marlee's mother wasn't there yet.

"Let me take you inside," Susie said after getting out of the van. "*Mami* said you can shower and change in the upstairs bathroom. She made me clean it yesterday."

"Oh, sorry." Marlee slipped her flip-flops off in the mudroom. "I told my mom about the no shoes thing so that she wouldn't wear socks with holes in them."

Susie laughed. "Company's allowed to leave their shoes on." She opened the door to the house, and the most delicious smells wafted toward them. "*Dios mío*, I'm in heaven."

Marlee nodded her agreement, even though she looked petrified.

Susie's mother walked out of the kitchen, wiping her hands on a dishtowel. She hugged Susie and then said to Marlee, "I'm so glad you were able to come for dinner."

"Thanks for the invitation."

Susie's father stuck his head out of the kitchen door. "Nice to see you again, Marlee."

"You, too, Mr. Torres." Marlee smiled at him and then back at Susie's mother. "My mom will probably be here soon."

"*Bueno*," Susie's mother said.

Susie's *abuelita* shuffled toward them with her arms open. "Nice to see you, *mi querubín*."

Marlee gave her a big hug. "*Mucho gusto, Abuelita.*"

Susie's mother turned toward Susie. "Go ahead and show her where to shower. I need you in the kitchen as soon as you get showered and changed. *¿Me entiendes?*"

"Okay." Susie ushered Marlee up the stairs and into the bathroom. She snuck a peek behind her to make sure her pesky brother wasn't listening in. She whispered, "Now, don't freak out later. I'm wearing a dress."

Marlee's mouth dropped open. "Really? Was I supposed to wear—"

"Shhh," Susie put her finger over Marlee's panicked lips. "You're fine. I'm surprising my mother by wearing the sundress she bought me at Walmart last week during our peace mission."

"Oh." Marlee nodded her understanding. "I'm not leaving this bathroom until you come back up for me, okay?"

Susie nodded and couldn't help the grin spreading on her face as she turned to go. What she didn't tell Marlee was that she was also wearing the dress to turn Marlee's head.

Susie ran out the front door and sprinted up the garage stairs to her bedroom. She showered in record time, blow dried her hair, and then put on her dress. She struggled with the back zipper but finally managed to pull it all the way up. She put her hair in a loose bun on the back of her head. She wanted her neck exposed to entice a certain blue-eyed pitcher from Clarksonville. After applying eyeliner and a subtle touch of eye shadow, she inspected herself in the mirror. She ran her hands down her hourglass figure, liking how the thin strapped black and white dress clung to her curves. Her mother said the dress looked tailor-made for her. When she'd come out of the dressing room that day at Walmart, she'd turned more than a few heads.

"Look out, Marlee," Susie said to her reflection. "You're about to be rendered powerless."

She threw on the pair of flats they'd found to match and practically skipped down the stairs. Marlee's mother's new Cadillac was in the driveway, so obviously, she must have gone inside. Susie headed into the house, keeping the flats on, and greeted Marlee's mother in the kitchen.

"Hello, Mrs. McAllister. I'm glad you found the house okay." Susie smiled her best future daughter-in-law smile.

"Being a realtor has its perks. I pretty much know every street in the North Country." Marlee's mother looked nice. She'd worn a light olive-green dress that flattered her light brown hair and slim figure nicely. Marlee definitely looked more like the pictures of her father Susie had seen.

"Let me run upstairs to see if Marlee needs anything."

Susie headed toward the stairs, but before she was out of earshot, she heard Marlee's mother say, "That dress is stunning on her. Oh, to be seventeen again."

Susie smiled at the praise. There were three seconds until Marlee's meltdown. Susie knocked gently on the door. "Hey, it's me." *Three, two…*

"Oh, man. I've been done forever." Marlee unlocked the door and swung it wide open. "How long was I—" Her mouth dropped wide open.

*One.*

"Everything okay?" Susie asked innocently.

Marlee gulped and looked down either side of the hallway. She grabbed Susie's hand and pulled her into the bathroom with her. She shut the door behind them, locked it, and kissed Susie with a passion they'd just begun to discover together.

*Mission accomplished*, Susie thought when they pulled apart. Marlee held her at arms' length and then stroked Susie's bare arms and shoulders.

"You are so freakin' gorgeous." There were tears in Marlee's eyes. "Oh. My. God."

Susie felt her face flush.

"I hope to God you found a private place for us for later." Marlee didn't wait for Susie to answer. "Let's eat really fast—turbo— so we can get out of here. Man, I need a cold shower."

Susie felt her face flush. "C'mon. It's time." She unlocked the door and opened it a crack. She looked back at Marlee, eyeing her up and down. She looked good, handsome even, in her khaki pants and tight blue oxford shirt that totally brought out her eyes. "Oh, and, uh, you're no slacker either. You look good enough to eat."

Marlee blushed to the roots of her blonde hair.

They headed down the stairs and into the kitchen. Marlee greeted her mother with a hug. Within ten minutes, the food was on the table, and the Torres and McAllister families were seated around it. Marlee sat in between her mother and Susie.

After they said grace, the conversation seemed to be limited to "pass the rice" or "this is some heatwave we're having," but inevitably, the conversation turned to Marlee and Susie.

"So," Susie's mother said to Marlee's mother, "what are Marlee's plans for college?"

"Well," Marlee's mother beamed, "she wants to study engineering. Right, honey?"

Marlee nodded but then probably realized she needed to actually speak, so she added, "Engineering or physics. Brockport has a really good physics program."

"Brockport?" Marlee's mother and Susie's mother said simultaneously, and then everybody laughed. Marlee's mother said, "I never heard you mention Brockport before."

Marlee shrugged. "I don't think we can afford Cornell. I mean, who knows if I'd even get in. Brockport will be way cheaper, and their softball team looks good from their website."

"I guess we have to explore all the options." Marlee's mother smiled.

Susie raised her eyebrows in wonder. Marlee must have done some research about Brockport without telling her. She reached under the table and squeezed Marlee's hand. Without taking her eyes off her mother, Marlee squeezed back.

"My Susie wants to study geology," Susie's mother said. "She wants to study global warming." Susie's mother managed to look proud. Who knows? Maybe she was. Maybe her mother's switch was finally flipping all the way over.

Susie raised an eyebrow at her father. He smiled ever so slightly as if to say he knew her mother would come around.

Thankfully the conversation turned away from Susie and Marlee. Marlee's mother asked Miguel what grade he was going into in the fall and if he liked school. Susie chuckled when he only gave one-word answers, but that was okay. At least he was behaving himself.

After discussing what Susie's father did for a living, he asked Marlee's mother about her career, so she gave a brief description of her job as a residential and commercial real estate agent in the North Country.

Marlee's mother then asked Susie's mother, "And what do you do?"

"I'm a nurse," Susie's mother said. "I used to work at the hospital."

"Used to?" Susie blurted before she could stop herself. "What do you mean 'used to'? ¿*Que pasó, Mami*?" Did stupid Mrs. Johnson fire her mother, too? Susie's anger boiled inside her.

"*Aay, aay, hija*," Susie's mother put out a calming hand. "I gave them my two-weeks notice yesterday. I can't work with those bigoted people anymore." She sat up tall and jutted her chin out to show everyone she was serious.

"Did you know, *Papi*?" Susie looked at her father. He nodded once. So, he knew. When were they going to tell her? "*Mami*, what are you going to do now?"

"I seriously don't know." Susie's mother sighed. "I'll land somewhere, I suppose."

An awkward silence grew around the two families. Marlee reached for and squeezed Susie's hand.

"I may be able to help, actually," Marlee's mother said. "I recently negotiated a very large commercial space for Dr. Webster's pediatric practice right here in East Valley. She's expanding her practice and may be looking for help. It's a long shot, but I can at least make introductions to help you get your foot in the door."

Susie's mother's face held a mixture of pride and gratefulness at the suggestion. She hesitated but finally said, "Thank you. I may take you up on that."

"I'm fairly certain Dr. Webster has a website. You could look it over, and if it's something you think you might like doing, I'll make a call."

"I—Yes, I would like that." Susie's mother smiled, and it was then that everyone at the table seemed to relax. Susie was happy to see that her mother was able to put her pride aside and accept help.

Once everyone had eaten, Susie's mother said, "Susie, can you find that website for me?" She pointed to her laptop in the living room.

"Dr. Webster's?"

Her mother nodded.

"Sure." Susie stood up and started to clear the dishes with Marlee's help.

"*Aay, no, hijas,*" Susie's mother said. "Miguel and I will get this."

Susie almost burst out laughing at the shocked look on Miguel's face. One stern look from their mother, and he started picking up plates from the table.

"Go ahead and find that website," Susie's mother said.

"Okay, *Mami*," Susie said. "*Gracias*." Susie tapped Marlee on the arm. "C'mon."

Before they headed into the living room, Marlee said to Susie's mother, "Dinner was really good. Teach Susie how to make that, okay?"

Everyone chuckled, including Susie's mother, who said, "She's the one who taught me." That got an even bigger laugh.

Susie was relieved that Marlee and her mother seemed to be hitting it off, or at least getting along. She led the way to the family computer. Luckily the computer was already on, and the internet was up and running. She was about to type the doctor's name into the search window when she noticed someone had already typed something there. She pointed it out to Marlee.

"Earth Science at Clarksonville," Marlee read off the screen. "Hit the search button and see what sites it brings up."

Several websites popped up. Susie clicked on the link that had obviously been taken before, and there it was—the high school internship page for the science department at Clarksonville Community College.

"My mother had that application sent to me," Susie said in a low voice, so she wouldn't be overheard.

Marlee pulled a chair closer to the computer and sat down. "I think you're right, Sherlock. I think your mother's switch definitely turned in your favor. You have more support in this house than you realize."

The relief that Susie felt was almost tangible. "You may be right, *mi vida*."

Just then, Susie overheard Marlee's mother say, "Our daughters are all grown up, aren't they?"

Susie snuck a peek into the dining room. Her mother's smile looked like one of resigned acceptance as she slowly nodded her head. "*Aay*, this is true. I have to keep reminding myself that she's not a baby anymore. They're both beautiful young women now."

Marlee must have overheard their conversation, too, because she put a hand on her chest and whispered, "And this beautiful young woman would like to be alone with you." She pointed to Susie.

"*Aay, Santo*. Me, too. After dessert, let's get out of here, okay?"

Susie found Dr. Webster's website, and she and Marlee liked the looks of it. Susie was proud of her mother for finally standing up for herself, and it would be *fantástico* if her mother could get a job so soon after sticking it to Mrs. Johnson.

After a delectable flan dessert, Marlee's mother said her goodbyes to the Torres family. Before walking her to the car, Susie told her parents she and Marlee were going out for a short drive. Susie was astonished when her mother actually gave Marlee a quick hug and told her how nice it was to meet her as if it was the first time.

Once they made it to the driveway, Marlee's mother told them not to stay out too late since Marlee had a long drive home ahead of her. They watched until her mother's car was out of sight and then dove into the van.

Marlee accidentally revved the engine. "Oops."

"Slow down there, *mi amor*," Susie said. "Let's get there in one piece."

Susie guided Marlee back to Sandstoner Fields to what she hoped would be their new private spot in East Valley. One day after a game, she noticed a dirt road leading from the parking lot to a big maintenance shed behind a tall stand of trees. No one would ever find them there. Maybe it wasn't as private as their hideout in the meadow, but it would do just fine.

Marlee pulled in behind the shed. "I never realized this was back here." She turned off the van engine, undid her seatbelt, and practically threw herself in the back.

"In a hurry, *mi vida*?" Susie gingerly climbed through the two front seats and sat down in the open space as best she could in her tight dress.

Marlee pulled her into a fevered embrace, one that Susie returned with equal passion.

"You're so hot in that dress," Marlee whispered.

Susie felt her face get warm and looked down, almost shy. "Thanks." She looked up again and saw the reflection of her own desire mirrored in Marlee's face. "You've got me tingling. All over."

"Me, too." Marlee leaned in for another steamy kiss, but Susie stopped her.

"Wait, *mi vida*. I have something for you first. If you want it, that is." Susie reached down into the front of her dress and into her bra. She pulled out a small wad of tissue. At the look on Marlee's face, she said, "No, I'm not stuffing my bra. That's the real me in there."

Marlee grinned. "What'd you get me?"

"Monday is our four-month anniversary. I've had four amazing months with you, but I want more."

"Oh, me, too. Years and years and years."

Susie unwrapped the tissue paper but clenched her fist quickly before Marlee could see what she held.

"Marlee McAllister." Susie opened her hand. Two gold plastic rings rested in the palm of her hand. "Will you stay with me forever?"

"Yes," Marlee said without hesitation. "A thousand times yes." She held out her left hand, fingers splayed, ready to receive the ring.

"These aren't real. They're just—"

"They're real enough for me." Marlee kept her hand poised.

Susie slid one of the rings on Marlee's ring finger, surprised at how well it fit.

Marlee took the other ring and reached for Susie's hand, but before sliding it on, asked, "Will you stay with me forever?"

Susie nodded and let Marlee slide the ring on her finger. They hugged for a moment until Susie said, "What is taking you so long to unzip me?"

With a growl, Marlee obliged.

~~~ The End ~~~

# Newsletter Signup

Sign up for Barbara L. Clanton's newsletter to stay on top of new (and revised) releases. She also likes to provide writing tips for newbie (or oldbie) writers and recommend books to read (other than her own, of course).

Sign Up on Barbara L. Clanton's Official Website:

www.BLClanton.com

# About the Author

Barbara L. Clanton

Barbara L. Clanton is a native New Yorker who left those "New York minutes" for a slower-paced life in central Florida. While in middle and high schools, she played any sport she could find—softball, volleyball, basketball, and field hockey. During high school she could even be found in the upstairs gym  playing handball with her friends. She played softball at Princeton University and was the team captain during their Ivy-league champion senior year.

Her career has been spent teaching mathematics at college preparatory schools in both New York and Florida. She also coached softball and basketball in both states as well. She was inducted into the ASANA's (Amateur Sports Alliance of North America) Hall of Fame as an amateur softball player.

Somewhere in adulthood, she picked up a new hobby. "Dr. Barb" plays the bass guitar and has been in several pop-rock bands, playing such notable events as Gay Days Orlando.

When asked why she started writing, she said she was writing the books she wished she had in high school to help her make sense of her "differentness." Although the world is evolving, it's still not easy to come out to yourself or the world. She hopes her books will help.

Barbara L. Clanton's Website:
http://www.blclanton.com


Barbara L. Clanton's Instagram:
https://www.instagram.com/barbara.clanton14


Barbara L. Clanton's Facebook:
https://www.facebook.com/BassGuitarGirl


Barbara L. Clanton's Goodreads Page:
https://www.goodreads.com/author/show/3072442.Barbara_L_Clanton


Barbara L. Clanton's Author Page on Amazon:
https://www.amazon.com/Barbara-L-Clanton

# Books by Barbara L. Clanton

## THE CLARKSONVILLE SERIES (Young Adult)

The Clarksonville Series follows four high school girls in upstate New York as they maneuver the difficult process of coming out to themselves, each other, and their families. And it doesn't always go well. The four friends have a mutual love of softball which helps them bond and find love. Each book is from a different character's point of view, but all four main characters are present in each book. There are currently eight books in the series.

### Out of Left Field: Marlee's Story
### (Book One in the Clarksonville Series)

High school junior Marlee McAllister lives and breathes softball. She's the pitcher for the Clarksonville Cougars in the North Country of upstate New York. With the season opener approaching, Marlee and her best friend, Jeri D'Amico, go to scout their rivals, the East Valley Panthers. The Panthers' star pitcher, Christy Loveland, took the All-county pitching title the preceding year. It is a title Marlee covets. Marlee and Jeri settle in for the game, but as the Panthers take the field, Marlee finds herself staring at Susie Torres, the Panther left fielder.

For reasons Marlee doesn't understand, she's drawn to Susie. Over the next few weeks, Marlee and Susie will slowly act on their mutual attraction. But suddenly, Susie pulls away without explanation, and Marlee realizes it has to do with Christy. Susie won't explain the bond she and Christy share, but whatever it is, it threatens Marlee's burgeoning relationship with Susie.

Struggling to maintain her grades, dealing with the ever-increasing estrangement from her best friend Jeri, and handling the pressures of the All-county pitching competition, Marlee also has to confront the bittersweet realities of what it might mean to be gay.

ISBN: 978-1-953734-04-4 (eBook)
ISBN: 978-1-953734-16-7 (Paperback)

## Tools of Ignorance: Lisa's Story
### (Book Two in the Clarksonville Series)

Lisa Brown is the starting catcher for the Clarksonville Cougars High School softball team, and she has a major crush on her pitcher Marlee. Lisa continues to carry her torch for Marlee, even when Sam, a rival softball player, flirts sweetly. However, Lisa becomes more confused than ever when Tara, the first girl she ever kissed and the first girl who ever broke her heart, resurfaces. Since Marlee doesn't know Lisa's alive, should Lisa give up on her once and for all?

Sam seems to have secrets of her own, but Lisa wonders if she should overlook them and allow her fledging attraction to grow for the pretty blonde, or should she fan the tiny flame still burning in her heart for Tara? Lisa faces these problems and deals with society's tools of ignorance in her quest for love and acceptance.

ISBN: 978-1-953734-06-8 (eBook)
ISBN: 978-1-953734-17-4 (Paperback)

## Going, Going, Gone: Susie's Story
## (Book Three in the Clarksonville Series)

Susie Torres planned to spend most of the summer before her senior year of high school with her girlfriend, Marlee McAllister, but that's proving to be quite challenging. Marlee works at D'Amico's restaurant, and Susie babysits for Mrs. Johnson, her mother's boss. Susie hates the job because she not only works like a slave but almost gets paid like one. Susie is desperate to take her physical relationship with Marlee further, but she knows she has to go at Marlee's slower pace. Complicating things is the attention that a pretty blonde softball player from another team shows Marlee, and Susie falls into a funk when Marlee seems to enjoy it.

On top of that, nothing she does seems to be good enough for her summer softball coach. Frustrated with life, Susie accidentally, on purpose, comes out to her mother. It would be an understatement to say that her mother didn't take it well. Can Susie deal with a girlfriend whose head has possibly been turned by another, an employer who treats her like dirt, a coach who doesn't respect her, and a mother who tells her she is unnatural? Can she get her life back on track before senior year starts?

ISBN: 978-1-953734-05-1 (eBook)
ISBN: 978-1-953734-18-1 (Paperback)

## Stealing Second: Sam's Story
## <u>(Book Four in the Clarksonville Series)</u>

Samantha Rose Payton likes girls, but her parents don't know that. And Sam would like to keep it that way because her parents are ultra-conservative Republicans. They live in a mansion and have servants and chauffeurs. However, instead of playing the dutiful debutante who plays the violin and still has a nanny at age seventeen, Sam would rather watch ice hockey on TV and play second base on her summer softball team. Having to hide her relationship with her girlfriend, Lisa, from her parents is becoming an agonizing struggle. Not only are her friends pressuring her to come out to her parents, but they are also trying to convince her to attend a very public gay pride festival at the local college.

At least she has her nanny Helene to confide in, but for how much longer? Sam is acutely aware that the time for Helene to move on may be fast approaching. And if that isn't enough, Sam's summer softball coach gives her no end of grief after an error-filled game and isn't afraid of making an example out of her. Will Sam remain the perfect princess her parents expect? Will her beloved nanny leave her forever? Will her girlfriend get fed up about being kept hidden? Will her friends continue to pressure her about coming out? Will Coach Greer make her life miserable? All of these questions are answered in Stealing Second: Sam's Story.

ISBN: 978-1-953734-07-5 (eBook)
ISBN: 978-1-953734-19-8 (Paperback)

## Out at Home
## (Book Five in the Clarksonville Series)

Marlee McAllister just wants to fit in. She didn't know she didn't fit in until Kate and Rita - the prettiest girls in the senior class - pointed it out. Even Marlee's grandmother declared that Marlee's too old for "this tomboy nonsense." All the other girls at school have long hair except Marlee. All the other girls wear something other than jeans, a t-shirt, and sneakers to school every day. Except for Marlee. All the other girls fit in except Marlee.

Marlee decides to grow out her short hair, buy femmy girly clothes, and pretend she has a boyfriend named Ronnie. Really, though? She has the most amazing girlfriend in Susie Torres. Susie is everything Marlee hoped for - sweet, sexy, kind, athletic, pretty. And best of all? She loves Marlee as much as Marlee loves her. Although their parents know about their relationship, not many other people do.

Marlee is out at home but not to anyone else. And if anyone else finds out she's into girls, Kate and Rita especially, the entire school and her grandparents will know within a day. Life as she knows it will be over.

Out at Home is the story of Marlee McAllister's life-altering struggle to fit in.

ISBN: 978-1-953734-20-4 (eBook)
ISBN: 978-1-953734-24-2 (Paperback)

## Tools of the Devil
### (Book Six in the Clarksonville Series)

Seventeen-year-old Lisa Brown loved going to church. Oh sure, sometimes she'd rather sleep in, but she liked the calming and empowering strength of her faith. Sundays revitalized her spirit when she thanked God for the wonderful things in her life, like her loving family and amazing girlfriend, Samantha Rose. One day she hoped to marry Sam, have a house and yard, and have babies together. One day.

But then it happened. That fateful Sunday, the guest preacher stepped behind the pulpit and spoke four words that would change Lisa's world forever. "Homosexuality is a sin," he said. Had she heard him right? When her mother put a hand on her forearm, she knew she had. Every muscle in her body tensed, and she forgot to breathe. What was happening?

The church she'd been baptized in, grown up in, and wanted to get married in had, in one instant, turned against her. Still not quite believing what she'd heard, she mumbled, "Ignorance is a sin, Reverend." Never one to back down from a challenge, she scanned the congregation but didn't find a single soul who looked upset by his statement. On the contrary, many nodded in agreement. Under her breath, she muttered, "Game on, people. Game on."

ISBN: 978-1-953734-21-1 (eBook)
ISBN: 978-1-953734-25-9 (Paperback)

## Going Under
## (Book Seven in the Clarksonville Series)

Susie Torres is a second-semester senior with devoted friends and an amazing girlfriend in Marlee McAllister. Susie's father has the kind of job that takes him away from home on frequent business trips, but lately, his trips seem to be longer and more frequent. Tensions rise at home when Susie's mother challenges him about that. At first, Susie and her younger brother Miguel hide in her room when their parents' frequent squabbles elevate to out-and-out yelling matches. But as her parents' war escalates further, Susie finds other ways to escape the tension.

A fake ID becomes a clear and easy way to anesthetize herself with alcohol. Her crumbling home life becomes momentarily forgotten whenever she swims in a sea of peaceful drunken bliss. Unfortunately, Susie doesn't realize that she is alienating everyone around her with her attempts to cope with her parents' possible divorce. Including Marlee. Her best friend Sam tries to warn her that her excessive drinking is driving away all of her friends, but Sam's well-meaning advice isn't heard. Will Susie finally realize that it is her own actions that are making her life fall apart around her? That her new love of drinking is getting in the way of everything good in her life? That her amazingly patient girlfriend isn't going to put up with much more?

ISBN: 978-1-953734-22-8 (eBook)
ISBN: 978-1-953734-26-6 (Paperback)

## Stealing Hope
## (Book Eight in the Clarksonville Series)

Sam Payton is a high school senior with a bit of an identity crisis. Raised in a well-to-do family, she dutifully plays the role of Samantha Rose Payton, the wealthy debutante. Now, almost one full year into her life-changing relationship with Lisa Brown, Sam is hit with many life-challenging events. Her best friend, Susie Torres, struggles with alcohol addiction and a wrecked home life as her parents go through a bitter divorce, and Sam tries to help her friend keep her head above water. In another struggle, two friends cross the line between friendship and intimacy—a line that should not have been approached. Sam finds herself trying to make them see how incredibly egregious the transgressions are for all involved. And to top it all off, Sam's mother is diagnosed with a serious illness.

Through the love of her parents and her girlfriend, Sam navigates these challenges the best way she can, all while trying to fulfill everyone's varying expectations of her. Sam struggles to break free of the preconceived roles she seems to be bound by to figure out who she really is. It ultimately comes down to whether Sam can make everyone see that she is both a softball-playing ice-hockey-loving lesbian named Sam as well as a classically-music-trained debutante named Samantha Rose.

**ISBN: 978-1-953734-23-5 (eBook)**
**ISBN: 978-1-953734-27-3 (Paperback)**

# THE WHICKETT SERIES (Young Adult)

## Art for Art's Sake: Meredith's Story
### (Book One in the Whickett Series)

High school senior Meredith Bedford is a social outcast. Her family recently moved from the Catskill Mountains to the sprawling suburbs of Albany, the capital of New York State. Shy and self-conscious about her acne scars, she stays to herself and tries to remain invisible. Her twelve-year-old brother, Mikey, has Down Syndrome, and she tries hard not to blame her troubles on him. Despite verbal and sometimes physical harassment, she survives because she has her art. She was selected to be part of the elite Advanced Placement art class and is quite good at capturing the emotions of her subjects in her portraits. Besides her family, art is the one thing that helps her cope with her outcast status.

One day, at a senior class meeting, she sees Dani Lassiter, president of the senior class and captain of the lacrosse team and knows that she must paint this enigmatic young woman. One class period later, Dani manipulates things to have Meredith as her partner for a history project. Meredith is suspicious of Dani's motives but takes a chance. And it pays off. Meredith slowly sheds her invisibility cloak and allows Dani in - a little at a time. They explore an old Victorian house for their history project and become close with Esther and Millie, the two older women who own the house and who've lived together for about forty years. But, when Dani reveals to Meredith that she is gay, Meredith simply can't deal with the news. How had she not known? What is it that won't allow her to come to terms with this unexpected news? Will Meredith control her own homophobia, or will she reject the one person who had taken a chance on her and made her feel human?

# Dani's Story
## (Book Two in the Whickett Series)

< Coming Soon >

## THE GRASSE RIVER SERIES (Young Adult)

### Quite an Undertaking: Devon's Story
(Book One in the Grasse River Series)

Devon Raines, a sixteen-year-old journalism nerd, was happily minding her own business when wham, her life was turned upside down. She struggled with grief when her grandmother died from a sudden heart attack. But it was at her grandmother's wake that she locked eyes with the most beautiful black girl she'd ever seen. No, Rebecca Washington was the most beautiful *girl* she'd ever seen, period. Would this beautiful dancer freak out if she knew Devon was gay and attracted?

Enter Jessie Crowler, Rebecca's basketball-playing best friend. Or were they only friends? Devon tried to hide her attraction for the ebony dancer, but would fate allow Rebecca to look her way? Would Jessie get in the way? Would the difference in skin color keep them apart? All this adds up to quite an undertaking in Devon's formerly quiet existence.

### Rebecca's Story
(Book Two in the Grasse River Series)

*< Coming Soon >*

## THE GIRLS' SPORTS SERIES (Children's Books Ages 9-12)

### Bases Loaded

Sixth-grader Mackenzie Kelly's first love was soccer until her best friend talked her into playing summer softball. Now Mack is eager to be on her school's softball team and dreams of playing in the Olympics with her idol, Cat Osterman. But first, she needs to bring up her failing English grade to stay on the team. When she learns softball has been cut from the Olympics, she's determined somehow to get it back into the Olympic Games so she can fulfill her dream.

*"I just wanted to let you know I received the book and I think it is FANTASTIC!"*
– **Jessica Mendoza,** *US Olympic Softball Team*

ASIN: B0094IT3RK (eBook)
ISBN 978-1-934452-79-0 (Paperback)

## Side Out

Seventh-grader Dina Jacobs feels like she's landed on another planet when her family moves from Long Island, New York to Indiana. She tries out for the seventh-grade volleyball team, and her new friend, Christine, introduces her to Olympic volleyball. Now Dina dreams of playing in the Olympics like her newfound idol, Logan Tom. Indiana doesn't seem so bad until Dina's Jewish faith crashes against her coach's win-at-all-costs attitude. Miserable, Dina is torn between staying true to her religious customs or putting them aside to play the game she loves.

ASIN: B005HM9CUU (eBook)
ISBN 978-1-934452-65-3 (Paperback)

## Live, Love, Lacrosse

Addie Coleburn, fresh out of the sixth grade, is spending the summer at her grandmother's house in Syracuse with her mother and brother. Kimi Takahashi, a girl who lives up the street, invites Addie to go to the park and play lacrosse. Addie hasn't the first clue what lacrosse is and would rather sit on Grandma's front porch eating potato chips, drinking sodas, and reading books. But then again, spending the summer dealing with her younger brother isn't that appealing, either, so she goes to the park with Kimi. Within a week, she's hooked on lacrosse. She's overweight and can't keep up with the faster, stronger girls. She has to find a way to lose her excess weight quickly or risk getting cut from the team.

ASIN: B09GPYMHDK (eBook)
ISBN 978-1-943837-50-2 (Paperback)